# A Hero Lies Within

# A Hero Lies Within

Patrice Wilton

This is a work of fiction. People and events portrayed are used fictitiously.

Originally released as a Kindle Serial, February 2013
Text copyright © 2013 Patrice Wilton

All rights reserved.
Printed in the United States of America.
No part of this book may be reproduced, or stored in a retrieval system, or transmitted in any form or by any means, electronic, mechanical, photocopying, recording, or otherwise, without express written permission of the publisher.

Published by Montlake Romance
PO Box 400818
Las Vegas, NV 89140

ISBN-13: 9781477805763
ISBN-10: 1477805761

# EPISODE ONE
# CHAPTER ONE

"Kari, can you come into my office?" Tom Delaney spoke in a hushed tone that Kari Winslow knew meant trouble. He stood behind her desk, looking none too happy.

Kari worked for the Palm Beach News as the morning and noon anchor, and Tom was one of the producers. That meant that along with editing the news, deciding on content, and doing numerous other tasks, he was also in charge of hiring and firing his staff.

"Yes, sir," Kari said. "I'll be right there." Her stomach jumped and her palms were damp, but she smiled at Tom, putting on a brave front.

She stood up, straightening her jacket and smoothing her skirt. She wore a lemon-colored Armani suit that she'd bought on sale at the end of the season last year. At least she still had enough pride to look like a competent TV news anchor, even if she didn't sound like one.

She followed Tom into his office and closed the door behind her.

Tom whirled on her. "What's going on with you, Kari? This is the third time this week you've flubbed a line. You're a professional, for Christ's sake!"

Her jumpy stomach did a butterfly kick. She looked into his eyes, hoping to see a little compassion. If it was there, it was well hidden. She considered her options: attack or defend. "I don't know what to say. Except that Jeremy—"

"Jeremy what?" he growled. "You can hardly blame him if you screwed up. All you have to do is deliver the lines. If you can't do that, we'll find someone who can."

Dammit, she needed this job, and if Tom fired her, what would she do?

On the other hand, she had blown her lines and deserved whatever happened to her. Not that it had been her fault. Not entirely. When Max Hammond, their evening anchor, had suffered a fatal heart attack, Tom had brought Jeremy Chandler in to replace him. Everyone in the news station had known she wanted Max's job. She'd been around the longest and deserved the promotion, but it had been offered, conditionally, to Jeremy instead. He'd moved from Chicago to join their network, and according to Tom, they were lucky to have gotten him.

Kari knew he'd committed to only a one-year contract to try out the market, but the network hoped to extend the contract to five years. As of now, the terms had not been agreed upon, so she had a limited time to convince her boss that she was the better person for the job. Trouble was, around Jeremy, she wasn't stellar. He unbalanced her, threw her off her game, and she had no idea why. For her to stammer and mispronounce a word was unthinkable. Unacceptable. She'd better shape up fast if she hoped for even a chance at the nightly news.

"All I can say is I'm sorry." Her chin went up, and she met his gaze head-on. "Jeremy stopped by to deliver a personal message to me—right before my noon report. I know he was trying to upset me."

"I don't care what he said. You can't let your emotions affect your work." Tom's ruddy face grew even redder, and she suspected his rising blood pressure was brought on by stress—a.k.a. her. "You've been here long enough for me to know that you're a professional, but something or someone is distracting you. Have you and Jeremy got something going on that I should know about?"

"Holy crap, Tom. No! I don't even like the man."

"Well, what is it, then?" He settled into his chair, folding his large, freckled hands over his wide girth.

"He's an ass. He thinks I'm an amateur who doesn't belong in the same room with him." Kari sat down in the chair opposite him, acting nonchalant, even if her heart hammered like a woodpecker on speed. She crossed her legs and leaned back too. "I miss Max. He got along with everyone; the newsroom had this easy, relaxed atmosphere. With Jeremy, it's just different. He rubs everyone the wrong way."

"You need an attitude adjustment. The station's offering him a five-year contract, and it's in your best interest to get along." Tom's bushy brows furrowed, and he glared at her. "Get your act together, Kari. I can't have you stumbling over your words anymore. And that's an order."

"I know. It won't happen again."

She'd make sure it didn't. It wasn't like there were dozens of TV networks in the vicinity aching to hire her. It was a small community of professionals, and the competition was tough. That was part of the reason she wanted the evening anchor job; it would give her better job security and a higher salary. Plus, it would provide greater visibility, more exposure. And maybe one day, her sister might see her and come home.

"One more thing," Tom said in a gentler voice, as if he'd read her mind. "This missing-children series of yours. You know I've always been a big fan, and it boosted our ratings at the beginning, but people are tired of it. They want a feel-good story."

"A feel-good story?" She felt sick inside. That was exactly what Jeremy had told her right before the broadcast—that the station was axing her special half-hour show. She'd thought he'd only said it to upset her.

"Come on, Tom." Her gladiator spirit rose to the occasion. She knew when to pick her fights, and this was one of those times. "I'm doing something really important here. I'm bringing attention to missing children and runaways, closed cases that the authorities have given up on." She fought back the feeling of panic. He couldn't do this. Her sister was still missing.

"Please reconsider, Tom. This series has done a whole lot more than boost our ratings. We've actually found a few missing kids since we started this show."

He shook his head. "Sorry. George and I talked about it, and we're in agreement. It's done."

"George? He never said a word to me." George Collins was Tom's boss, the executive director, and he'd even congratulated her on a good show after her weekly broadcast last Friday evening.

Her temper flashed. "This isn't right. We've brought children home. How 'feel-good' is that?"

"Look, I know you have a personal motivation to keep this series alive, but we can't let our emotions get involved with our decision making. The show has lost its oomph. We need something to engage our viewers, and it's not stories about runaways. Nobody gives a shit anymore."

Kari's already bouncy stomach plummeted, and a dull but familiar pain spread inside her. She held on to the edge of the desk to steady herself. Gladiators didn't buckle. They held their ground. "You really mean this." She stared straight at him, letting him see her determination, but her mouth trembled. "Don't you? You're really cutting the show?"

"I'm sorry." Tom looked away. "I know how much this means to you, but yes. We're starting something new the first of the month."

Kari said nothing, deflated beyond words. Tom stood and opened his office door, signifying that she was free to leave.

She headed to her desk, sat down for a moment to check her computer for messages, and ignored the curious glances from her coworkers. She kept her head averted, not allowing them to engage her in conversation. Let them think what they wanted—she wasn't going to give them fuel for gossip. Determined not to show any weakness, she kept her chin high as she walked past the reception area and out the door.

Once she was inside her car, her chin quivered. Her hands shook. Her entire body trembled. How could he do this? She had to keep her show on the air. She had to find more runaways so that the parents, the families, could finally rest. They had to know. She had to know.

After several minutes, she'd calmed down enough to start the car. She had learned long ago that some things were out of her control, and dwelling on them did no good at all. If the show was cut, if she was fired, life would still go on, whether she ever found her sister or not.

She'd figure things out. She always did.

Passing a Publix on her way home, Kari decided to make a quick stop. The lack of food in her refrigerator didn't matter, but she was almost out of wine, and if she had ever needed a glass, it was today.

She pulled into the parking lot, grabbed a cart, and raced up and down the aisle, mindlessly tossing in frozen meals, a package of skinless chicken breasts, a steak, and a salmon fillet. Since she hated taking time out to shop, she tried to make this once-, sometimes twice-a-week experience as painless as possible.

Strolling over to the produce, she added asparagus, a head of broccoli, and a couple of packages of prepared salads to the cart. Passing the fruit, she grabbed a pint of strawberries and a small bag of cherries, then made her way to the wine counter. She picked up a couple of her favorite bottles, one red and one white, then checked out and headed home.

She lived on the fourth floor of a relatively new building in CityPlace, West Palm Beach, which had nearly every convenience imaginable, except concierge service. After parking in the garage, she entered the lobby and was dismayed to see only one elevator available—the other in service for someone moving into the building.

Balancing the bags and her handbag, she watched the numbers as the elevator crept downward from the eighteenth floor. Patience was not one of her strong suits, especially not today. She punched the elevator button again, as if that might hurry it along. Just then, the occupied elevator reached the lobby level and the door opened.

"Hold that elevator," she heard a man shout.

Before she could move, he rushed forward, wheeling two suitcases, one balanced on the other, and a dog carrier. The dog was one of those small yippy things, and it barked ferociously when Kari tried to slide past.

The man's suitcase bumped into her, and the bag holding the wine slipped out of her hands, hitting the ceramic tile. Both bottles broke, splashed her legs, and coated her new Manolo Blahnik heels.

"Oh my God!" She let out a small cry. Could her day get any worse?

"I'm so sorry. Did I do that?"

"Your bag bumped into mine." She glanced up from her once-beautiful shoes and met the eyes of the man who'd ruined them.

Her heart sped; her mouth went dry.

There was a churning in her stomach, and a yearning so intense it shook her to her core. Her hands released their grip, and the remaining grocery bags fell to the floor. Her mouth opened once or twice, but no words came out.

Jake. Back from war.

Not only had he ruined her shoes, he'd ruined her life.

"Kari." His eyes registered shock. "What are you doing here?"

"I could ask you the same." Anger surged through her. "This is my building, my home. You're not welcome here."

He didn't say a word, just arched his brow and gave her a hint of a smile.

His amused expression made her realize how foolish she seemed. She stiffened her spine and lifted her chin. He couldn't hurt her. Not anymore.

"It's good to see you again," he said, offering his hand.

She didn't take it, which didn't seem to faze him at all. He gathered up her groceries and handed her the bags. "I'll get the mess cleaned up."

Bitterness choked her. She'd always wondered how it would feel to see him again, but she'd not been prepared for this. Not today. Not ever.

"When did you get back?" The last she'd heard, he was in Iraq. She'd figured that was a good place for him to stay.

"I was at Walter Reed for several months, but here in Palm Beach, only a few weeks."

"So you were injured, then?" For many years she'd wished him a painful death, but obviously he'd survived in spite of her.

"Yes. I was luckier than most."

"I see that. You look…" She was at a loss for words. He was still as beautiful as she remembered, dammit! Why couldn't he be missing a piece or two? "So are you visiting someone?" she asked hopefully. "You wouldn't own a poodle."

"No, I'm moving in. And yes, by default, I guess, Muffin is mine."

"You can't." A feeling of panic rose in the pit of her stomach. "I live here."

"And now so do I." He smiled once more, and Kari blinked, feeling the oxygen sucking out of her. His devastating good looks, his natural charm, the ease and grace that he'd inherited at birth, were still as intact and powerful as they'd been in his youth. Those same qualities that had once attracted her now infuriated her.

It had taken her years to stop hating him and only a few minutes to bring it all back.

"You owe me a new pair of shoes." She knew it was a ridiculous thing to say, but it was better than the terrible words she longed to hurl at him. Silent accusations had been her bed partner for years. Like, why had he moved on so quickly—how could he have stopped loving her so fast? And the one that stubbornly teased her brain—what if she had confronted him that day and told him the truth?

"They're Manolos and they're ruined."

"I'll be happy to buy you a new pair. Although I think I prefer you in flip-flops." His gaze roamed over her. "When did you cut your hair so short? I liked it long, bouncing around on your shoulders, or up in a ponytail."

"I haven't bounced in a long time." She glared at him, remembering how happy they'd been until her world fell apart. "That girl's gone."

"Maybe we can work on that." He picked up the soggy bag that had once held two bottles of wine. "I'll replace your wine too."

"Forget it. I don't want anything from you. Not now. Not ever." She lifted her chin and stared into his eyes. "I don't want you here, Jake. I'm not comfortable with you around."

"That's too bad, because I'm not going anyplace."

"Why the hell not? You're good at moving on."

"And what's that supposed to mean? You're the one who wouldn't answer my calls."

Her fingernails dug into the palms of her hands. How dare he? He knew nothing—nothing—of what had happened to her. "Don't go there."

"I'm not going anywhere. I'm going to be your neighbor whether you like it or not."

"I don't." Her shoulders went rigid, and her entire body fought for control. She wanted to lunge at him and beat her fists against his chest, but if she went anywhere near him, her fragile hold on her emotions might snap.

He ran a hand over his face, shaking his head. "Listen to the two of us. We're acting like a couple of kids." His eyes crinkled with his smile. "Remember how we used to go at it when we were young? Always fighting and making up. Let's put our grievances behind us and agree to be friends."

"Impossible." She stepped around the broken glass, needing to put distance between them until she got her breathing under control. "I'll get someone to clean this up."

"Hold Muffin. I'll get someone."

She eyed the quivering snowball with little pointy teeth, snarling at her. "Thought you hated small dogs."

"Long story. I just figured he had a right to live."

"I didn't say he didn't. But with you?"

Someone from security had heard the commotion and showed up with a bag and a broom. "We'll take care of this," he said, then proceeded to do so.

Jake held the elevator door for her. "Go ahead. I'll take the next one."

She stepped inside. "Good idea."

"What's your apartment number?"

"Don't call me. I live with someone." She pushed the elevator button and leaned back against the wall, whispering, "You and I are done."

The elevator door slid closed.

*Oh God, oh God, oh God! Jake!* She couldn't bear it, but what could she do?

The idea of living in the same apartment building, being near him, was unthinkable. Not with the history between them, and he didn't even know the half of it. He had no idea why she'd suddenly cut him out of her life, and she didn't plan to tell him either.

As she entered her apartment, her knees buckled, causing her to sink into a chair, then put her head in her hands. The pain came crashing back. It swept over her in one long, undulating tide—the highs, the lows, years of loving him and losing everything that mattered.

She got up from the chair and went to the kitchen. She poured herself a glass of white wine from the near-empty bottle in the fridge, kicked off her shoes, and sat down on the sofa. She took a big sip of the chardonnay, hoping it would take the edge off yet knowing one sip wouldn't cut it.

Why, of all the places in this city, had Jake ended up here? Had he sought her out? Did he know she worked for PB News? Perhaps he'd seen her when he'd been home on leave, or his father might have mentioned it. Had he hoped that they might pick up again where they had left off? Could he really think it would be that simple?

Probably not. And if he had, he certainly would know better now. He'd rattled her so badly that in a matter of minutes, she'd been reduced to a snippy, unsophisticated, immature child, telling him he couldn't live here, that it was her home and he made her uncomfortable. It made her sound so silly and weak, even territorial, and she was none of those things—just protective of her space, as well as her heart.

In fairness to him, some of the terrible things that had happened had not been his fault. But Jake had changed who she was and helped make her what she'd become. Her youthful joy, the hope of a bright and happy future, had been ripped out of her, and she'd been left with nothing.

How could she pretend indifference when she felt so much?

Today, in the lobby, it had been his fault she'd made a fool of herself. His fault she had to live with her guard up, always wary that someone might get too close and shatter her mended heart.

After sucking down the remainder of her wine, she sniffed back her tears, picked up her ruined shoes, and tossed them in the bin. She'd made a big deal out of ruining her precious shoes, but in reality, she didn't give a damn about them or any of the designer merchandise she surrounded herself with. It was all a front, her entire persona, hiding the real Kari from the world.

She opened her patio doors and stepped outside. Her two-bedroom condo in CityPlace sat across the bridge from the glorious mansions in Palm Beach. She loved the fact that outside her door were several restaurants and bars, a big movie theater, shops and boutiques, all situated around a lovely and quaint town square.

Many people were milling about during the predinner hour. For several minutes, she mindlessly watched the activity, trying to distract herself from the flood of memories threatening to overtake her fragile state of mind. She spotted a few couples heading out for dinner, a group of young women apparently having a girls' night out, and several teenage boys with their hats on sideways, pants falling down, waiting in the square where musicians were setting up for a local show.

She went back inside, heading for the bedroom, unzipping her skirt, when the telephone rang. The caller ID showed it was Sean, so she eagerly answered it. He was the perfect boyfriend: intelligent, interesting, charming, and absent most of the time. She was proud of the fact that he was an award-winning freelance photographer, and thrilled that his career was as important to him as hers was to her.

"Sean! Where are you?"

"Hunan, China, but we leave tomorrow." His New Zealand accent accentuated when he spoke quickly, as he did now. "We're doing some shots on the Mengdong River, and then at a place called the Fairyland of Peach Blossoms. It's been really crazy for the past few days; that's why you didn't hear from me."

"Tell me everything. I miss the sound of your voice."

"No time. I'm rushing right now, but I'll be in Beijing in a few days and can call again then."

"Sean. Don't hang up just yet. Can't we talk a little longer?"

"Sorry, honey. I'll have more time in a couple of days."

"Okay." She whispered, half to herself, "I need you tonight."

"What was that?"

"Nothing." For just this once, she'd like to unburden herself, but she knew and accepted the fact that he lived with one foot out the door, as did she. "When are you coming home?"

"I can't say for sure, but it'll be within the next couple of weeks. Maybe sooner."

"Good. I have so much to tell you." She hesitated for a second, then blurted, "I miss you."

"Glad to hear that." His voice deepened. "When I get home, we have things to discuss."

"Like what?" she said, suddenly on guard.

"Things that should be discussed in person."

"Sean. Tell me." She wondered if he wanted to change the relationship. End it or step it up a notch. Neither prospect appealed to her.

"You'll know soon enough."

"Okay. Be mysterious. See if I care."

"I miss you too." His voice sounded different, almost romantic, and it made her heart yearn.

"Give my love to Beijing," she said, keeping things light.

He laughed, and they said good-bye.

She headed for the bathroom to take her shower, feeling more unsettled than ever. Sean was a darling, but they spent so little time together that she never completely knew where they stood. They were lovers, but were they in love?

While the warm water washed over her body, her thoughts returned to Tom's sudden decision to cut her runaway series. Every instinct in her wanted to fight him on this, but management had made a decision and there was not a damn thing she could do about it. She would get him his "feel-good" stories. Hell, if Tom wanted her to bend over and show her backside to the world, she'd do it. Whatever it took to make the boss happy.

# CHAPTER TWO

As soon as Kari stepped out of the shower, she heard pounding on the door. She threw on a robe and peeked through the peephole. It was Jake. *Holy crap! How'd he find me?*

She cracked the door open an inch, enough for him to glimpse her face but not her pink silk robe that didn't quite reach her knees. "I'm not dressed."

"That's okay." He waggled his eyebrows. When she didn't respond, he wore an apologetic smile and waved a brown bag in his hand. "I brought you a bottle of wine. And some shoes," he added. "You're going to love them."

"I told you not to. Please go away." She was about to shut the door on him, but he had his foot in the way. "How did you find me?"

"Easy." His eyes roamed over her, sending a flutter of alarm charging through her system. "You're in the directory."

"Oh. Of course." She tried to muscle the door closed, but he had other ideas.

"Come on, Kari. Open up." His deep blue eyes glinted with amusement. "Don't you want to see your shoes?"

"No." Curiosity got the better of her. "Where did you get them? Kmart?"

"Downstairs. Told you I liked you better in flip-flops. You were nicer then."

"I was young. Gullible." She bit her lip to hold back the pain. "I'm not that person anymore."

"I bet you could be." He sang loudly, "Kari, Kari, come out, come out, wherever you are."

"Get lost, Jake. Don't be an ass." She glanced around the corridor, hoping no one would witness this embarrassing drama. "I don't want you around. It's bad enough that you live in my building."

"Is your boyfriend home?" He tried to peer around her. "I'd like to meet him."

"No. Now go away. I've had a rough day."

"Want to talk about it? You used to tell me everything."

"Don't you get it?" she snapped. "Take your wine, your flip-flops, your dog, and your arrogant ass and go for a long walk off a short pier."

He grinned. "Kari Winslow, the successful news reporter, has such a gift for words."

"Piss off." Did he really think that she'd have anything to do with him after all that had happened? But then, he probably had more questions than answers, and that's why he was here.

His grin deepened. "Even better." He shouldered the door. "Let me in. I can't wait to hear what you're going to say next."

"Leave me alone." She used both hands to push at the door. "Do you want me to call security?"

"Are you serious? Come on, Kari. I just got back into town. Be nice. Please?"

"I am nice, and I have a boyfriend. His name is Sean."

"I'll leave the moment he gets home. Promise."

Jake was doing it again. Being his charming, utterly irresistible self.

"Why are you so insistent? We don't have anything left to say to one another."

"Sure we do." He pushed the door wide. "What's it been? Damn near fifteen years. I'd say we have plenty of catching up to do."

"I have nothing to say to you, at least nothing you'd want to hear."

He ignored her comment. "Go get dressed," he told her, "and I'll get the glasses."

"I'm not getting dressed, and you're not staying." She held her robe at her throat, making sure she was properly covered.

Jake marched past her, walked into her kitchen, and rummaged around her drawers until he found the wine opener.

"What the hell do you think you're doing?" She reached for the corkscrew, but he lifted it over his head, taunting her.

"Give that to me," she snapped, "and get out."

"You want it, come and get it." He waved the corkscrew near her, and she made a grab for it and missed.

"Why are you doing this?" she hissed. "Why don't you leave me alone?"

He put the wine opener on the counter, then wandered into the living room and sat down, looking for all the world like he planned to stay. "I want to know why you're so darn mad at me. What did I do to you?"

"It doesn't matter now. But trust me, I have a very good reason."

"Whatever it is, I'm sorry."

Her eyes met his, then slid away. He might look like the man she'd once loved, but he was different too. Older, sadder, wiser. His face was etched with deep creases now, and his eyes looked as if they'd seen too much.

Before she sent him on his way, she had one question demanding an answer. "Jake, why did you go?"

He looked confused for a moment, and she left him to ponder the question. Would he answer why he had left her or why he had gone off to war?

"I wanted to be a hero." He glanced her way. "I wasn't one."

She bit her lip and stepped away.

"I should go."

She nodded and followed him to the door, intending to lock it the moment he left. "What's up with your dog?"

"It was Tiffany's dog; that's Dad's new wife. He was hit by a car, and she wanted to put him down. I offered to do it for her and decided to bring him here instead."

"That's very sweet of you."

"I'm not sweet."

"Right. I remember." She swallowed hard. "I'm sorry about your mother. I sent flowers."

"I know. I thought you might come to the funeral."

Kari opened the door for him. "I wasn't family. There was no reason for me to be there."

His eyes glittered. "You could have been. The way I remember it, we had a plan. You're the one who stopped talking to me. Wouldn't answer my calls."

Kari licked her lips. Her throat was dry, and she had a tightness in her chest. She blinked, afraid that that pricking sensation could mean an onslaught of tears. No! She wouldn't cry. Not for any man, and certainly not for him.

She answered, "The plan I remember didn't include me."

He opened his mouth to deny the accusation, she was sure, but he was cut off by the ringing of the phone. They held each other's gaze before she ran to answer it.

"Sean!" she gushed. "I'm so glad you got a chance to call me back."

"You sounded out of sorts. Want to talk about it?"

Her back was turned, but she heard the door close behind her. She released a long, shuddering breath, and felt the oxygen in the room return. Phone in hand, she sank down on the sofa to cozy up for a long chat.

∽

Kari fell asleep well past midnight, still stirred by seeing Jake and by the other, more important events of the day. A few hours later, her alarm went off. She rolled out of bed, showered, and applied her makeup with expert care. Once dressed, she poured herself a to-go cup of coffee and drove the fifteen minutes to the station.

As the 5:00 a.m. broadcast began, she gazed straight into the camera, feeling her confidence return as she reported her first story.

"Here's one for my 'Can you believe it?' list. A man walked into a Fort Lauderdale bank Friday morning and showed a teller a note written on his company's letterhead, saying he had a weapon. The unmasked robber walked away with an undisclosed amount of cash. With his face clearly displayed on the bank's security camera, police say an arrest is imminent."

The broadcast broke for an ad, then she came back with the next item of interest.

"The body of a man was pulled from the Atlantic Ocean, four miles east of Sebastian Inlet State Park, after he fell off his sailboat…"

At six, Kari gave her second morning report. When she finished, she hurried to Tom's office, hoping to catch him before her noon report. "Has Tom come in yet?" she asked the receptionist.

The young woman nodded. "Yes, about fifteen minutes ago."

Kari marched over and rapped sharply on the door.

"Come in," he called.

She poked her head in. "Hi, Tom. You got a minute?"

"For you? Anytime."

He stroked an unlit cigar the way a mother would her baby's cheek. Kari knew he was having a hard time with the no-smoking policy.

"Tom, I've been doing some thinking." She drew in a quick breath. "You know I'm reluctant to give up on the missing-persons series, but I'm a team player, and if happy stories are what you want, then you'll get them from me."

He frowned and rubbed his jaw. "I know having your series axed came at you pretty quick." His gaze slid away.

"Jeremy has already offered to fill the spot, and George has agreed."

"No!" Kari took two steps closer. "How can George do this?" She was breathing hard, fighting for her professional life. A burning sensation behind her eyelids threatened tears, and she willed them away. "I earned that spot. I deserve it. Viewers expect to see me each week. They've been with me since the beginning, three years now. I helped the ratings, not Jeremy."

"Kari, sit down and we'll talk about this."

"Tom, this isn't right. First you cancel my series, and now you want to replace me?" She took a breath to calm herself. "I can do this, Tom."

"Aren't you forgetting who's boss?"

"You haven't given me a chance," she wailed, hearing the desperation in her own voice. After a second, she unclenched her hands, sucked in a breath, and forced herself to relax. "I have an idea," she said, "but it's not properly fleshed out yet. It's something big—that much I can tell you."

"What is it?"

"Give me a day. I'll have the whole thing worked out by then, and I'll run it past you. Please don't tell Jeremy it's his, not until you hear me out. I've put my time in—three years, Tom. Can't you give me a couple of days?"

"Forty-eight hours, and it better be good."

She knew something was up. The producers had already made up their minds without speaking to her first. "What has Jeremy got?"

"I'm not at liberty to say. He's working on something hot, he assures me." Tom put his hands behind his head and leaned back in his chair. "You do have an idea, right?"

"You bet I do." Kari stood and had to grip the table to keep her knees from buckling. "Bring George in too. He's going to want to hear this."

Perspiration trickled down her spine. She'd be cooking her own goose if she couldn't deliver. "I assure you that whatever Jeremy has, mine is going to be bigger."

# CHAPTER THREE

Jake spent the first night in his new home sleeping on a king-size box spring and mattress that occupied the middle of the floor. His father had offered some old furniture that had once belonged to Tiffany, but he'd rather stick needles in his eyes than live with anything of hers. With the exception of Muffin. The three-legged mutt could stay.

After seeing Kari's apartment the night before, Jake had a much better idea of what he didn't want. What he couldn't understand was how someone as emotional as she was could live in an ice palace like that. Not the Kari he remembered. She'd have made off-colored jokes at such a place. Everything was white on white. White leather sofas, white shag rug in the center, with a large, square, marble coffee table. Stark white walls broken up only by two colored prints and a bunch of framed awards she must have received during her so-called illustrious career. There were no personal pictures lying around, only a small wall unit with some hardcover books and a few CDs. A fifty-inch flat-screen TV perched on a wall across from her sofa and love seat, and she had a round glass dinette table with four chairs next to the kitchen. One gangly plant stood in a corner, looking as if it were ashamed to be there. The condo was about as inviting as a museum, and just as lifeless.

Knowing what he didn't want made him run out to buy the complete opposite. This morning, he'd driven the car his father had lent him straight to Rooms To Go and bought himself a shitload of furniture. He'd made the salesgirl very happy, purchasing an entire bedroom suite, comfortable, laid-back living-room sofas and chairs, and a solid wood dining table with six plush chairs. It was the perfect one-stop furniture store, with table lamps, rugs, wall pictures, and even TVs thrown in for good measure. Better yet, he could expect delivery within the week.

When he had returned from his shopping spree, he'd felt like a warrior returned from battle. It had been exhausting work, but satisfying, now that it was behind him.

Muffin licked his face, and he put the poodle back on the floor. "Not sure how much walking you want to do, old boy, but I bought you a new lead and some toys."

Jake emptied the plastic bag full of doggie toys on the floor and watched Muffin take a mouse in his mouth. He shook the little thing and growled, then used a front paw to hold it down. His wet nose began pushing it around the floor.

"Okay, buddy. Let's go for a quick walk, and then you can come back and play some more. I don't have all day to sit around and talk to a dog, you know."

He carried Muffin down the elevator, and they walked around CityPlace, stopping for coffee at Starbucks. It was midmorning, too late for breakfast but early for lunch. They sat outdoors, and Jake broke pieces of a blueberry bagel and fed the dog under the table. He'd considered ordering a blueberry muffin, but having a dog named Muffin and eating one just didn't seem right.

The dog started barking and pulling at the leash. Jake glanced up and saw Kari. His guts knotted up, and he wasn't sure what he felt. Anger, definitely, curiosity, sure, but that wasn't all. Too much had been left unsaid. Their love affair had never had closure, and he for one wanted to know why she'd ditched him without an explanation.

"Your dog is out of control," Kari said as she walked past them, heading inside for her beverage.

When she came back out, she would have walked past again had he not loosened his grip on the dog's leash. Muffin lunged at Kari and nipped at her feet, causing her to drop the cup from her hand. Slowly, she turned her head and looked at him.

"What is it with you and your mutt?" Her eyes blazed. "Do you get some warped pleasure out of ruining my shoes?"

He grinned and reeled Muffin back in. "Today it's only spilled milk."

"It was a latte, and now you owe me one." She glanced down, noting a splash on her expensive sandals. "And shoes. Not flip-flops either."

He could practically see fumes rising out of her cute little ears, and bit back a grin. "How else was I going to get you to say hello?"

"Hello," she sniped. "Now what about my low-fat, french vanilla latte?"

"No problem. You take care of Muffin and I'll get it."

She glanced at the dog straining at the leash, eyeing her. "I'm not hanging around your dog. He doesn't like me."

He grinned. "Probably thinks you're after his life story."

"Ha, ha, ha. Very funny." She picked up her cup from the ground. "I'm getting another. Fork over five dollars."

He handed her a ten. "I'll have a coffee. Black."

"You expect me to get it?"

"Please."

Her eyes narrowed. "Why would I do that?"

"Because you're nice."

"Not to you, but I'll make an exception if you promise never to bother me again."

He smiled. "Promise." Crossing two fingers under the table, he added, "Scout's honor."

"One black coffee, coming up. Doesn't sound very interesting, though."

"We didn't have a Starbucks in the desert."

"Nice line. Can I use that?"

"Just get me a damn coffee and stop pretending to be cute."

"I am cute." She sashayed to the counter and returned with her latte and his plain coffee. "There you go. Black." Kari plopped his coffee on the table. "I kept the change."

"You deserve it. I've never been waited on by someone so sweet."

She gave him the middle finger and turned to go.

"Why don't you stay, enjoy your latte? Muffin wants to apologize to you. Don't you, Muff, ole boy?"

Muffin growled at her and bared his sharp little fangs.

"Clearly. I can see that." Kari's expression was colder than an ice chip. "But I can't stay. I've got to get home and work."

"Sure. I've got things to do too." He looked her over. "Take care, Kari."

Jake took Muffin upstairs and put out dried food and fresh water. Then he was off again. He wanted to hit the car dealerships this afternoon so he could return his father's car to him and have his own set of wheels. After spending an hour or two looking around, he ended up with a two-year-old, precertified Jaguar in mint condition.

It was late afternoon when he drove the Lexus back to his father's, and when he stepped out, he heard the sound of laughter and conversation around the pool.

"Jake, is that you?" his father called out. "Come join us. Brent finally arrived. Took long enough."

Tiffany yelled, "Bring the pitcher of margaritas from the fridge."

"Hell, Jake, bring two pitchers," Brent called out.

His weariness vanished. He hadn't seen his younger brother in years, but then, that was hardly Brent's fault. The Iraqi war botched a lot of relationships, but he'd been responsible for this one.

"Brent?" He walked out to the pool. "Hell, it's good to see you. You still fighting those fires in California?"

"Yup. I've been lugging around the Grumman tanker for eight long years now. It's a heavy load to bear." He grinned. "I'm trading it in for something a whole lot sexier and technologically advanced."

"I'm not sure what any of that means, but shit, man. You look good. I'm glad you managed a visit." He punched his brother's arm.

"You won't believe what Brent is up to now," their brother Nick said. He was sitting at the table, drinking a beer, while his wife, Cindy, was in a lounge chair, feeding their baby.

Nick jerked his beer can in Brent's direction. "He signed up."

Jake could hear the criticism behind the words and wondered what had crawled up Nick's ass. Nick was a VP for a banking firm, and he and Brent rarely saw eye to eye. Even as kids, they had been polar opposites.

Jake ignored Nick and turned toward his father. "What's he talking about?"

His father grinned with pride. "Brent joined the army six months ago. He's finished his MOS and basic combat training, and has started flight training. Wants to be a warrant officer and fly the new high-tech choppers."

Jake looked at Brent. "Come on, you can't do that. You've got a great career. You love what you do."

"The job will be waiting for me—no need to worry about that." Brent fidgeted with his collar, as if it were too tight. "Look, Jake, I'm not going to sit around on my butt any longer. It's time to teach those sons of bitches a few lessons. They started this damn war, and it's time we finished it." He took a slug of beer. "Things are slowing down over there, and I need to get involved."

Jake released a long breath. "What you need is to rethink this. Hell, what you do is dangerous enough, and California just keeps getting beat up, year after year."

"I know, and that's never going to change. Blame it on global warming or whatever, but it's just a reality."

Jake searched his younger brother's face. "You're a highly trained professional. Why would you want to walk away from all that? Christ, a man of your talents is needed here, in this country. Forget the Afghans. Let them fight their own damn battles."

"What the hell?" Brent shook his head. "How can you of all people say that?"

His father answered. "Jake didn't mean that the way it sounded. He did the right thing by going overseas. You will too."

"Like hell I didn't mean it," Jake snapped. "I sure as hell don't want to see Brent giving up his career, maybe his life, fighting for a country that doesn't give a shit."

Everyone's mouth dropped, and he could almost feel the shock waves reverberate in the air. "Look, let's shelve this conversation for now. Last I heard, there's to be a big party here tonight. Why doesn't one of you run me home so I can shower and dress? This discussion can wait until morning."

Brent met his gaze. "I'll drop you home, but don't try to talk me out of it. My mind is made up."

Jake nodded. "Okay. No more words on this subject. But you're a pig's ass if you go off to war."

"Get your own ride."

John Harrington raised his hands. "Sons, put it to rest. We have all weekend to speak our minds. Tonight, we're here to celebrate Jake's return."

Jake flung an arm around Brent's shoulder and whispered, "We're not done yet," as they walked away.

Brent waited until they were in the car to speak his mind. "Look, I understand your concern, but I've got to go. You saw what happened to Shane. I'm not going to sit back and let them do that to my friend." He rubbed his jaw. "He tried to get me to sign up when he did, but I thought he was crazy. Fucking bastards tortured him. Cut off his hand, for Christ's sake." His voice was grim. "I know what I've got to do."

"You made the right choice for yourself, and Shane made the right choice for him."

Shane had been Brent's best friend since childhood. They'd taken off right after high school graduation and hitched a ride to California to be surfer dudes and maybe get a lucky break in the movies. They'd both ended up working for CAL FIRE, Shane as a medic, Brent flying the choppers.

Brent flexed his hands. "Dammit to hell. Shane came home damn near a year ago and hasn't been right since. After he got his prosthesis, he left rehab and nobody knows where the hell he is."

"You haven't heard from him? I can't believe he wouldn't let you, of all people, know his whereabouts."

"Not a word in six months. I have a feeling he might have come back here." Brent crushed his empty can of beer with one hand. "I'm going to spend a day or two checking around."

"All the more reason you should stay put and not go off to war." Jake tried to be the voice of reason, but he wanted to knock some sense into his brother and beg him to change his mind.

"I have a personal reason now." He swallowed hard. "When he wouldn't follow orders, they chopped off his hand."

"I know how you feel, but that is still one piss-poor reason to join the military, brother."

"What about you? You left because of Cathy."

*Cathy.* A familiar pain shot right through him. The years had dulled it, but it was an ache that resurfaced with the mention of her name, a triggered memory, or catching sight of a woman who reminded him of her. He welcomed the ache, as he didn't want to lose his memories of this beautiful woman he'd once loved.

She'd been his fiancée. She'd worked in a nearby brokerage house, and after two years of dating, he'd popped the question. Before the wedding, she took a trip to England to see her parents and was there in July 2005 when a terrorist group in London planted bombs on three subways and a bus. Fifty-two people died. Cathy was one of them.

Jake nodded. "I did what I had to do, but that doesn't make it right."

"And I have to do the same," Brent answered softly.

## CHAPTER FOUR

Kari did have work to do if she wanted to save her series, but instead of using her creative energy to find a solution, her mind wandered to Jake. Maybe time had somewhat mellowed her deep-rooted turmoil, but it still simmered below the surface.

When her sister had disappeared, she'd remained behind to hold her family together until they found her again. Jake had gone to college, as expected, and although she missed him terribly, she knew he had to leave. He called every day, and things were almost fine until her period was late. Anxiously, she watched and waited, while days turned into weeks, then months, and still it never came.

Her parents were so distraught over Alaina, and Kari didn't have any close friends she could confide in about such an important decision. Jake had been her closest friend, but he was no longer calling as often as he should. She could see him drifting away. She was nearing her third month when she knew she couldn't wait any longer. If she had to have an abortion, the decision had to be made soon. But the very idea of not having Jake's baby reduced her to tears. She couldn't imagine anything sweeter than having his child. She loved him so much and already loved the baby who was growing inside her.

When she told Jake, he'd want the baby too, she was sure of it.

Since her parents were so distracted, they didn't question why she was going to see Jake in California for the weekend. She flew out on a Friday, intending to spend the weekend in his arms. After landing at LAX, she rented a car and drove to USC, eager to surprise him.

It was a surprise, all right. She found him walking arm in arm with a pretty, long-legged blonde who looked at him with hero worship in her eyes. Kari had been about to call out to him, when the girl slipped her arms around his neck and kissed him. Blinded by tears, Kari followed the two of them, stopping short when she saw him enter the girl's dorm. An hour later, he left her room.

She ran as fast as she could, through the campus grounds and back to the parking lot. She gunned her rental car and flew out of the parking lot without a backward glance. She headed straight back to the airport, sobbing and wiping away tears. Traffic was heavy, and she couldn't see…then…

Kari's reminiscing ended abruptly when she heard a double knock on her door. Feeling out of sorts from her unpleasant memories, she winced when she saw Jake's face through the peephole.

She opened the door a crack. "You again?"

"I have a favor to ask."

"Well?"

"Can I come in for a sec? I don't want to discuss it in the hall. It will only take a minute, and then you can decide if you want to help me or not. I'll never bother you again if your answer is no."

That sounded good to her, so she nodded and opened the door. "You've got one minute."

He told her about his brothers being in town, and that Brent had joined the army and was training as a chopper pilot. She wished he'd get to the point.

She folded her arms and tapped her toe. This story was taking longer than a minute, and she was sorry she'd let him in. "Cut to the chase. What's the problem?" His face was grim, the devilish smile subdued for once. "Jake? What is it?"

"My brother's buddy was captured and tortured in Iraq." He grimaced. "They cut off his hand."

"How awful." She put a hand to her chest and closed her eyes for a second.

"The kid was rescued, and after months of rehab and a new prosthetic, he takes off. Been missing for six months."

"What does this have to do with me?"

Jake turned to her. "If we found Shane, Brent might not go off to war."

"If he's enlisted, it's likely too late."

"I realize that, but Dad might be able to pull some strings."

"So, you want me to help you find Shane?"

"I figured that you might know where to start. You've been at this for some time."

"It didn't help with Alaina." She sighed. Her conscience would not let her walk away from a missing person. "But I can do some quick research for you."

"If you don't mind, I'd be grateful."

She nodded. "I don't like to see people disappear. He served his country and shouldn't be ignored. I would like to find him too."

Jake sat down, and she clicked on her computer. "This may take more than a few minutes," she told him. "Do you have something else to do?"

He glanced at his watch. "Yeah. Dad's throwing a big bash for me tonight, and I need to shower and get dressed."

"Go on, then. I should have something for you later."

Jake's face brightened. "Hey, why don't you come? I know my father would like to see you. There'll probably be plenty of people you know."

"Thanks, but no thanks. I have enough on my plate. I promised my boss something in the morning, and I haven't got a clue what I'm going to give him."

He stopped with one hand on the door. "Anything I can help with?"

"No."

"Okay." He shrugged and opened the door. "If you change your mind, you know where we live."

∽

Jake hated parties at the best of times, but after the conversation with his brother, he was certainly not in the mood. To make things worse, Tiffany had invited a friend to the party and tried to line him up. The woman was pretty enough but had a high-pitched giggle and nothing to say. After ten minutes of trying to make conversation, he made his excuses to mingle.

A few of his father's friends were eager to get his perspective on the war, but he kept his comments short and moved along, greeting one face after another. If he could slip away somewhere quiet, just for a few minutes, he might get his act together. He could hardly breathe. The people, the faces, the questions were all suffocating him. The blackness was coming on, and it was pulling him into a bottomless pit that he imagined was hell. Once he was there, nobody could reach him.

Someone bumped into him, and he flinched.

"Sorry," the fellow said. "You okay?"

"I'm fine. Fine." He hurried away, and a second later, his brother Nick was at his side. "You don't look like you're enjoying this. Everything okay?"

"Yeah, I'm all right. Just not good company." He shrugged. "Feel like I'm going to explode. Crazy, huh?"

"I told Dad this wasn't a good idea," Nick said.

"I'll be okay." He glanced away. "I need some time to slip back into all this." He gestured to the sprawling house, the pool, the people on the oversize terrace. "I'll get there, eventually."

"Well, if you ever need to talk…"

"I'll let you know."

He walked away from the pool area, where a large outside bar had been set up, and he headed for a secluded spot on the property. His father's home was on the far end of Jupiter Island, and hidden from the road by a mammoth hedge, heavy foliage, and lush landscaping. The road divided the island, with homes on one side of it facing the Intercoastal Waterway, and homes on the other side, like his father's, facing the ocean. The beach was miles of coastal sand dunes and mangrove swamps.

From where he stood, he could hear the sound of the waves breaking along the shore. Jake would have liked to stay there all night but knew he couldn't. After taking a few deep breaths, enjoying the smell and taste of the salty air, he left his place of refuge.

He returned to the pool area and headed straight for the bar.

"Thought I might find you here."

Recognizing the female voice, he turned slowly. "Hi, Kari. So you came after all."

"Is that a problem?" She tilted her head, and the fading sun seemed to light her face.

"No, not at all. I'm sure there are a lot of people here you'd like to meet." He glanced around, nodding toward the mayor and the governor, who were chatting like old friends. "Want an introduction?"

"That won't be necessary. We've met on numerous occasions." She smiled, nodding as the two politicians looked her way.

"Did you solve your problems at work?"

"No. I hoped I might hear something interesting tonight that would spark an idea." She folded her arms and made a face. "If not, I might be the one moving out of the apartment, or out of the city, for that matter."

"That bad?"

"I'm hoping not. That's why I'm here."

Jake spotted his father marching toward them from the other side of the pool. Even at a distance, Jake recognized the purposeful stride, the set jaw, and the look of concern on his father's face.

"Jake," his father said when he reached them, "what's going on? Nick said you weren't feeling well."

"He shouldn't have said anything. A headache, that's all." Jake put a hand on Kari's back, urging her forward. "You remember Kari Winslow."

"Hello, Mr. Harrington."

She smiled and shook his hand, and Jake noticed how tiny she was standing next to the general. She looked like a little pixie with her short blonde hair, big green eyes, and petite stature. His father, on the other hand, made an imposing figure—tall, with the bearing of a person used to command.

"I watch you every morning on the news," he said to Kari. "How's that old rascal Tom doing?" He didn't wait for an answer but carried on in his deep baritone voice. "Ask him why he hired that dick Jeremy for the evening news instead of another pretty young woman like you."

"I will, sir." She grinned. "I'll be sure to ask him just that."

He suddenly looked past her, waving his hand to someone. Jake glanced in that direction and saw Tiffany weaving her way through the crowd to join them. His father grabbed his young wife's hand, drawing her forward.

Jake's tension returned with her arrival. Tiffany wore a body-hugging white dress that ended well above her knees. Her long legs were slim, toned, and tanned. He looked away.

"Tiffany," his father said, "this is Kari Winslow, an old friend of Jake's."

"Nice to meet you." Tiffany flashed a toothy smile. "Aren't you the woman on the morning news? I just love that cute new anchor who took over for the old guy—Jeremy somebody."

"Jeremy is a welcome addition to PB News. We are very lucky to have a man of his talents," Kari said. Jake thought her smile looked forced.

Tiffany continued to gush about Jeremy. Kari interrupted her to say, "I'd love to talk more, but we mustn't monopolize all your time. I'm sure you need to mingle."

"Oh, it's all right," Tiffany said, tossing her long blonde hair off her shoulders. "I'd like to get to know you better. I also have a friend here who wants to get into show business."

"Not now, dear," his father said. "Let's see to our other guests." He put an arm around her waist and guided her away.

Jake shook his head as he watched the newlyweds walk away, and then he turned to Kari. "So, what do you think of my stepmother?"

"Perfectly charming," she said, with no expression whatsoever.

Jake shot her a skeptical look.

"Okay, no wonder you moved out," she answered. Their eyes met, and they busted out laughing. "Let's get something to drink." She spoke to the bartender and came back with two glasses of champagne.

They found a couple of unoccupied lounge chairs, and Kari tilted her glass in his direction. "To Muffin. May he live a long and happy life."

Jake nodded and touched his glass to hers, noticing the instant she saw the scars on his hands. She drew in a quick breath, and her body became perfectly still.

"Jake," she said softly, "I didn't know you were burned. What happened?"

He was sick and tired of every conversation reverting to either his injuries or the war. But he couldn't ignore her genuine concern.

"It's nothing," he said. "I was in the wrong place at the wrong time. It was a convoy, and the truck in front of us ran smack over a land mine. Bodies went flying, but I got away with only a few burns."

"I'm so sorry."

"Don't be. I'm luckier than most of the enlisted men and women who come home."

She was silent for a second, then said, "You won't be going back again, will you?"

"No. I've been discharged."

He put his glass down and rested his head on the lounge chair, looking up at the sky. It was a beautiful, balmy night. The stars danced above the swaying palm trees, and the moon was half full. It was nice. If he were back in Iraq right now, he'd be either bored out of his skull or in sheer terror, fighting his way through some damn ambush. Strange that he should miss it. He used to dream of home when he was away, and now that he was back, he dreamed of Iraq. He needed his head examined, that's what he needed.

After a minute, Kari spoke again. "It must be hard seeing your father with another woman."

"If he's happy, it's okay by me."

She didn't look like she believed him. "I'm kind of glad my dad went quickly after Mom passed away. He would have been lost without her."

"I always liked your mom."

"She liked you too."

He stayed quiet for some time, remembering all the times he'd come to pick her up after school and how warm and friendly her mother had been. Always wanting him to come in and sit down, asking him about his football games, as if she really cared. Other memories came to mind too. Like making out with Kari in the backseat of his Trans Am. They were good memories, of a more innocent time—when he believed the world was worth fighting for.

He pushed out of the chair. "Let's get out of here. Go for a walk on the beach or something."

"Good idea."

They walked to the edge of the property, where a gate led to a private, narrow path to the beach. They took off their shoes and wandered down to the water's edge, letting the cool water splash over their ankles as they talked and walked.

Jake was glad she'd come to the party tonight. He'd left Kari when her life was falling apart, and obviously she'd never forgiven him. It hadn't been his fault, not all of it, anyway.

His father had chewed his hide when Jake had suggested delaying college for a year for Kari's sake, and in the end, he had done what his father expected of him. Felt like crap about it, but he'd gone off to USC while she'd been stuck at home, helping her parents search for her runaway sister. He and all of her friends had moved on with their lives, but her dreams had been put on hold.

He was glad to see that she had a career she cared about and a man close to her heart.

## CHAPTER FIVE

Kari watched as Jake skimmed rocks into the water, the way he'd done when they were kids. How strange it was to be here on the beach with him again. So much had changed, and yet so much was familiar.

"You're still pretty good with that," she said almost grudgingly, not wanting to be free with her compliments. She wasn't a dewy-eyed teenager anymore, lusting over the football hero. She'd come here for one reason, and one reason only. She needed a story to sell to her boss, and after wracking her brains for hours, she hadn't come up with a single idea.

"It's a skill set one never loses." He was looking at the sand, searching for the perfect flat stone. "Like riding a bike."

"Yeah? Well, it's been a while, but I think I could still take you." She picked up a perfectly shaped stone before he saw it and tossed it sideways, like a Frisbee, watching it skip along the water before sinking.

"Nice. But you haven't seen anything yet." Picking up a stone, he blew on it, then whisked it through the air. When it landed on the water, it easily hopped half a dozen times.

He didn't say a word, just smirked.

"Okay, okay, you're still the best," she grumbled. "How could I ever have doubted it?"

"It's human to err," he said with a wink. "You ready to give up? You know you can't win."

"Who said?" She jutted out her chin. She bent to pick up another stone but stopped as a bittersweet memory replayed in her mind. "Jake, does this remind you of something?"

He glanced at her face, then kicked at the sand and stuffed his hands in his pockets. "You mean the last day we were at the beach together?"

"Yes." Her heartbeat quickened. Not with excitement, but the way it always did when she remembered that day. "We were here."

He looked away from her, his gaze sweeping the long beach. He didn't speak for a few seconds, and she wondered what he was thinking. Did he remember it, all of it, the joy and the sorrow, as vividly as she did?

His eyes returned to her, and he answered her unspoken question. "I remember everything about that day."

"We made love." She flicked her hand in the direction of a dune. "And we were so scared somebody would come along and catch us."

"Which made it all the more exciting." His mouth turned up in a half smile. "Of course."

"Of course." She took a few steps toward the water, blinking rapidly. She had to force down a sudden lump in her throat, not wanting Jake to know how much the memory saddened her.

"And then I took you home, and we found out..." His voice trailed off.

"That my sister was gone." Kari sucked in a painful breath. "Mom and Dad were going to take her to rehab the next morning. She'd promised to get clean."

"Was there ever any word after that day?"

"No." She bit her lip, remembering the years of endless searching, following thin leads, the dwindling hope. "Dad quit his job and spent his life savings trying to find her. Eventually, both of them gave up." She looked up at him. "I know it's not likely, but a part of me is still waiting for her to come home."

"I'm sorry I had to leave. Dad would have disowned me if I didn't take that football offer."

"I know. You would have been a fool not to accept." She shrugged and forced a small smile. "It was my tragedy, not yours."

He pushed his hands deeper into his pants pockets.

She studied the waves breaking on the shore. Anger, hurt, the bitter taste of betrayal—all those long-dead emotions rose to choke her. She swallowed hard, not wanting them to surface tonight. When she was alone, it was okay to remember, but around him, she had to carefully guard her emotions.

"Kari, why did you stop answering my calls?"

She couldn't speak right away. Bitterness tasted like bile, and she had to force it down. "I saw you," she answered when she could.

"What are you talking about?"

"After you'd been gone for a couple of months, I came to see you. To surprise you."

Jake shot her a look. "What happened?"

"You were walking arm in arm with some pretty coed. She was laughing, looking at you the way I used to." Kari swallowed the lump in her throat. She glanced at him. "That's what hurt. It took me forever to get over you, and you forgot me in a few months."

"You're wrong. I don't remember the girl." He sounded sincere, which made the situation even worse. "I loved you, Kari. I wanted us to be together."

"I followed you, and I saw you go into her dorm room. You didn't come out for at least an hour."

"Maybe we were studying," he said, and shrugged.

"Maybe you were having a good time, more likely."

"I'm sorry." He glanced at her. "I cared about you. I was just a kid, though."

"Doesn't matter." She felt cold suddenly, and rubbed her arms.

He removed his hands from his pockets and took hold of her arms, forcing her to look at him. "I wish things had turned out differently."

They held each other's gaze, and then she pulled away. "Me too."

She heard steps from behind, and she turned to see a pretty woman approaching.

"Jake. Tiffany asked me to come get you. Your dad has a little speech prepared."

Kari glanced at the two of them. "I should head out." She turned to walk away, but Jake reached out and grabbed her arm.

"Kari, this is Maria. A friend of Tiffany's."

"Nice to meet you," Kari said. Maria was beautiful, with flowing dark hair and a lush, curvaceous body. She nodded to Jake and quickly walked away.

Why had she wasted time speaking with Jake instead of working the crowd? Their past made no difference now. Her career was at stake, and that was what she needed to focus on, not rehashing memories and reopening old wounds.

Although her intention was to leave as quickly as possible, she couldn't ignore the people she knew and those who recognized her. Besides, someone might still spark an idea.

She chatted up a few people, then stopped as John Harrington began his speech. He welcomed Jake home and spoke proudly of his son's accomplishments. Then, surprising everyone, he put an arm around his younger son Brent, announcing he would be leaving soon to fly helicopters in Afghanistan.

Two men, brothers, would go off to war to fight for freedom, perhaps never to return. How many stories were there like that? Brave men and women willing to sacrifice all. Heroic in mind, if not in deeds. They were the everyday heroes, the ones who never made the news. Unless… unless…

A ripple of excitement trickled down Kari's spine. *That's it!* She had it. Her new series would be bigger than she'd imagined. Better than she'd told Tom.

# EPISODE TWO
# CHAPTER SIX

Kari had spent most of the night working on her proposal. She didn't report the news Saturday mornings, but still, she bounced out of bed at 6:00 a.m. after only a couple of hours' sleep. Once she showered and dressed, she gulped down a coffee and ate half a bagel, then headed to the station. She wanted to be there when Tom walked in.

The moment she saw him enter, she jumped up to greet him. "My forty-eight hours isn't up, but I've got something." She grinned. "It's good."

He indicated for her to follow him. They entered his office, and she waited for him to sit. "Do you want George here, or should I give it to you now?"

"You seem pretty confident about this. Let's hear it."

"Okay." She swallowed, noticing her palms were damp. So much to gain—keeping her series, possible advancement in her career—if it turned out to be as big as she thought it would.

"My idea is a hero series about the unheralded soldiers who have fought for our country, the 'everyday heroes.' As you said, the viewing audience wants hopeful, feel-good stories. They want to hear the good stuff, not the crap that happens over there. It'll be stories of incredible bravery and humanity." Her voice rose with excitement as she envisioned the depth and passion such stories would bring. "This is going to be big, Tom."

"I don't know." Tom leaned back in his chair and put his hands behind his head. "I mean, I like the idea, and it is a timely piece, but we promised Jeremy he could take over for you."

"I don't understand. You promised you'd give me a chance."

Tom closed his eyes for a second and didn't answer. Then he sat upright and looked into her face. "You can get the stories, right?"

She chewed on her bottom lip, wondering how to answer. She could pull this off, given time, but how much time would they grant her? Still, what choice did she have? Her career was at stake.

She lifted her chin and nodded. She exuded confidence when she answered, "I will get them, and that's a promise. How soon would you need them?"

"I could let you do another couple of weeks with your missing-persons series, but we want to introduce this new project by the first of the month."

"I can do that," she answered quickly. She'd work twenty-four/seven to get her new series up and running. "The time frame will work for me."

"Okay, see that it does. Keep me posted."

"Yes, boss. I'll do that." She backed out of the room as fast as she could, worried Tom would change his mind.

Her heart pounded fast with excitement as ideas raced through her mind. Instead of going home right away, she decided to make use of her time at the station and research local war heroes and set up some appointments. She encountered a few hang-ups when she told them she was from PB News and wanted to tell their stories. She tried a different approach with the others on her list, inviting them to appear on her show.

"What would I have to do?" one asked.

"Nothing, except show up and answer some prepared questions. We're looking for feel-good stories, about either you or someone you served with."

He laughed and hung up. She glanced at her phone, wondering what she'd said to elicit such a response, but after several hours, she had her answer.

No one wanted to talk to her. They all said the same thing—she shouldn't be soft-pedaling the news.

Kari rubbed her brow, trying to finger away a headache, then reached into her desk for a couple of Tylenol, tossing them down with a sip from her water bottle. She'd been so sure that it would be easy to find strong, emotional stories, week after week, but how was she to find them if no one would talk?

She tidied her desk and headed to the parking lot and her Mercedes. She'd almost made it when she heard Jeremy call her name. He was standing by his Lexus, wearing a well-cut designer suit that fit his frame perfectly. He was at least six foot two, possibly taller, lean instead of muscular, with dark, wavy hair, a tan that probably came from a tanning booth, and teeth so perfect and glaringly white she was damn near blinded. Everything about him seemed fake.

The last thing she wanted was for him to drag her into a conversation. She considered getting into her car and driving away, but he was walking toward her.

"I had a call from Tom," he said. "Guess congratulations are in order: you get to keep your Friday-night show. I know the time slot is important to you."

"Thanks. But remember, I worked hard for it." She continued walking toward her car, but Jeremy stepped in front of her, forcing her to stop.

"You're welcome to it," he said in a warm, friendly tone that didn't fool her a bit. "I offered to take over when Tom mentioned he canceled your runaway series, but in truth, I don't have time for it myself. The nightly anchor job carries a lot of responsibility."

She gritted her teeth. "I'm sure it does." She turned to leave. "I'm glad it all worked out."

"Look," Jeremy said, putting a hand on her arm. "I feel as though we got off to a bad start. Since we're going to be working together for the next few years, why don't we bury the hatchet and agree to get along?"

"Next few years? Does that mean you've signed the five-year contract?"

"Not yet, but we're negotiating."

She sighed inwardly with relief. "Fine. Hatchet buried." She could be just as phony as he could when she set her mind to it. She gave him her cool, professional smile. "So what's holding things up?"

"Minor details. Should be ironed out by the end of next week."

She swallowed hard and had a sour taste in her mouth. "I would have thought Palm Beach would be a step backward for a man on the rise like you."

"Not in the least. As you very well know, this is a substantial marketplace, and as head anchorman, I'll get all the visibility and experience that I'll need for the next step."

"Uh-huh." She kept her head held high, squared her shoulders, and looked him dead in the eye. "You know I turned down a cable news station a couple of years ago."

"Why would a smart girl like you do a dumb thing like that?"

"Personal reasons. But my day will come." She'd put her career on hold to take care of her mother and would do it again in an instant.

He flashed his smile, making her blink. "I'm sure it will. So now that you know my plans and I know yours, why don't we help each other along the way? No reason for us to be competitive, now, is there?"

"No, not at all." Since his contract was still not signed, she had a few days to change their minds.

"Glad we got that settled. Now, how about dinner sometime?"

She bristled. Who was he kidding? Did he really think she could be bought off with a dinner? If so, he knew nothing about her and how hard she intended to fight for his job. "No, thanks. I'm busy."

"Every night? Come on. Neither of us works on weekends."

"I have someone special in my life."

"You're not scared of me, are you?"

She rolled her eyes. "I'm not scared of you, Jeremy. I'm just not interested in having dinner together."

"Most women would beg for the chance."

She laughed. "You probably think I'm dying to sleep with you."

His brown eyes lingered purposely on her mouth. "What do you think all the vibes between us are about?"

She wrinkled her nose. "I'd rather sleep with my dead grandmother."

"Now who's the comedian?"

"Will you go away if I tell you I'm absolutely not interested and never will be, even if you were the last man on Earth?"

"No, you'd have to do better than that." He grinned again, and his unshakable confidence made her insides tangle up.

She snapped, "I have a boyfriend, and you aren't even in the same ballpark with him."

He cocked an eyebrow. "Believe me, I'm in everybody's ballpark."

"Excuse me." She pushed by him and got into her car, slamming the door.

As she drove away, Kari frowned. She wished she hadn't mentioned Sean, because very few people knew about him. She liked her private life to remain just that—private.

She put Jeremy out of her thoughts and focused on what was important. How was she going to get the stories she needed for her new series within two weeks' time?

## CHAPTER SEVEN

Jake groaned as he rolled out of bed. He'd spent the night at his father's rather than drive after several drinks. He also wanted to spend the weekend with his brothers. They might not have another opportunity for years.

He took his coffee outside, drank it quickly, then dove into the pool. He swam half a dozen laps, allowing his long strokes to glide through the water until he found his natural rhythm. He'd always loved the water, and the monotonous activity helped him relax.

When he came up for air, he spotted Tiffany standing inside the glass door that led to the pool. She was watching him. He climbed out of the pool, grabbed a towel, slung it over his shoulders, and headed inside.

Nightmares had stolen his sleep, and he'd had a massive headache all morning. The swim took all that away, but his good mood evaporated when Tiffany cut off his retreat.

"You could teach Maria and me to swim like that," she said with an invitation in her eyes. "I'm only good at the breaststroke."

"I don't think so." He slammed past her and took the flight of stairs two at a time.

In his bathroom, he peeled off his wet trunks and checked out his back in the mirror. It was not a pretty sight, but it could have been a hell of a lot worse. He'd been riding in the back of a truck, part of a six-vehicle convoy, when the first truck ran straight into a land mine. He could still see the searing glare of the explosion, still hear the concussive blast and the screams and shouts of the other marines.

They'd flown him to the nearest treatment center, Landstuhl in Germany, and when he'd been stabilized, he'd flown home. The nearest burn center was in Tampa, and he'd been hospitalized there for many months. That was when the real torture began, but compared with losing a limb, he'd take the burns and skin grafts anytime. He made it out whole and alive, and that was more than could be said for others in the convoy that day.

He showered and dressed, and when he got downstairs, his brothers were up and his father was flipping pancakes.

"Hey, lazy-head," his father said. "You ready for my special banana pancakes?"

"Sure am. I've been up for hours. Did fifty laps this morning when you all were cutting z's." He helped himself to another cup of coffee.

Brent looked up. "Holy shit. I've got a hangover so big my head feels like it's going to explode."

Nick groaned. "Yeah, well, you weren't up all night with a baby who decided to throw a crib party."

Cindy, Nick's wife, walked into the room carrying the sleeping baby. "She's tuckered out now after crying half the night. I had to wake her up to feed her."

Jake ran the back of his finger down his niece's soft cheek. "She's a beauty. Good thing she takes after you and not her dad."

Cindy smiled at him. "You say the nicest things. Nick should take lessons." She had the baby supported on her chest, and with one hand poured herself a coffee.

"Why don't you let Jake take Caitlin?" Nick said. "Give you a chance to have some breakfast."

"Sure." She glanced at Jake. "You want to hold her?" Cindy offered the baby.

"Not just yet." He had never been around an infant this small and was afraid his big hands would be too rough for the soft, newborn skin. "I'm afraid I might drop her."

A memory flashed in his mind of small children playing in the street, their mothers sitting in a nearby coffee shop, right near an Iraqi police station. It was an innocent, everyday scene, until a car bomb exploded, scattering body parts everywhere.

He shook the vision out of his mind. "Maybe I will, just for a sec." He took the sleeping child into the crook of his arm and kissed the peach fuzz on the top of her head. "I think she's smiling at me."

"Young babies don't smile," Tiffany said, taking a seat at the table. "She's probably passing gas."

"No, she smiles," Cindy stated with a mother's conviction.

Nick took Caitlin out of Jake's arms. "I never thought a baby could make a man burst with pride, but she's the best thing that's ever happened to me." He cradled the baby, rocking her gently in his arms. "No dates until she's twenty-one, but anything else she wants, it's hers."

Cindy laughed. "Good luck with that." She leaned down and kissed Nick's cheek.

Jake felt something stir inside him. Not envy, but almost an embarrassing love for his two brothers. Tears stung his eyes, and he coughed to cover his emotions. Hell, if they knew he was choked up, they'd really think he was a pansy, and he'd never hear the end of it.

"You know, Dad, I better hold off on those pancakes. I have to run home first. I have a couple of things to take care of, but I'll be back by noon."

Maria walked in at that moment, wearing a bikini. She smiled at the men. "Good morning, everyone. Did I hear someone mention pancakes?"

Brent lifted an eyebrow and gave Jake a meaningful glance. "Sure you don't want to stay a little longer?"

Jake nodded, stealing a quick look at what he'd be missing. The luscious Maria filled that bikini like nobody's business.

She spun around and looked at him. "You're leaving?"

"Just for a few hours. I'll be back for lunch."

She pouted. "Okay, but hurry back. I hear you're a very good swimmer."

"I'll do that." His brothers looked at him as if he were crazy, but he couldn't tell them he had a dog at home. He'd left Muffin plenty of dry food and water, a cage to sleep in, and a mat on the balcony to do his business, but he couldn't leave the little guy alone for long.

Half an hour later, he entered the apartment, and the dog did happy circles around him and tried to jump into his arms.

·

"Hey, Muff." He picked the dog up and cradled him for a few minutes. "How was your first night in your new home? Nothing much to destroy, is there, boy?"

Jake took him downstairs, figuring they could take a short walk and grab breakfast. He found a place where he could sit outdoors and have his bacon and eggs, and wolfed it down like a starving man. Muffin had his own helping of bacon.

As he sat, he tried to call Kari twice, eager to learn if she had any news for him regarding Shane. He also hoped she had her own problems sorted out so she could help him with his. It was a selfish thought, but if it kept Brent out of harm's way, he would go to any length.

He paid his bill and picked up Muffin, thinking about that conversation at the beach the night before. So she had seen him with one of the cheerleaders. Hell, he didn't even know which one. He'd dated a couple of girls that first semester, but they hadn't meant anything to him, and it all could have been avoided if Kari had only let him know she was coming. Their lives might have turned out so differently. He might never have gone to war, and they could be married with three kids by now.

∽

When Kari returned home, she noticed that Jake had called several times. She had done a preliminary search for Shane, which had come up empty, but hadn't had a chance to dig deeper.

She was about to call him back, when he knocked on her door. Kari sighed, knowing it was him without looking, and thinking she might need to change her address after all, just so she could go about her business.

She opened the door. "You need to call first. I can't have you dropping in all the time."

"I did call. Twice." He walked in, and Muffin sniffed Kari's legs, then licked at her toes. At least he didn't bite her.

"Stop that, Muff," Jake said, tugging at the dog's leash. "Am I interrupting anything? Is your boyfriend back?"

"No, I just returned from the news station."

He took a seat without an invitation. "Did you figure things out?"

She kicked off her shoes and took the opposite chair. "I did. Last night when your father was talking, I had a light-bulb moment." She grinned. "For the past few years, I had a successful runaway series and I reunited young people with their families. Of course, I had hoped to find Alaina, but that never happened. Anyway, Tom, my producer, told me the other day that he was cutting the show, saying people wanted 'feel-good stories,' and gave me forty-eight hours to come up with something else."

"That was short notice."

"You got that right." She licked her lips. "I was under the gun, but I came up with a brilliant idea, if I do say so myself. A returning-war-hero series."

He looked perplexed. "What is that, exactly?"

"Stories about enlisted men and women who did something brave or heroic and never received recognition."

Jake didn't say a word, but he didn't look excited about the idea.

"You don't like it? You don't think it'll work?"

"It might. I don't know. What kind of stories do you plan to tell?" He picked Muffin off the floor and petted him. "There're plenty out there, but they're not exactly upbeat, if you know what I mean."

"Come on. There must be thousands of good stories. Stories of outstanding bravery or surviving the odds. That's what I'm looking for."

"Well, every man and woman who returns is a survivor. Right, Muff?" He nuzzled the dog's neck. "Go talk to them. You want the truth—there's plenty of that."

"Jake, I tried calling several people today. They wouldn't talk to me." She sighed. "I'm not looking for recipients of the Medal of Honor. I'm only looking for something newsworthy. Heroic or otherwise. They didn't have to throw themselves in front of a tank. Although"—she paused and tapped her lip—"that would make for a good story too." She leaned forward. "You must remember someone who deserves honoring. Just a name. That's all I need."

"Can't think of anyone offhand."

"I have to have this up and running by the first of the month." She rotated her shoulder muscles to shake off a growing anxiety. "I thought this would be easy, with all the servicemen and women returning right now. Figured I'd have my pick of stories." Yet no one was talking. What *did* happen over there? "I have very little time."

When he didn't reply, she pulled her chair a few inches closer, her eyes searching his. "You must have contacts or know how to find them."

He ran a hand over his unshaven jaw. "Sorry. I can't think of anyone 'hero worthy.'"

"But you *must.*" She knew she shouldn't badger him, but he'd done two tours, for heaven's sake. He had to know something. And, dammit, he'd lied about that pretty coed, and likely there'd been plenty of others. He owed her. Big time.

"Nope. Sorry."

She sat back in her chair and raised her eyes to the ceiling. If he wouldn't help her, where would she get her stories in such a short amount of time?

"Hey, this is probably not a good time to ask, but did you have a chance to research Shane's whereabouts? I know you've been busy."

She stood and began pacing. Muffin yipped at her, but she ignored the dog, too agitated to stay in one place. "No, I'll get to it, don't worry. But if I do this for you, can't you help me with my problem? Is that too much to ask?"

"I wish I could, but I can't."

Kari looked into his eyes, trying to reach inside him for something. Anything. It was like facing a brick wall, there was so little emotion in his eyes. Down at the beach, he hadn't shown any real remorse either, not for leaving her, cheating on her, and breaking her heart. "I looked up local heroes on the Internet, and most everybody hung up on me. You'd think I was asking for security secrets, not for nice stories about heroic feats."

Jake looked down at his lap, his eyes on Muffin. "My memory is fine with things that took place before the war and since, but some of the stuff over there is all screwed up in my brain."

"Just try, please? A name, that's all I'm asking."

"A lot of people aren't going to open up to a journalist. We had our fill of them overseas. People were being killed, women and children slaughtered, bombs exploding, heads flying. Saw a child cut down right in front of one of them, and this big-ass news reporter didn't do a damn thing to help. Just kept the film rolling."

"That was his job, Jake."

He looked everywhere but at her. "I'm not saying what journalists do isn't risky—it is—but they don't get their hands dirty. The enlisted men and women are the action heroes, putting their lives on the line every minute of every day. And not for a story, either. They do it for all sorts of reasons—some good, some bad. They don't expect commendations or medals; they don't expect much at all."

"Jake. This is why I want to tell their stories. Someone should."

"Is it for them? Or for you?"

Kari felt as if she'd been hit in the stomach. She backed away. "You think so little of me?"

He looked ashamed for a minute, before meeting her gaze again. "Forget it. I'll look for Shane myself."

## CHAPTER EIGHT

Jake picked up Muffin and left, feeling even less a hero than ever before. She might be upset with him, but he was doing her a favor. When it came to live action in Iraq, his mind was full of holes. Flashes came to him like staccato fire, not the whole picture. He'd try to drudge up a name or two later to help her, but right now, his priority didn't concern rescuing Kari from the situation she'd put herself in.

He jumped in his car and drove it as if a demon chased him. Unfortunately, his thoughts kept up. He'd hurt Kari again, and that hadn't been his intention, but hell, he was right about journalists. They didn't do—they observed. Sometimes they slanted the news. If he were to talk about the war, which he was not ready to do, he'd want to make sure the truth was told. Not some damn fairy tale with a happy ending.

He had a bigger priority than her stories, a last chance to convince Brent not to go to war. The kid was tough, but he had no idea what was in store for him. It drained a man and took his soul. Although Jake had never been to Afghanistan, he'd heard from marines who had that it was a harsh country. It could kill a man.

When he arrived back at his father's house, everyone was at the pool. He went upstairs to his old room and put on his swimming trunks and a white T-shirt to cover his back. He wasn't trying to hide his injuries; he just wanted to forget about them.

"Hey, everybody. I'm back." He shrugged off his guilt, not wanting to think about Kari. She'd land on her feet, he was sure.

"Jake, hi." Maria held her bikini top over her breasts, and he noticed the ties were undone. "You missed out on some great pancakes this morning."

"I'm sure I did." His gaze roamed over her. She had a ripe, lush body, all curves and ass. "You look like you're getting burned."

She smiled. "Want to put some lotion on my back? If it's not too much trouble?"

Brent grinned at him. "If it is, I can do it. Front and back."

Maria laughed. "Back will be fine, and Jake's already got the bottle in his hand. You snooze, you lose."

Jake sat down next to Maria and squeezed out a generous amount of lotion. He rubbed his hands together, then slowly applied the cream to her shoulders and her back, going lower with every stroke. When he reached her bottom, he gave it a light smack and she giggled.

"What was that for?"

"For being so damn tantalizing." He jumped up and dove into the pool.

When his head came up, he saw the knowing grins on everyone's faces. "Come on, guys. Stop lazing around and sucking up beers. Who wants to play volleyball?"

Nick tossed him a ball and jumped in. Brent followed. They started a lively game, which included smashing the ball at each other and a whole lot of splashing.

Later, Tiffany brought out a pitcher of margaritas while his father got the grill going. The three brothers climbed out of the pool to towel off.

Jake grabbed a beer from a cooler and tossed one to each of the men.

While the women brought out the food, the men sat around sipping their brews, enjoying a lively conversation spiced with a healthy dose of brotherly bickering. They ate grilled steaks, corn on the cob, baked beans, and potato salad, followed by bowls of mango ice cream. It was a perfect lazy, peaceful day.

The kind of day when one could forget about war, forget that life could change in an instant, that many everyday warriors would never return or have one more afternoon to enjoy with their family and friends. This could be Brent's last.

Jake could feel himself sinking deeper, his mood shifting to black. He had so many things to say and so little time to say them, but wisely kept them inside. Finally, the sun gave way to the moon, and Cindy put Caitlin to bed. The women retired indoors.

The men talked football, the draft picks, and the usual bullshit that a father and his sons were comfortable with. The men Jake knew, including his family, didn't talk about their feelings or let on if they were hurting. They just sucked it up.

But Jake couldn't hold back any longer. Between the alcohol, his exhaustion, and the comfort of being with his family, his tongue loosened.

"You ever grab a burning man from the back of an AAV—that's an amphibious assault vehicle—and seen the man torn in half?"

The group went silent.

"Happened to me. There was an ambush, and these marines were seriously burned. The medic tried to get them out, and I stepped in to help. I took hold of this poor bastard by the arms and gave a tug. I wanted to slide him out gently, and his torso came away from the rest of his body. Damnedest thing I ever saw."

Jake tipped back his beer as only the sound of cicadas interrupted the silence.

"Well, that's a real pleasant memory," Brent finally said. "Thanks for sharing."

There wasn't much to say after that.

∼

Jake spent the greater part of the following morning in a do-or-die effort to talk Brent out of flying for the military. Career-wise, Brent wasn't losing anything, but what concerned Jake was the danger his brother would face every minute in that harsh, formidable country.

Brent had a late-afternoon flight, and Jake and his father drove him to the airport.

During the drive, Brent turned to him. "I know I'm going to ask you something that won't be easy, but I have nowhere else to turn."

"You know I'll do anything for you," Jake answered. "Ask away."

"Find Shane for me. What's left of his family is here. He's probably not too far away."

"I'll do my best, but you've been looking yourself for several months now. I probably won't have any better luck than you."

"I was concentrating my search in L.A., figuring he would have gone back to California after walking out of Walter Reed. I left no stone unturned, which leads me to think he's here."

Jake nodded. "I'll search, Brent. On one condition."

"What's that?" Brent's chin lifted as he faced him.

"That when you go off to fight the Taliban, you remember to come back home."

"Yes, sir. You bet your ass I will."

Jake and his father hugged Brent and said their good-byes, and with a heavy heart, Jake watched Brent head for the security checkpoint.

Jake didn't stay long at his father's house, as he needed to get back to his apartment and Muffin. They went for a nice walk around the town center, and, as usual, the three-legged little guy was the center of attention. Although he'd lost his leg only a few weeks before, he managed to bounce along just fine, wagging his tail, making people smile. He loved everyone, with the possible exception being Kari.

Jake grabbed a takeout dinner and headed back upstairs to his condo. Instead of hitting floor number three, he punched four instead. He had said some unkind things to Kari, even if half of it had been true. Still, it nagged at him and he wanted to clear the air.

He knocked, and she opened the door a crack. "Was there something else you forgot to say? Besides my being a user, what more is there?"

"I was harsh on you, and I'm sorry." Muffin yipped and bared his teeth.

She began to shut the door.

"Kari, I didn't mean to insult you. I was just pissed. You seem to want something from me that I can't give you."

She didn't reply, just looked at him with her big green eyes that could never hide her emotions. Right now, they expressed her disappointment in him.

"Let me in so we can talk."

"No. I don't want you here. Never again. I mean it this time. I'm through with you. Please don't call or knock on my door again."

"Shit. Give me a break. What did I ever do to you that was so bad?"

Her pretty features hardened, and her eyes threw daggers. "Leave and don't come back."

Muffin jumped out of his arms and ran inside Kari's apartment. She stepped away from the door, and Jake ran in, trying to chase the animal down.

"Muffy, come here. Be good."

Kari grabbed a broom from the laundry room and tried to corner the mutt, but he kept growling and lunging at her. Finally, she tossed the broom at him and ran for the couch. She stood on the pillows. "Get him out of here, Jake. Jesus! Between work, you, and your dog, my life is going insane."

Jake bent down on one knee and snapped the leash on the dog.

"Go. Get out. Please just get out." She burst into tears.

Jake went over to Kari and put a hand on her arm, wishing he could hold her instead. His throat tightened and his chest hurt; he hated the sight of her tears. "It's okay now. Come down from there."

She shook her head as tears ran down her cheeks.

He put a friendly arm around her waist, trying to calm her down. "Please, Kari. Don't cry."

She blinked and sniffed back tears. She swiped her cheeks and finally stepped down. Tears filled her eyes once more, and she began to sob.

He put an arm around her shoulders and gave her a hug. "There, there. I don't know why you're so upset, and I'm sorry for all the mean things I said. I didn't mean them. I know you're a very caring person. Your problem is that you care too much."

Her sobs grew louder.

"Look, even Muffin is kissing your toes. We all love you. Nobody thinks you're a user, or a heartless journalist. Nobody who knows you, that's for sure."

She sniffed.

"Kari, forgive me, please?"

"How can I? You wouldn't have said it if you hadn't thought there was an element of truth."

"I know you'd do pretty much anything to protect your career, but nothing dishonorable. I can tell you're passionate about this subject, and if I can I'll even help you find some stories."

Kari lifted her head to look at him.

"Jake, do you mean that? You'll help me?"

"Yes. Dad and I took Brent to the airport, and I'm a little down at the moment. Don't want you mad at me too."

"I guess that means I'll have to see you again. Doesn't it?"

He smiled. "We could do it by e-mail, but it wouldn't be as much fun."

"I don't want to have fun with you." She wiped her eyes again. "Even if we do this, we can never be friends."

"Why, Kari? Why do you hate me so much?"

She didn't answer, only shook her head, and he could see tears spring to her eyes.

"I let you down once," he said in a low voice. "I won't do it again."

He picked up Muffin and headed for the door. "Where's your boyfriend? How come I never see him around?"

"He's a freelance photographer. Travels a lot."

"Look, I have an idea. Since you're alone tonight, why don't I take you out for dinner? It'll give us time to talk things through, maybe figure something out."

He could sense her resistance.

"Purely business. I swear."

"I guess we could."

"I'll pick you up in an hour. We'll figure it out together. I promise."

# CHAPTER NINE

Jake knocked on Kari's door at seven sharp. She'd put on a skirt and blouse and looked casual but pretty. They took the elevator to the lobby, discussing the pluses of living in an area where a car wasn't needed to go to dinner or a movie. Everything was right outside their door.

"So what's it going to be?" Jake asked. "Seafood or steak?"

"How about City Cellar? It's got a varied menu. We can make up our minds when we get there." Kari walked along at a fast pace, looking like a woman on a mission. He knew she was stressed.

He didn't know what had caused her meltdown earlier or what had happened in her past, but he didn't want to pry any more than he wanted her to meddle in his personal affairs. The past was what she said—better left behind.

Hell, the future had enough problems.

He'd help her if he could, but he couldn't promise anything. He had loved Kari once and still felt bad for the way things had ended between them. If he could get her a story or two, it might help even the score.

They had to wait for a table, so they had a drink at the bar. A few people recognized Kari and came over to speak to her but mostly left them alone. "Does that happen often?" he asked.

"All the time." She ran a finger up and down the stem of her martini glass. "It's a small price to pay to be a local celebrity. Truthfully, I'd miss it if it went away."

"Well, we're going to see that doesn't happen, right?"

"We're going to try." She sipped her cosmopolitan, then pushed it aside. "So tell me about your memory loss. How does it work?"

"Wish I knew." He scratched his chin, wondering what to tell her. "I remember most things fine, but when it comes to Iraq and the events that led up to combat, it gets haywire. Like, when I'm in a nightmare, things flash at me. I don't see the collective whole, only bits and pieces."

"Can you separate what's real and what's not?"

"No." He glanced around the bar, avoiding her eyes. "That's bad enough, but worse is when I feel this terrible darkness coming on and know I can't climb out of it." He took a sip of his scotch. "Wouldn't wish it on anybody."

"Are you on medication?"

"Doctors at Walter Reed put me on Prozac. It doesn't help much." He shifted uncomfortably, wanting to change the conversation but eager to keep the line of communication open. "The moods come and go, and I have learned to just ride them out."

"That's awful." She put a hand over his, then quickly removed it. That simple touch warmed him. He always felt so cold inside.

"Don't you wish sometimes that you could turn back time and make different choices?" she asked with a sad smile. "If you could, would you still have gone off to war?"

"That's a tough question. I'm not sure how to answer."
"Off the record."
"At the time, I didn't feel I had a choice." He told her about his fiancée and how that was the catalyst that sent him off to war. "I went because of Cathy, and to do anything less would have been unthinkable. But now, knowing everything I do, I'm not sure I agree with our decision. It was supposed to be a quick in-and-out, then bring the troops home. Obviously, it didn't turn out that way. The war moved from one troubled area to another."

"My feelings are mixed also, but I just report news and keep my opinions to myself. Still, we have to live with our decisions and learn from them." She took a sip from her drink, then added, "Like when I didn't go to college. We didn't find my sister, and my parents practically spent every last cent trying. We did what we thought best, and now it's too late for regrets."

"Let's lighten up this conversation, shall we?" He took a sip of scotch, then pushed away his glass. "Tell me more about this interesting boyfriend of yours. How did you meet him, and how long have you been dating?"

"He's a globe-trotting photographer and worked on *Planet Earth*. He's got an amazing career." She smiled. "We've been together for two years. I interviewed him for a special report. And as they say, the rest is history." The buzzer started flashing, indicating their table was ready. "Have we paid for our drinks?"

"I'll get it. You get the table."

They were seated at a cozy round booth that offered both privacy and a choice view of the room. As they perused the menu, Jake continued the conversation.

"Two years is a long time, and yet you don't spend much time together."

"It works for us."

"What about a family? When you were young, you always loved kids. Couldn't pass a baby without getting all goo-goo-eyed."

"Jake, I don't want to talk about it, okay? Let's leave it at that." He could hear the heat in her voice. "All I have now is my career."

He opened his mouth to speak, but a couple walked over. "Ms. Winslow," the man said, "I'm John Doyles, and this is my wife, Nancy. We watch your morning news, and we're big fans of yours."

"Thank you, John, Nancy. This is Jake Harrington, an old friend." She gave them both a warm smile while shaking their hands. "It's so nice to hear that you enjoy *Palm Beach News*."

Nancy nodded. "We do, except for that new anchorman. He's too slick, if you ask me."

"Now, Nancy. You don't want to offer an opinion like that," John said.

Kari's smile grew bigger. "I appreciate your coming over to say hello. What are you having so I can buy you a drink?"

"That won't be necessary," John answered before his wife could speak. "It's been a real pleasure meeting you." The couple walked away.

"You introduced me as an old friend," Jake said. "I hope to be friends going forward. With Sean too. He sounds like an interesting person."

"He is, and he doesn't have many friends here. Not with his traveling and all."

The waiter came over, and they ordered dinner. While they waited for the food to arrive, he told her about Nick's promotion to VP at his bank. Told her about Cindy and the baby. She got quiet again, so he shut up.

The waiter brought their appetizer—a dozen oysters and two plates. Kari squeezed lemon on the oysters, put spicy sauce on her plate, and dove in. He followed suit.

"Love these Blue Points." She slurped one down, and he watched her lick the edges of her mouth. She was getting ready for the second.

"I didn't realize that eating oysters could be so sexy." He grinned. "Maybe we should order another dozen."

She gave him an annoyed look. "Don't flirt with me."

He went back to eating, feeling as though he had to tiptoe around her—it was like walking on friggin' eggshells. He hadn't meant anything by the comment and had to be careful about every little remark. Maybe she felt guilty having dinner with him.

Better to stick to business and keep his thoughts to himself. "I might know someone who can help," Jake said. "He was in the burn unit at Walter Reed."

"Do you keep in touch?"

"Not really, but I can get his number."

"Thanks. I appreciate your trying to help me." She looked over his shoulder and nodded to someone behind him. "Excuse me for a moment." She got up and walked over to a table in the corner, where a middle-aged couple sat. She shook the man's hand and greeted his wife.

When she returned, Jake frowned. "Who was that?"

"Congressman Charlie Burns. Don't you know him? He has quite the reputation about town."

"I haven't been home long enough to know all the local gossip and wouldn't be interested if I did." His mood was sinking fast, and he could feel the blackness coming. It normally started with a slight headache, and then his vision blurred. He rubbed his eyes as if to clear them.

"Are you all right?" she asked.

"I'm fine, but I hope that rack of lamb arrives soon." As he spoke, the waiter arrived with their dinner. He ate quickly and tried to keep the conversation lively, but it was an effort that showed.

"You're not well," Kari said. She raised a hand, caught the waiter's eye, and asked for the check. "I'll get this. Go on home." She touched his arm. "I'll call you tomorrow."

He had difficulty getting to his feet, and she jumped up to help him. "Wait, Jake. I'll walk you back."

He pushed her hand away. "I'm all right. I need air. That's all."

While she waited to pay the bill, he fought his way out of the restaurant and to the street. By now, there was a dull roar in his head and he could see vivid flashes before his eyes. He stumbled to a park bench and put his head in his hands.

He sucked in deep breaths, trying to keep the flashing memories at bay. Pain shot through his temple as a kaleidoscope of colors exploded in his brain. He opened his eyes, and Kari's face appeared.

"Jake." She touched his shoulder. "Come on. Walk with me."

"Go, Kari. I'll be all right in a minute." He didn't want her here. He needed a dark room and to be alone.

"No," she answered stubbornly. "I'm going to see you home." She put an arm around his waist and pulled him up.

"If you don't move of your own accord, I'm going to call for help."

He walked slowly, with her support. Eventually, they reached the apartment building and she led him inside. "Give me your key," she ordered, and he fumbled in his pants pockets.

"Here." His fingers shook as he handed her the key. Shame washed over him. He was pathetic, weak. Not half the man he used to be.

She opened his door and helped him through. Muffin jumped up in excitement, nearly knocking Kari off her feet. She staggered, and the poodle snarled, trying to nip at her.

"Muffin. Behave." Jake put his hand down for the dog to lick, and Muffin left Kari alone.

"Jake? Where's your bed?" She glanced around the empty apartment. It was completely bare.

He nodded to the mattress in the master bedroom. "That's it for now."

She took his arm and led him toward the makeshift bed. "You need to lie down until you feel better. I'll stay with you."

"Are you propositioning me?" He gave her a lopsided smile, which took great effort.

Kari groaned. "Lie down and I'll undress you."

"That sounds like an offer too good to refuse."

"Don't try any funny stuff. This wouldn't be a trick, would it?"

He grimaced. "I wish it were." He lay down and closed his eyes. "Sorry about dinner. There's no rhyme or reason to the flashbacks. I just see stuff. Sometimes it's a jumble; other times, it seems so real."

"Like what?"

"I saw the face of a marine, a young woman with a small child at home. She used to cry every night for her daughter." He ran a hand over his face. "Don't know what she was doing there."

"What happened to her?"

He opened his eyes, and Kari's face came into focus. "I'm not sure. But I remember some of it." He blinked. "The village was destroyed."

He pushed himself up and tried to stand, but his legs were useless. "You might want to write this down. My memory might be coming back."

## CHAPTER TEN

"I can do better than that. I have a tape recorder in my bag."

"In a minute. I still need a minute."

"Do you want some water?"

"Thanks."

She returned with a full glass of ice water and handed it to him. He downed it at once.

"Another?" she asked.

"No, I'm good."

"Can I make you comfortable?" She knew she was acting like a mother hen, but the thought of a story had her mind doing cartwheels. Perhaps Jake might remember more than he realized, and if it had a happy ending, she could use it. She didn't even care if Jake accused her of "using him" again. They had agreed to help each other, and he'd offered to get her stories.

"Would you like me to help you out of your clothes? Do you have a robe to slip on?"

"I'm fine. Stop fussing." He had his knees up to his chest, resting his arms on top. "The weird stuff has subsided, but it drains me. That's all."

Kari kept one eye on the dog as she sat next to Jake. Muffin was very protective of his master, and she wasn't in the mood to tangle with him.

Muffin put his head on Jake's thigh and rested it there.

"Does this stuff happen often?" she asked Jake.

"I used to get them every day, but now several days go by and I'm fine."

Her conscience niggled at her, but she wrestled with it and won. "I have the tape recorder up and running. What do you remember about the marine?" she asked gently. "What's her name? What was she like?"

"Jamie Parsons. And I remember how tough she pretended to be, but at night, we could all hear her cry for the little girl she'd left behind." He sat up on one elbow and looked at Kari. "She'd have these red, puffy eyes in the morning and say she had allergies. Didn't fool anybody."

"I can only imagine how difficult it was for her," Kari replied. "Probably thought she'd never see her child again."

"Yes, but a lot of men were in that same position. For whatever reason, she signed up for the Marines and should have realized that this could happen. Not that I didn't feel bad for her, but it came with the job."

She didn't offer an opinion, so he carried on. "Anyway, we were stationed near a town with a lot of civilians, and it was pretty tough on her because there were lots of kids, orphans mostly. They didn't have any shoes or proper clothing. We'd see them running down the streets, begging for money, and some of the marines would give them gum or chocolates, whatever they had in their pockets."

"That must have broken her heart."

"Yes, well, one little girl was about the same age as her daughter. Can't remember her daughter's name. But this girl had one leg shorter than the other. She walked with a limp and was skinny as a skeleton. Her hair was long and natty, but she had the saddest, sweetest face you could ever imagine."

He closed his eyes for a moment, and Kari wondered if the memory was going to trigger another episode.

"Don't talk about it if it's too hard. You can always finish the story another time."

"No. I'm fine." He took a couple of deep breaths and ran a hand over his face. "I just got another one of those visions. I should be used to them by now."

He didn't say anything for the longest time, and she was afraid she'd lost him again. He had a frozen look on his face and slumped back down.

"What is it?" she said sharply. Fear leaped inside her chest. She didn't know how to handle a person with stress disorder and was afraid that if she questioned him, his condition could get worse. Even though she'd once hated him, she didn't want to see him hurt.

He blinked and looked up. Blinked again. Finally, he pulled himself together and managed to sit up. "I'm okay." He swallowed hard. "Sometimes when she was off-duty, Jamie would take food to this little girl's family. She'd even buy clothes for the girl on the black market. Then, one day, we were on patrol and nearly blown off our feet by a huge explosion. Suicide bomber in the marketplace."

"Jamie? Did she live?"

"I'm not sure, Kari. But I think so."

"Do you remember anything else?"

"No, that's all."

She licked her lips, as her mouth was bone dry. "Good job, Jake. You remembered quite a lot."

"This is just bits and pieces, stuff that's in my head and needs to come out. I don't want you to use it, okay? My memory can't be trusted."

"That's fine, Jake." She clicked off the recorder. "I'm sure that you have dozens of memories buried inside that head of yours." She touched his hand. "You'll get there, eventually. You're one of the strongest men I know."

"I'm not feeling too strong right now. If you don't mind, I think I'll call it a night. I'm exhausted, and I'm going in to the office tomorrow. First day back."

She stood. "Will you be all right by yourself?"

"Sure. I'm tough, remember?"

"I'm glad your memory is coming back, even if it's not complete. It's a good start."

"I'd like to hear the tape again; it might jog something else. Can you leave it?"

She nodded. "Sure thing. Good night, Jake."

## CHAPTER ELEVEN

The following morning, Kari headed straight for Tom's office to tell him she was working on a story and promised more to come. It wasn't a lie, exactly, because she *was* working on a story, one that might help jiggle Jake's mind and open it up. With any luck, he'd soon remember other names and events that had ended well.

"I'm glad to hear it," he said. "Once you've made headway on the first story, we'll go over it together. Don't let me down on this, Kari. I've already told Jeremy he's not getting the spot, and he didn't take it well."

"He said he was happy I was keeping that time slot, since he's joining our team as the nightly newscaster." She locked eyes with Tom. "He said he was signing a five-year contract. I thought I might still be in the running once his first year expires."

"I never said that. You assumed as much."

"Tom, I'm qualified. I have a huge following in this town, and I've upped our ratings on every show I've been on."

"I know." He chewed on the end of his unlit cigar. "It's true, but I don't think you're ready for the nightly news. He's older, more experienced—that's why we chose him." His voice was kind when he stabbed the knife further in.

"If Jeremy agrees to the conditions of the contract, the job is his."

Her stomach knotted, but she knew when to back down. "In that case, I wish you both the best of luck. As far as my new series is concerned, it's going to be better than good. That's a promise."

She left his office and headed for the studio. She had only a few minutes until she went live with the noon show. She'd show Tom and Jeremy, and the entire studio, that not only did she deserve the number-one anchor spot, but she was the best person for the job.

As if her thoughts conjured him, Jeremy appeared at her side, keeping pace as she strode quickly down the hall. "Hey, I saw you talking to Tom. So what have you got planned for your Friday nights?"

"You'll know when you see it." She didn't turn her head.

"There's no need for secrets. I'm on your side, in case you didn't know, and I'm willing to help."

"I don't need your help, but thanks." She glanced at him. "By the way, if you ever find that you need some kind of assistance, no matter how small, I'm the person to go to." She gave him a curt smile. "Now that we're friends, of course."

"Shame about your runaway series. I know about your sister, and I guess you were hoping she might contact you if she was watching. Guess that dream's gone."

The blood drained from her face. She could almost feel it seeping from her pores, and tears were close behind. She wouldn't cry. No way would she give him that satisfaction.

"You really are a prick, aren't you?"

There was a nasty gleam in his eyes. "Don't get too full of yourself, Kari. I've decided to sign the contract." He added for emphasis, "A five-year contract. You can have your Friday-night special."

She watched him walk away. Taking a deep breath, she tried to gain control of her emotions. He wanted to upset her, and he had. What she couldn't figure out was why. If he signed the contract, he had already won. She was no threat to him, so why did he act as if she were?

∽

Kari had a few ideas for a couple of shows and couldn't wait to get home and research them more thoroughly. She'd discovered several organizations online that would tie in with her returning-war-hero series, and she was eager to set up interviews. She'd also started a file for Jake with a list of numbers and transitional houses where Shane might have sought shelter. She intended to deliver the list to him today.

As good as her intentions were, a frantic call from her best friend, Lisa Davis, put her plans on hold.

"David's having an affair," Lisa cried over the phone. "I don't know what to do."

Her husband was a doctor, and they had been married for eight years, with darling twin boys.

"No, Lisa. He wouldn't." Kari couldn't believe it. David was a kind, gentle man. Not exactly exciting or much to look at, but a loving father and husband. Or so she'd thought. "Are you sure?"

"Yes. The phone rang this morning when I was getting out of the shower. David was in the bedroom, and I heard him answer. He was whispering and it made me curious, so I opened the door a crack and listened."

"Well, you only heard one side of the conversation, so you might have misunderstood."

"I heard enough," Lisa answered. "He said he was leaving for the hospital in a few minutes and he'd call her back. Then he said, 'Love you' and hung up. He wouldn't say that to anyone, not even his own mother. Not like that. It was the tone of voice he used to use when he was romantic with me."

"Oh, Lisa, honey. I'm sorry. What are you going to do? Did you confront him?"

"No. I couldn't. I stayed in the bathroom until he said he was leaving. I just said good-bye through the door, then I broke down."

"Look, why don't you come over for a few hours? Bring the boys. Better yet, if you need a place to crash for a few days, consider my spare bedroom yours."

"Thanks, Kari," she sobbed. "I'll see if I can get a babysitter on short notice. I don't want to bring the kids, not like this. I can't let them see me cry."

"Whatever works best. But come, okay?"

A couple of hours later, Lisa knocked on her door. It was obvious from her tear-streaked face that she was still a wreck. Kari had a bottle of chilled wine waiting, and she sat her friend down, poured them both a drink, and comforted her as best she could.

"Don't call David tonight and don't go home. Let him worry," Kari suggested.

"I can't do that, can I? What about the kids?"

"They'll be fine. I'm sure everyone can survive one night without you."

"I don't know. I should at least let him know I'm here. In case something happens."

"Yes, that's best."

Lisa used her cell to call David, saying she wouldn't be coming home that night. "He wanted to know what was wrong. Can you believe it?" She gulped her wine and looked at Kari with reddened eyes filled with sadness.

"Men are fools. What can I say?"

Lisa sat back down and looked at her. "Have you ever really been in love? I don't mean what you have with Sean. You guys are great together, but I mean the heart-stopping, can't-breathe-without-you kind."

"I do love Sean, but I know what you mean." Kari thought of her youthful feelings for Jake. "I was passionately in love once. That was a mistake, never to be repeated." She clearly remembered the euphoria, the heady bliss of falling in love, and all its alluring magic. But she also remembered the sick despair, the emptiness, when it ended.

"Why? What happened?"

"After my sister disappeared, he left for college. I knew he had to leave, and I didn't resent him for going, but he moved on a little too quickly. I went up to see him, and he didn't know I was coming. Found him with a pretty coed, even saw him go into her dorm." She felt a pang even now, simply remembering it. "I was two months pregnant, and I had come to tell him." Kari shook her head. "I headed back to the airport without confronting him, and I was crying so hard I couldn't see the road. There was an accident, and I lost the baby."

Lisa put her hand over Kari's. "Oh my gosh. I'm so sorry, sweetie."

"Yes, well, that was a long time ago."

"Maybe if you had told him…"

"I know. I felt like I hated him for a long, long time, but he wasn't to blame. It's just that I don't ever want to feel that kind of helplessness again. I don't want to love someone that much."

"I think that's sad," Lisa said. "Love is the greatest feeling in the world."

"Yes." Kari studied her friend's face. "But is it worth this kind of pain?"

"Definitely. No doubt about it. You really need to find the right guy. I don't think Sean's the man for you."

"Of course he is. He's perfect."

Lisa shook her head. "He's never around, and when he's gone for months on end, you don't seem to miss him that much."

"I'm busy, that's why." Kari stood. "I'm starved, and I know a great place for dinner."

They went downstairs to a Greek tavern, knocked back a few ouzos, then returned home, arm in arm.

Back at her place, Kari told Lisa about her problems at work. "They cut my show."

"Your runaway show?" Lisa gasped. "They can't do that! It's the best thing on TV. And you've helped find kids who have been missing for years."

"They can and they did. Tom, the producer, said it was losing ratings and everybody was tired of it. They want something new. Something fresh."

"What are you going to do?"

"Give him what he wants." She told Lisa about Jake returning from war and moving downstairs and how they were going to help each other.

Lisa's eyes grew round and lit up with glee. She snapped her fingers and grinned. "You still have feelings for this guy. He's the one."

Kari shook her head in denial. "Forget it. He ruined my life."

Lisa smiled gently. "We've been friends for many years, but you never told me about him before."

"It's not something I talk about, but you shared your grief tonight and I shared mine." She stood, ready to call it a night. "Are you ready to face your husband in the morning?"

"I am. I'm not giving him up. He's worth fighting for."

"I agree. You have too much to lose and far more to gain." She firmly believed that some marriages were worth fighting for, especially when children were involved. "David's a good man, even if he has made a terrible mistake. I'm sure he loves you still."

Kari made the sofa bed for Lisa and promised to keep in touch. She'd lost too many people in her life; her friends were all she had.

# CHAPTER TWELVE

Jake returned to work, feeling like a duck out of water. His specialty had been corporate law, and he'd always enjoyed the challenging work, putting in the long hours necessary to get himself on the partner track. But he wasn't sure that had the same allure as before.

As he walked down the hallway toward his old office, his colleagues greeted him. Some of the women hugged him; most of the men gave him hearty handshakes. A few slapped him on the back, until someone remembered he'd been in the hospital with serious burns, and then backed off, afraid to touch him in case he crumpled like a dry leaf.

Jim Sheridan, one of the senior partners, walked into his office and dropped off a stack of files. After a cordial greeting, he said, "Thought you should spend the next few days familiarizing yourself with some of your old clients. Take as much time as you need to get back up to speed." He studied Jake for a second, as if unsure how to proceed. "Everyone around here is behind you a hundred percent. You did a fine thing for your country."

"Thank you, sir."

"You'll want to catch up on what's been going on here for the past four years. If you have any questions or concerns, just ask."

"I'll be sure to do that." Trying to act nonchalant, Jake flexed his hands behind his head and said, "It's good to be back, sir."

"You don't have to 'sir' me," Jim answered with an affable grin. "You certainly never did before."

Jake felt a prickly heat on the back of his neck. "As long as I don't salute you, we're fine."

Jim only laughed and cocked a mock salute on his way out the door.

Everyone left him alone, which made it easier for him to sort through the files. But several hours in, he was tired of reading and wondered what the hell he'd ever found interesting about corporate law. After the lethal situations he'd faced in the past few years, and the adrenaline surge as he made split-second, life-or-death decisions, this was about as exciting as a day at the dentist.

The longer he sat in his small office, the more claustrophobic he felt. Sweat broke out on his face, and his breathing became erratic. He sensed his panic and got up, walking around to calm himself. When that didn't work, he left the office and walked across the street for a tuna sandwich and two cups of coffee and felt almost normal by the time he returned.

He told himself that this was to be expected. The counselors at the burn center had told him he was bound to suffer anxiety attacks and that settling back into home life and his job could take time. He understood that in theory but had thought he might be exempt. After all, he loved his work. Or had, before his fiancée had been killed and he'd gone off to war.

He sat down at his desk, but instead of picking up the next file, he tilted his chair back and stared out the window. His civilian life wasn't going quite the way he'd pictured it. While overseas, he'd thought about meeting someone, falling in love again, and a life full of promise and laughter and children. But terrible shit had happened over there, and he wasn't the same man anymore, and didn't deserve the life he'd envisioned.

He read for another hour, then was done. He was baked and had lost focus. Previously, he had rarely left the office before seven, but today he left at three, knowing they'd cut him some slack. He'd work his way back, but it might take a little longer than he'd figured.

When he got home, he took Muffin for a short walk, then hurried back, remembering he'd set up a delivery time for his furniture between five and eight that night. He grabbed a quick shower and dressed in a pair of shorts and a T-shirt, opened a beer, and headed out to his balcony. He sat in a cheap fold-up chair, the only chair in the house, to wait for the furniture to arrive.

He'd drunk only half his beer when he heard a buzzing at the door. He checked his watch. Right on time. He jumped up to answer.

"Kari. What are you doing here?" He hadn't expected to see her tonight. It was bad enough knowing he wasn't quite right in the head, but he didn't like anyone witnessing it. Especially her.

"I have a file for you. It's got a list of agencies that deal with missing persons, a list of hospitals and vet facilities, and transitional housing where Shane might stay. And I wanted to talk. See if you remembered anything else." She waved a bag of delicious-smelling food in his face. "I brought Thai. You haven't eaten yet, have you?"

"No, I was planning on frozen pizza." He took the file and leafed through it. "Thanks, Kari. I appreciate this."

"Did you listen to your tape?"

"No, I never got the chance." He ran a hand over his face. "I did remember some stuff, didn't I?"

"Yes. Go get it." She took a step in, even though she hadn't been invited. "Why don't we listen to it together? I'm hoping it'll jog your memory and open the doors for you." When he didn't respond, she asked, "You want to come up and eat at my place, since you don't have a table or chairs?"

"If you don't mind, I'll take a pass. The furniture's arriving any second."

"Jake, what's wrong?"

He wouldn't look at her. "You saw me. Pretty damn pathetic, aren't I?"

"No, not in the least. It's going to take some time, Jake, and you're doing fine. I'm not going to use your stories, so you don't need to concern yourself about that." She touched his arm. "Do you really want to eat frozen pizza when we have chicken pad thai, shrimp panang, and beef curry?"

"You drive a hard bargain." He glanced around at the bare room. "Guess we can make a picnic of it on the floor."

"What about Muffin?"

"He can have some too." The dog danced around his feet, sniffing at the bag in Kari's hands. Jake got the plates out of the cupboard, and Kari laid the food out. "Want a beer?" he offered.

"Sounds good." She opened the containers and got the large spoons out.

He'd just popped the lid on her Corona Light when his cell phone rang. "We might have to wait. Furniture's here."

"At least we'll have chairs." She put the covers back on the containers to keep them warm.

Two men carried everything in and assembled it in record time. Living-room sofas, coffee tables, lamps, an entertainment center, free TVs included, and a dinette set now occupied all the empty spaces. The only thing missing was Jake's king-size bed and wardrobe. It would arrive the following week.

Once they left, Kari assessed the place, nodding her approval. "This is very nice. Good job. It's comfortable, and I like the warm earth colors and plaid pillows. It's masculine and comfortable-looking. Suits you."

"Not designer stuff like yours, but it'll do me." He picked up a plate and handed her one. "I'm starved. Let's eat."

They wolfed down the food, and Muffin seemed to enjoy his too. While he put the dishes away, she packed what remained. "I'll leave this with you. I'm sure your fridge is empty."

"I have beer, bread, peanut butter, and coffee. What more does a man need?"

She smiled. "Takeout menus?"

"Got those." He glanced at her. "Now that I have a TV, want to stay and watch some?"

"I still have some work to do, and I'm expecting a call from Sean."

"Don't want to miss that. Does he call every night?"

"When he gets the chance. Sometimes he's in places where he can't."

"Like in the middle of a jungle," Jake said. "Bet he can't call from there."

"Or in a crocodile-infested swamp."

"Or with a bunch of Pygmies. Bet they don't have phone service either."

Her lips twitched. "What if he's hanging with chimpanzees?"

"Couldn't call."

She was walking to the door and laughing. He put his hand on her shoulder and turned her around to face him. "I enjoy being with you."

She shook off his hand. "You just don't know many people. It takes time, Jake. You'll settle in soon. Find yourself a nice girlfriend."

"Why do you insist that we can't be friends?" His eyes looked into hers. "I would like us to be."

"I have Sean. That's why."

"Is that the only reason?"

"Isn't that enough?"

He swiped her bottom lip with his thumb. "Sauce." He stuck his thumb in his mouth and licked it off. "Nice."

Her eyes widened. "Why did you do that?"

"No reason." He leaned in closer, close enough to breathe in her scent. "Maybe if you stayed a little longer, I'd remember another story."

"Don't tempt me." Her eyes searched his, and her cheeks grew pink. "I have to go." She staggered away from him, and without a backward glance, she ran out the door.

"Wait!" He found her keys and took off down the hall after her. "Kari, you forgot your keys."

She punched the elevator button and stood with her arms wrapped around her, tapping her toes and looking upset.

"What's wrong?" he asked.

"You wanted to kiss me," she whispered, sounding horrified.

"But I didn't." He wondered what she'd do if he pulled her into his arms right now. He'd like to find out. She might like it better than she thought.

The door slid open, and Kari gasped. "Sean!"

Jake felt a disappointed punch in his stomach. So this was the missing boyfriend. He was tall, thin, with wavy, sandy-colored hair and a strong, lean face, currently covered by a couple days' growth of beard. Nothing much to look at.

He carried a camera bag and had a small suitcase, which he knocked over when he saw Kari. "I decided to surprise you with a quick visit."

"Oh my gosh!" she squealed. "I'm so glad you're home."

"Get in here," he grinned. "I want to give you a kiss."

Kari glanced at Jake. "Sean, this is Jake Harrington. He just moved in."

"Nice to meet you," Jake said, extending his hand. The two men shook, then Jake stuck his hands in his pockets and backed off.

Sean held the door open, but Kari didn't enter.

Jake spoke quickly, sensing her confusion. "Kari was telling me you're a photographer and always on the move. Must be hard working out of a suitcase."

"Not so hard when you love what you do." Sean shrugged. "Job suits me fine."

"I'll bet it does. Traveling to exotic lands, taking photos, winning awards, working on the *Planet Earth* series," Jake said. "Nice work if you can get it."

"True," Sean said. "Although it's not always the most glam job in the world. I spent the last month in Asia. Don't know about it being exotic, but I did get some beaut pictures on my walkabout. Sent them to *National Geographic*."

Kari finally stepped into the elevator and put her arm around her boyfriend. Her eyes met Jake's. "He's amazing, he really is. Spent two whole years traveling around the globe. Worked on *Oceans*, didn't you, darling?"

"That was dinky di. A bloody good time." Sean grinned. "She's always been my biggest fan," he told Jake, giving Kari a light kiss. "Did you miss me?"

Jake saw Kari's face, and he knew without being told that she was not a woman in love. She could think what she liked, but he remembered how she'd looked at him all those years ago, her eyes shining bright, full of passion and wonder and joy. It wasn't there.

He turned to go. "It was nice to meet you, Sean. Enjoy your stay."

Fighting the urge to smile, he walked off.

∽

Kari was delighted to see Sean, and yet she wished he'd let her know he was coming so she could have stayed home and greeted him properly. She gave him a quick kiss on the cheek as soon as they entered the apartment.

"Is something wrong?" he asked. He lifted her chin and looked into her eyes. "You didn't seem all that happy to see me."

"Of course I am." She hugged him. "You just surprised me, that's all. As I mentioned on the phone, I have a lot on my mind and a few problems to sort out."

Once he was settled and unpacked, she poured them both a glass of wine. They sat together, and she told him about her problems at work. He listened patiently, patting her knee every so often. "Good thing I got home," he said, pulling her head down to his shoulder. "You need a lot of hugs, that's for sure."

She let herself relax and accepted his cuddling. She was a self-reliant woman, but there were times when it simply felt good to be held and comforted. And if ever there were such a time, this surely had to be it.

She prepared him a light meal, since he hadn't eaten, and they talked for hours. Sean was his charming, intelligent self, and she knew she was lucky to have him. As the evening progressed, moving closer to the time they'd share her bed, she wondered at her lack of enthusiasm. What was wrong with her tonight? She'd always enjoyed him in bed. Their sex life was more than adequate. Not head-banging, earth-shattering lovemaking, but certainly very nice.

She gave herself a mental kick. Whatever she was feeling, she needed to put it under wraps.

EPISODE THREE

CHAPTER THIRTEEN

Jake entered his apartment, shaking his head. What the hell did she see in that guy? He was too skinny, he had hair down to his shoulders, and his eyes bounced around, never focusing on a person. Full of himself too. But hell, he shouldn't judge the guy on one brief meeting.

He opened the patio doors, wondering if he'd be able to hear Sean and Kari speaking. He sat down in his lawn chair and put Muffin in his lap. "I met Kari's boyfriend tonight. Yes, I did." He scratched behind the dog's ear, knowing it was difficult for the little guy to scratch himself with a missing limb. "She seemed more confused than excited, if you ask me."

Muffin turned his head and licked Jake's hand. He whined a little when Jake stopped scratching, so Jake gave him a good rub all over. "They have a strange relationship, that's all I can say. I mean, if he loves her so much, why hasn't he married her after two years? Huh? Tell me that."

Jake grabbed a bottle of water from the fridge and returned outdoors to drink it. He didn't want her sleeping with Sean tonight. And he didn't want her getting hurt. She'd gone through enough pain in her life and lost enough people who were important to her. Jake considered himself a good judge of character, and Sean might be an all right guy, but he wasn't the right man for her.

He guzzled his water and tilted his head to look at the stars. He wondered what had caused her to dislike him so much. Seeing him with another girl had to have hurt, but enough to hate him forever?

He wanted her forgiveness and to become friends again. It might not be too late. If he could get her her stories, sooner rather than later, she might like him a lot better.

∽

After the wine was finished and the kitchen cleaned, Sean went into the bedroom to take off his clothes. Kari followed him and stood watching for a minute.

She had no real reason not to sleep with him, and even bringing up the subject was awkward, considering they'd been lovers for the past two years. They weren't attached at the hip, but they were in a committed relationship. She loved him, not the earth-shattering kind of love she'd once felt for Jake, but close enough. It had been only a few nights ago that she'd missed him and wanted him home.

"What are you waiting for?" Sean unzipped his pants and let them drop to the floor. "If you're not in that bed in the next couple of minutes, I'm going to grab you and toss you in."

She knew he was joking and that he expected her to jump onto the bed, happily waiting for him to undress her, one button at a time. But she wasn't in a playful mood.

"I'm sorry, but I don't feel well tonight."

He stopped undressing and looked at her. "What's wrong, honey?"

"I'm having my period. I've had cramps on and off all day."

"Oh, you poor sweetheart." He walked over and took her in his arms. "Well, I guess I'll have to be content with just holding you tonight, won't I, love?"

"Actually, my cramps have been unusually painful lately. Would you mind sleeping on your side of the bed?" She kissed him lightly. "Please? Just tonight. I'm sure I'll feel better tomorrow."

She hoped so. Maybe tomorrow she'd be more like her normal self and be all over Sean. After all, it really was the perfect relationship, and she sure didn't want to be romantic with anyone else. Jake in particular. Whatever warped feelings she had for him, they couldn't be romantic, not after all they'd been through. She wished she could move past it, but how could she?

"You've been standoffish all night. What is really going on? Is it Jake? Have you two got something going on that I should know about?"

"No. Nothing. We used to date," she blurted, without giving it proper thought, "but that was a long, long time ago. We're barely friends now. More acquaintances than anything. Before I ran into him last week, we hadn't spoken in years."

Sean crossed his arms over his chest. "Then why were you with him tonight?"

She licked her lips and noticed her mouth was dry. "I've been trying to get some stories from him. For my new series, the one I told you about—my hero series."

"But he's not a hero, is he?"

"Not decorated, if that's what you mean."

"It is." Sean rubbed the side of his nose. "So how is he going to help? You need stories about veterans who are newsworthy. Men and women who went above and beyond the call of duty. From what you're saying, that lets your bloke out."

"Any person who risks his life for his country is a hero. Besides, Jake doesn't have to tell me about himself. He can feed me stories about men and women in his unit. He did two tours, so he must have witnessed many heroic acts."

"You want some feel-good stories, why not ask me? Think about some of the experiences my team and I have gone through. Freezing our asses off in Antarctica, living in a hut in the bloody Amazon to get exactly the right shot."

"I know, but—"

"We went to the ends of the earth, putting ourselves at great risk to reveal these habitats to the world." He smiled. "I should think that would be newsworthy enough for your weekly segment. The viewers would love it."

She swallowed hard, not wanting to hurt him. "What you do is incredibly special, and I have the highest admiration for you and your filming crew. But I pitched the idea of returning war heroes to my producer, and he thinks it's a timely piece. I want something with guts, and this will be an emotional, heart-wrenching series." She was getting a headache from all this. "My viewers know what to expect. And I'm going to deliver it to them, big time."

Sean looked unhappy. "Still think you could use me."

Kari smiled gently. "And I will. Tomorrow night, if I'm up to it."

His eyes lit with amusement. "Now you're talking like the Kari I know and love. Sleep well. I hope you're feeling better in the morning."

"I'm sure I will."

"What time will you be home?"

"The usual. I'm free for a couple of hours in the morning; then, after my noon report, I'm all yours." She gave him a tender smile. "We'll do something special. Want to go to the museum? Go to Miami? Catch a show?"

"I'll figure out something. It'll be a surprise."

"Sounds good." She quickly undressed and slipped into bed, curling up into a ball.

He slid in next to her but kept his distance.

She felt like such a shmuck, but she was sure she'd be her old self again tomorrow. As long as Sean didn't rock the boat, their relationship could continue for years. She didn't want anything from anyone else. All she wanted was to advance her career, find her sister, and have a comfortable existence.

Simple wants, really.

∽

Kari was out of the house before Sean was awake. When she returned a few hours later, delightful smells filled the apartment, making her tummy rumble. She sniffed her way into the kitchen, where Sean had coffee brewing and pancakes on the electric grill.

"Hi, hon." She dropped her handbag on the table and kicked off her high heels. Sean was in the middle of flipping pancakes.

"Good morning, luv," he said.

"Pancakes, yum. This is a nice surprise." Standing behind him, she wrapped her arms around him and kissed the back of his neck. "Did you sleep well?"

"I did. Must have been exhausted from that long flight." He poured her a cup of coffee, adding exactly the right amount of cream. "I'm sorry I wasn't more understanding last night. It kind of threw me for a loop, that was all."

She felt bad for lying to him about her period, but she simply had not been in the mood. Making love out of guilt would not have been right either. "I know. It was bad timing." Not wanting to risk getting syrup on her clothes, she escaped to change. When she returned in a pair of shorts and a T-shirt, Sean was setting their plates on the table. She replenished her coffee and sat.

"I want to make last night up to you."

He looked pleased by her words. "Good. The pancakes have a secret ingredient this morning. See if you can figure it out." He dropped a kiss onto the sensitive skin between her shoulder and neck, sending a tingle throughout her body. "I don't think you'll ever taste a better pancake again," he whispered into her ear.

"Hmm. Can't wait." She buttered the pancakes and poured syrup on top. She took a bite, anticipating the delicious taste. The one good thing about always eating lean was the pleasure of tasting something totally forbidden.

Three bites in, her eyes widened as she bit into something hard.

"Holy crap." With her tongue, she quickly separated the hard object from the mushy pancake. She pulled it out, hoping she hadn't broken a tooth. "I almost swallowed it."

Then she saw the object that was hiding in the pancake. A ring.

"Oh, no. You didn't…" Open-mouthed, she stared at Sean. Her stomach churned as waves of emotions battled inside her.

"I was going to give it to you last night, but you weren't in the mood. I hoped you might be a little more agreeable this morning."

"Sean, sweetheart." She felt her heart squeeze. She didn't want to hurt him, but she had never considered this. At least not right now.

He sat down in the chair next to her and took her hand. "Kari, I love you, and I want you to be my wife."

"I love you too," she answered softly. "I'm sorry, but this is such a surprise. We've never talked about this." His hopeful expression faded. She put a hand over his and gave his cheek a kiss. "We're both career people, remember?"

"I'm tired of living the life of a nomad. I want to settle down, in one place, with you."

She bit her lip as tears sprang to her eyes. "Oh, Sean. I don't know what to say."

"Say yes." He ran a hand up her arm. She enjoyed his touch. But her body was telling her one thing and her head another.

She stood and wrapped her arms around his neck, kissing the top of his head. "I care about you very much. I love what we have together, but I can't say yes." She searched his eyes, and hesitated before speaking again. Hurting him was the last thing she wanted to do, but if she accepted his marriage proposal feeling as she did, they would both be miserable.

"Sean, darling, I can't. I'm not ready to marry you. Or anybody. Can't we just go on as before?"

He stood as well. "Is it Jake?"

She threw her hands in the air. "It's not anyone. If I were going to marry someone, it would be you." She gave him a pleading look. "Can you at least give me some time to get used to the idea?"

"Are you sure you want it? You made me sleep on the far side of the bed, didn't want me touching you at all. Perhaps you're just not as into me as I thought. Isn't that more like the truth?"

She gave him a gentle smile, but it pained her heart. She wished she could take it back and make him happy, but she had to be true to herself. "I've been into you for the past two years, in case you didn't notice." She looked into his eyes, hoping he realized this wasn't easy for her.

She spoke quietly, aching inside. "There are still so many things that I want to do."

He looked sad, and when he spoke, even his voice seemed to have lost its charming lilt. "And I'm ready to stay home and raise a family."

"I'm sorry." She reached out to him, but he avoided her touch.

He dumped his plate of pancakes into the bin. "Lost my appetite. I'm going to pack."

She kept silent, fearful she might cave and say the wrong thing, causing them both years of unhappiness. With a heavy heart, she helped him pack his personal belongings, then stood at the door and watched him leave.

## CHAPTER FOURTEEN

By eleven, Kari was back at the station, dressed and ready for her noon report. She read the lines well enough, tossed in a smile or two, but even without the TV monitor, she knew her usual spark was missing—as if someone had pulled the plug. It wasn't an easy broadcast for her, but she made it through.

When she returned home, she changed back into gym wear and went for a long run. She pushed herself and her endurance, running faster and farther than her normal routine, a just punishment, she figured, for hurting Sean. When she'd been young, she'd always wanted marriage and kids, but after the miscarriage, the doctors had said she had scar tissue and might have trouble conceiving again.

With her family life in disarray, she decided to focus on her career. She had made it clear to Sean that she didn't want a family of her own, and he had been in agreement with that, so his proposal had truly thrown her for a loop. If he had prepared her better, perhaps she could have given it serious consideration. But who was she kidding? The end result would still have been the same. With sincere regret, she'd still have had to say no, because marriage was not what she wanted, what she needed. The entire idea of having a husband and children quite terrified her. The thought of losing them had her stomach heaving and stole her breath.

Still, she had a burning need inside her, and nothing, not even work, ever took it away.

As soon as she got home, the phone rang. Seeing it was Jake, she picked up.

"Kari, I know you're busy for the next few days, but when Sean leaves, give me a call. I want to see you about something."

"Sean left."

"What?" Jake cleared his throat. "He left already?"

"Yes." She mopped her brow with a hand towel, still dripping with sweat. "He won't be coming back."

"I'm sorry, Kari. I hope he didn't get the wrong impression about us."

"No. I set him straight about that." She looked at herself in the bathroom mirror, almost wishing she could push out more tears. It wasn't normal not to feel heartbroken after breaking up with someone you were supposed to love. It had taken her years to get over Jake, and she'd shed a river of tears. "He proposed this morning, and I turned him down."

"Shit."

"I couldn't marry him." She forced herself to sound normal, even though the air around her seemed suffocating. "I'm not the marrying kind."

"Why not?"

"I thought I wanted it once, but not anymore." She closed her eyes and held back a flood of emotions that she wasn't prepared to deal with. She had no room in her life for anything besides work. Work was safe, while love was... frightening, painful, and too emotionally exhausting.

Maybe Jake had sucked all the love right out of her, and she'd never be able to experience it again. Or perhaps she was so damaged, so afraid, that she could never chance having a family again. She cared about people, yet at the same time she held them back, afraid when they got too close.

"I loved him," she said. "Just not enough."

"You have a lot of love to give, Kari. This just means he wasn't the right man for you." Jake spoke in a low voice, and she had to strain to hear. "I saw that right away, even if you didn't."

She sniffed. "He was a good man. He deserved better."

"I know you don't want me as a friend, but if you ever do, I'm right here. I'm never going to disappoint you again. I promise, Kari."

"No promises, please?"

"Okay. No promises. But I know something that will make you happy. I remembered something. It might not be the best story, but I'll let you decide."

"That's great, Jake. I'm so glad your memory is returning."

"I looked at your file and appreciate the effort you put in." Jake spoke quickly. "I'm going to check on a few of the places tonight. If you're not doing anything, maybe you'd like to come along for the ride and I can tell you what I remember."

"I'd like that. I have to work for an hour or two, but after that, I'm free."

"I'm still at work. I could pick you up around five."

Kari devoured the Internet and found a fascinating story about service dogs and the military. One thing captured her interest—companion dogs were used for servicemen and women suffering from PTSD.

She thought about Muffin and Jake, wondering if he had inadvertently stumbled on the best possible cure. After reading the article and making notes, Kari knew she had a solid story, one that Tom would approve. Tomorrow, she'd work on getting in touch with one of the vets, who had a borzoi for a companion, and see if he'd agree to an interview on television.

It was a few minutes past five when Jake knocked on her door.

She had a big grin on her face when she answered. "Hey, Jake, come on in."

He looked around. "Am I in the right place?"

"What do you mean?"

"You're not usually so happy to see me."

She laughed. "Oh, it's not that. I've just had a wonderful afternoon and found the best story."

"I should have known," he said with a smile. "You're all rosy and flushed. It had to be something more exciting than me."

"It is. I'll tell you about it on the ride." She grabbed her handbag and followed him out the door. "So where are we going?" she asked when they reached the elevator.

"I have the list."

"Do you have recent pictures of Shane? He's probably registered under a different name."

"Brent emailed me some. The photos are a bit dated, but he's still recognizable."

"I think we should start with the ones closest to home and work our way farther afield. Sound good to you?"

He nodded. "I've done some research too. Did you know there are somewhere between one and three hundred thousand vets homeless in this country, and half of them are in Florida alone?"

"I had no idea the numbers were so high." She shook her head. "It's shocking."

"I know. All those vets wandering our streets with no place to go…" He sighed. "Our government isn't doing enough. They are trying and have recently put some money behind the effort, but still, we have men living in tents in the woods and camping in vacant lots behind major stores."

"I imagine the situation will get worse." When he used his electronic key to unlock the Jaguar, she stopped and gaped. "Wow! This is yours?"

"Uh-huh. You like it?"

He opened the door, and she slid into the cream-colored leather seat. "I love it. You rob a bank or something?"

He laughed. "No, I dipped into my savings account. Haven't owned a car in over four years, figured I could treat myself."

"It's beautiful, and you're right."

He got behind the wheel and revved the engine. "I thought we might start at the VA hospital. If he's in this area, he's probably an outpatient there."

"So tell me your idea for a story. What did you find?" Jake asked en route to the hospital.

She told him about Operation Wolfhound and the borzoi dogs. "According to the article, dogs have proven highly effective for veterans with PTSD, more so than medication and talk therapy. The training is very expensive, but at no cost to the veteran. Anyway, I'm going to see if I can set up an interview or two with someone who has a borzoi companion."

"I'm sure you will. Who wouldn't want to talk to a beautiful woman like you?"

"A lot of people, it seems." She glanced at him. "He's not a borzoi, but I think Muffin is therapeutic for you. He understands your moods too."

"I thought you hated Muffin."

"He's growing on me."

"So, what do you think our chances are of finding Shane after six months?" Jake ran a hand through his hair. "Kid's like another brother to me."

"Our search has just started." She added softly, "If he was treated at all, the hospital will have records. We'll find him, Jake."

She shut up right then, realizing she'd heard the same words herself from well-meaning friends and acquaintances when her sister disappeared. But all the platitudes in the world didn't change a thing. When people didn't want to be found, they wouldn't be.

Or they were already dead.

The VA hospital was a huge, pink building between Beeline Highway and Military Trail, and Jake knew it well. He had used it for outpatient treatments for his burns. He marched in, shoulders back, head high, like a commanding officer who would not take no for an answer. He pulled out his ID and handed it to the middle-aged black woman working in admissions.

"I don't know who I need to talk to, ma'am, but I'm looking for someone who was released nearly a year ago. His name's Shane Dawson, and he was a United States Marine, a medic, serving in Iraq. Could you tell me if he's a patient at this hospital?"

The woman handed him back his ID. "I can't give you that information. I'm sorry."

"Ma'am, I understand that your records are confidential, and I respect that, but our families were close, and they've asked me to help find their son. He's gone missing."

"I'm sorry I can't help you, but I do know someone who might be able to. His name is Roy Foster, and he runs the Stand Down House. It's a transitional-housing complex for vets. If anyone can help you, he can."

"Thank you, ma'am. Where can I find this Roy Foster?"

The woman wrote the name and address on a slip of paper and handed it to Jake. "Good luck with your search."

"Thank you very much. You've been most helpful."

"God bless you." She beamed at him like a proud mother.

Kari grabbed his arm as they walked to the car. "This is a good start. I have a positive feeling about this."

"It's a little late to call Foster tonight, but I'll be sure to chat with him tomorrow. Let's see if we can hit a shelter or two."

They drove to the first one on their list and had no luck. Same with the second. It was almost eight when Jake decided to call it a night. "You must be starved. Want to grab a bite to eat?"

"I have a couple of steaks in the fridge. Interested?"

"Sounds good. No need to twist my arm."

Once they were home, Kari busied herself making dinner but then received a frantic phone call from a reporter in need of her help. Jake took over grilling the steaks as she dealt with the minor catastrophe. She'd learned not to be rattled when stories fell through, or sources clammed up, or videos she'd hoped to use for a certain segment proved useless. It was all simply part of her job. The life of a newscaster was never easy, because stories kept changing and fresh news kept popping up. Even at dinnertime, which was the main reason she relied on frozen foods or takeout.

Jake walked back into the kitchen. "You like it rare or well done?"

"Medium rare, please." He returned to care for the steaks, and she put the salad on the table and took the baked potatoes out of the microwave. She sliced the potatoes and puffed them up, then yelled to Jake. "Butter or sour cream on your potato?"

"Load it up. All the trimmings."

She loaded his potato but used only a little butter on her own. She finished sautéing the mushrooms and was ready to go as Jake waltzed into the kitchen, carrying the platter in one hand like an experienced waiter.

"Perfect steaks, if I do say so myself."

"They look great." She took the platter, plopped the steaks on the two plates, and topped them with mushrooms. They sat at her small dining table and sipped their wine before digging into their meal.

"I'm eager to meet Roy Foster tomorrow. Sounds like he knows where vets hide out."

"I'll be interested in hearing what he has to say." She cut into her steak. "Good job. Pink but not too bloody.'

He cut a slice too. "You've been very patient tonight. Don't you want to know what I remembered?"

"Of course I do." A bite of steak was halfway to her mouth when she put the fork down. "I'm all ears."

"Once again, the story is clear to a certain part, then it gets fuzzy." He bit into a perfectly grilled bite of steak, chewed slowly, and finally swallowed.

Kari still hadn't taken a bite. "Now that you've got my attention, you're going to leave me hanging?"

He grinned. "Eat up. I'll tell you soon enough."

She took several bites, eager to finish dinner so she could hear what he had to say. Feeling his eyes on her, she put down her knife and fork. "Why are you looking at me funny?"

"I'm not," he answered. "I was thinking about the story."

"No, you weren't." She looked away.

"What did you imagine I was thinking?"

Kari was saved from a reply. The telephone rang, and she jumped up to take the call. She kept it short, telling the person on the other end that she'd call him back.

"Sorry," she said to Jake when she returned. "It's about the early-morning broadcast. Something's come up."

They both finished eating quickly, then carried their dishes to the kitchen. She popped a store-bought apple pie into a warm oven while he rinsed the plates and put them in the dishwasher. He turned to retrieve their wineglasses from the table just as she turned to put the steak sauce and butter in the refrigerator. Their hips accidentally bumped.

He didn't move; neither did she. "Jake. There's that look again."

He didn't answer, but his cobalt-blue eyes darkened and a muscle in his cheek twitched. Butterflies zoomed around her stomach. "What?" she whispered, sounding breathless to her own ears.

"Why did you get rid of Sean?"

"I told you. I'm opposed to the idea of marriage." She licked her lips. "I'm really going to miss him, though. He's a wonderful guy, and we had a lot of fun together." She knew she was chattering, but she didn't like the look in his eye.

He shifted his body and seemed way too close. "You're not going to miss him," he said in a low voice.

"I'm not?" She blinked rapidly, trying to come to her senses. "Why not?"

"Because you have me now."

She pulled away. "Jake, I'm trying hard to forget the past and put it behind me. I told you before—we can never get close, not like before."

His mouth lifted at the corners in the briefest of smiles. "You don't believe that any more than I do. We still have a connection."

"The connection is our past. Not our future." Kari refused to look him in the eye. She felt weak and knew if he touched her, she might unravel. "Please, don't."

"Don't what?"

"You know what I'm talking about."

He lifted her chin. "Why are you scared to look at me? What are you afraid of?"

"Nothing. I'm being sensible." She met his eyes. "Look what I did to Sean. I sent him packing. That's what I do if people get too close."

He smiled. "Okay, if that's what you think. I won't pressure you, but I'm not running away either."

## CHAPTER FIFTEEN

Jake backed away and took a seat at the table. Kari cut him a large piece of the pie and poured two cups of coffee before taking a seat next to him. "I'm so happy that your memory is coming back. Even if you can't recall everything at once, you will in time." She smiled, relieved that that moment between them had passed. She preferred feeling normal to being emotionally stirred up. "It's all tucked away in your memory bank somewhere, the good and the bad. You just have to dig through the muck to get to the good stuff."

"Easier said than done." He took a sip from his coffee, then put the mug down. "What's encouraging, though, is that the flashbacks are lasting longer and I'm seeing more of the whole picture, not just pieces of it."

The idea of a story had her on full mental alert, adrenaline coursing through her veins. She turned on the recorder, wondering how much he remembered and if it would be usable.

"Bear with me, as I may not remember the exact sequence of events. But I'll tell it the way I remember. That's the best I can do." He tilted his head back and closed his eyes. "There was a young medic with us. Lieutenant Gary Marshall, twenty-seven years old."

She leaned forward to listen but let him lead the pace.

"It was a routine day at the base, when suddenly the guys on guard duty began to shout. A truck had just sped through a checkpoint a hundred yards away, heading for the compound. It was only about twenty feet away when the damn thing blew up. It must have been loaded with explosives; it blew right through the gates, tearing a huge hole in the wall. Anyone within a hundred feet of the wall took a hit."

"How awful," she whispered.

"Marshall was hit, but he didn't seem to know it. Blood covered half his chest, but he dragged half a dozen men to safety before collapsing."

She didn't feel good about this story. "Is there something personal, something nice, that you can tell me about this young man?"

"Sure." Jake closed his eyes, seeming to struggle with himself, his thoughts. She watched his face contort, his eyes lose focus, and his shoulders shake.

"Jake, are you okay?"

He didn't answer right away. "Just got these damn images flickering in my brain. Sights, sounds, smells." He got up and started pacing. "I hate this shit."

"Look, why don't you relax for a while? Forget the story. You can tell me some other time."

"No. It's okay. I'll finish. Where was I?"

"Gary was hit and collapsed."

"Right." Jake rubbed the spot between his brows. He sucked in a breath and then released it. Finally, he looked at her and said, "He made it out alive. Carried a sonogram of his unborn son next to his chest. Says his baby saved his life."

Kari was silent for a long moment. It was almost too perfect to be true. "That is a great story," she whispered. "We will have to corroborate it, of course, but it has that strong emotional appeal I'm looking for." She touched his hand. "I'm sorry if the memories disturbed you."

"It's better than not remembering anything." He rolled his shoulders. "I'm getting used to the flashbacks, and I know what to expect."

"Maybe your stories will help you heal. Remembering the good stuff might put your mind at ease."

"You might be right." He took a big bite of his pie. "You not having any pie?"

"No, I don't eat desserts. It would mean I'd have to work out more." She grinned. "No time for that, I'm afraid."

"What *do* you have time for?"

"Work, exercise, occasionally I meet up with friends, but I have very little time to play."

"That's a real shame. A woman like you…"

He'd shifted his weight toward her, and there was an open invitation in his eyes. She wanted to taste his lips more than anything in the world. One kiss. Just one. But she had only just broken up with Sean, and it didn't seem right. It was almost like cheating on the man she had loved for the past two years. And yet no other man had ever made her feel the things Jake did. No man ever would.

"A woman like me needs her sleep." She yawned. "Sorry, but I have to be up so darn early every day. I'm usually toast by nine or nine thirty."

He glanced at his watch. "And it's already ten." He wolfed down the remainder of his pie and carried the plate into the kitchen. "Thanks for everything." His eyes met hers. "I enjoyed tonight."

She walked him to the door. "Good luck tomorrow. Hope you get some good news about Shane."

"I'll call you and let you know what happens." He put a hand on her elbow and leaned in to kiss her cheek. "Good night."

"Good night."

As much as she wanted to kiss Jake, she knew it would be a mistake. Letting her emotions get involved would be disastrous. She needed to be strong, but everything inside her felt weak. She had to fight this attraction. It would eat her alive.

# CHAPTER SIXTEEN

The next morning, as Kari walked into the station, her feet hardly touched the ground. She had a spring in her step and a new confidence she didn't bother to hide. "Tom?" She knocked on his office door, then opened it without waiting for a reply.

"Come in," he said, not looking up.

"I already did." She stood quietly, waiting for his full attention, but she was nearly bursting out of her pink power suit.

He glanced up. "You got something for me?"

"I've got something, all right." She handed him her written report. "Read it and weep."

"You're pretty full of yourself this morning, aren't you?" He raised his bushy brows. "It must be good."

She grinned. "It's wonderful."

"Go do your news, and we'll talk after I've looked through it." He turned his attention back to the mountain of paperwork in front of him, but she wasn't fooled. The moment she left, he'd be all over her report. The man could sniff out a good story from a pile of dung.

"Will do, boss." She gave him a mock salute and left with more confidence than she'd felt in a long, long time.

Her news reports went smoothly, and when she came out of the studio, Tom beckoned her into his office, George joining them this time.

"We've looked at the Lieutenant Marshall story. It looks good, Kari." Tom spoke first, looking at his boss. "George is concerned that you might not be able to get it up and running in time. Do you have anything else we might be able to use?"

"I have two ideas." She quickly told him about Operation Wolfhound and said she'd try to set up an interview. "Also, we have a local hero who'd make a compelling story. Roy Foster runs the Stand Down House, a transitional home for vets. He's been working with the government to get homeless vets off the streets for the past twenty years. I would like to interview him live. I think it would be an excellent way to kick-start the hero series."

George nodded. "I like it. We're taking a leap of faith here, mostly because there are so many details to work out and very little time." He looked her in the eye. "But it's a very timely piece and has merit. What I need to know is, can you do this?"

"I can and I will." Kari spoke firmly. "Thank you for giving me the opportunity. I won't disappoint you, sir."

She left the office on a high, but once she got back to her desk, reality set in. She needed to interview Mr. Foster and see if she could get him on board, as well as corroborate Jake's story in less than two weeks. She'd need to produce at least fifteen minutes of video that would include stock footage of military bases and small villages in Iraq, and perhaps a reenactment of the scene that Jake had described. It was a tight schedule, but possible.

She called Jake on his cell, eager to share the good news.

"My producers are excited about the story you gave me, and I also told them about Roy Foster and the Stand Down House. I'm hoping I can convince him to come on the show."

"That's great. I'm meeting him today. Want to come?"

She glanced at her watch; there was never enough time in a day. "I can't. I still have a million things to do here. Need to research Marshall's story and possibly get a tape up and running."

"I'll let him know that you'll be calling."

"Thanks. I appreciate that."

∞

Jake liked Roy Foster at once. The man had come off the streets himself and had struggled with his own addictions. He knew what other vets were going through and refused to give up on them.

Back when Roy had needed it, there hadn't been a proper recovery program set up for vets. Roy designed such a program and established a nonprofit organization to run Stand Down House, which had five buildings that provided rehabilitating vets with a temporary home. The VA hospital referred patients and helped fund the project, but Roy Foster made it happen.

After seeing the facilities and some of the people involved in running them, Jake got as excited as a kid did at Christmas. This was just what he needed—a worthy cause to invest his time in, something more important than corporate law for the rest of his life.

They tossed ideas around about how to save the new generation of vets, not only in Florida but also across the nation. They both agreed that they needed to find a way to get the government solidly behind the idea of "no man left behind." Every city in the country needed a place, or many places, for vets to stay and recover, to receive the treatment as well as the respect they deserved. No way should men and women who served their country be tossed to the wolves, expected to fend for themselves.

After they talked the subject to death, Roy showed Jake where the homeless vets usually camped. They searched the nearby woods and deserted parking lots for Shane, but nobody had seen him. Still, Jake felt as though he was one step closer.

His father had invited him to dinner, so he returned home to shower and change, then made the short drive to Jupiter Island. When he pulled up in front of his father's home, he noticed a car he didn't recognize parked in the circular drive.

Loud voices and laughter greeted him as he entered. Disappointment slowed his steps, as he realized his father was entertaining. He wanted to speak to his father about getting involved in this project, but that talk would have to wait.

"Jake? Come over and meet our guest," his father called out.

His mind was humming with ideas, and he wanted to go upstairs and do some research. Making small talk with Tiffany's friends had no appeal whatsoever, but respect for his father won out.

He walked into the dining room and came to a dead stop. A stunningly beautiful woman was sitting next to Tiffany, and Tiffany grinned when she saw his reaction.

"Jake," she said, "I want you to meet Monica Lewis, my best friend in the entire world. She's a model and lives in South Beach, but she's been in Europe for the past year."

"Hi, Jake." Monica gave him a big smile as he walked over to the table and politely shook her hand.

His father looked at him with an amused expression. "Tiffany has been telling Monica all about you and making plans for the four of us. She'll be staying with us for a week."

Tiffany reached across the table and squeezed Monica's hand. "I've missed her so much, and I'm trying to convince her to move closer." She giggled. "Maybe you can help, Jake," she added slyly.

Jake frowned. "I don't think I can do anything to encourage her. And what exactly have you been telling her about me?" He grabbed a bottle of red wine and poured himself a glass.

"All things good." Mischief glinted in Tiffany's eyes. "I told her about you being wounded in the war, and she was hoping to see you in uniform. Weren't you, Monica?"

Monica slid her gaze up and down Jake's body. "Nothing sexier than a man in uniform."

His father coughed and sputtered, hiding his grin behind his napkin.

"Sorry, ladies, but my uniform is officially retired." He glanced at his dad. "Why are you laughing, General?"

"No idea." Jake watched his dad pat his wife's leg under the table.

Jake wished he were back at Kari's, back in Iraq, anywhere but here. "I'm sorry I won't be able to spend more time with you," he said to the women, "but I have a lot going on this week. I'm back at work and have a lot of catching up to do." He spoke to his father. "Kari and I are trying to find Shane."

"That's a shame," Monica said. "I was hoping to get to know you better."

He looked at her, thinking he must be half crazy. She obviously was up for a good time, and if he were half the man he'd been before the war, he'd be all over it, but he had no interest. Zero.

"Look, I'm sorry to disappoint the two of you, but I'm certain I can squeeze in a dinner."

"Why don't we go change and enjoy the pool spa?" Tiffany said. "A nice, hot, soothing spa, a bottle of champagne, some good music. Wouldn't that be fun?"

Jake glanced at his father and raised an eyebrow.

Tiffany grabbed her husband's hand. "We'll all go in, won't we?"

The last thing Jake wanted was to be in the spa with two half-naked women. "I don't have a swimsuit here," he said. "I packed everything before I left."

"No swimsuit required," Tiffany murmured, and laughed when he blushed.

"It is around my 'stepmom,'" he answered, giving her a pointed look.

If only he could close his eyes and magically be back in the desert with his comrades, he thought. At least he knew what to expect when he was there.

Not wanting to look like a complete wimp, he agreed to bring the champagne and glasses to the pool. The women ran off to change into their bikinis, and Jake and his father sat in chairs on the deck, close enough to enjoy the view and pour the champagne.

"You doing all right, son?" His father gave him the briefest of glances. "If you ever want to talk about it, I'm here for you. And if you think it could help, you could also get some professional counseling now and then."

"I'm fine, Dad. At least, I'm working on it." Eager to change the subject, he said, "I met an interesting vet today—"

The two women appeared, interrupting the conversation. "Hi, boys," Tiffany called out, strutting toward them.

She had a knockout body, but her friend was built like a Victoria's Secret model. Jake sighed with real regret. It was a hell of a shame that he was only a shadow of his former self. The things he could have done with Monica in his self-absorbed youth might have inspired a best-selling novel. Now the thought terrified him.

Kari's image floated to mind. She didn't frighten him—he just didn't deserve her.

∽

Kari called Jake the following afternoon and asked him how his meeting had gone.

"How did you know about Tiffany's friend?"

"What friend?" A little knot tightened in her stomach.

"Oh, you're talking about the man from Stand Down House. Sorry, I thought you meant Monica, a model friend of Tiffany's."

"No." She swallowed the sour taste in her mouth. "Tell me more."

"Well, there's not much to tell. She lives in South Beach but was over in Europe for the past year."

"Oh, how nice." She knew her voice was cool as a Popsicle, but she didn't give a damn. He gave a short laugh.

"Wish it were. Unfortunately, Tiffany and Monica have made plans, which include me, to go out every night the rest of this week."

"I can't imagine anything worse than hanging out with a South Beach model."

"It's not as great as you'd think."

"I'm sure you'll tough it out."

"Actually, I have a more serious problem than her. I had a handyman come in this morning to remove that built-in unit in my master bedroom, and he found water damage that hadn't been taken care of properly. Now I need to get a mold inspection before I can paint. I want it taken care of before the furniture arrives next Monday." Jake hesitated for a second, then continued, "Dad invited me to stay there for a couple of days, but I turned it down."

"Why?"

He cleared his throat. "I'm not up to this whole double-date thing. I can barely tolerate Tiffany, and Monica is just as bad. I need an excuse to escape."

She thawed a little. "How can I help you?"

"I agreed to dinner on Saturday, and I was thinking maybe you could call me in the middle of it, say you have some kind of emergency or whatever, and I'll have an excuse to leave and come back here."

"Why don't you just tell them you're not interested?"

"You haven't seen these two in action."

"Okay. I'll help save you."

"Thanks, Kari. I owe you."

"Call us even. You've made my bosses very happy."

"Great. Glad I could help." Jake rushed on, "Since my place may have mold damage, I might have to get out for a few days. Go to a hotel or something."

"Are you hoping for an invitation?" she asked. "I warned you about getting too close. You don't want to do that."

"No, I wasn't suggesting that. Would you be able to take Muffin for a few nights?"

"Don't push it."

"Poor Muff. He might have to go to a kennel. Unless…"

"Unless what?"

He chuckled. "If you let me stay on your couch, Monica would think I was sleeping with you and it'd get her off my back."

"We'll figure out something simpler to cool her heels," Kari said firmly. "But not that."

# CHAPTER SEVENTEEN

Jake spent part of the afternoon calling shelters where many of the homeless drifted in and out. He had a possible lead, and that evening decided to check it out.

He walked into the Broward Outreach Center and was greeted by a woman of an uncertain age. Her hands looked young, but she had old eyes and a face that spoke volumes about the hard life she'd led. Her brow was wrinkled, feathery lines fanned out from her eyes, and deep gouges ran from either side of her nose to her mouth.

"I'm Jan Tanner," she greeted him, "and you must be the man I spoke to on the phone."

He nodded, digging his hands into his pockets. "So, you think my friend Shane Dawson was here for a while?"

"I'm sure of it. He registered under that name. We have two hundred beds, but I remember most faces and names. Your friend Shane was here for a few weeks at the end of last year. He could have stayed longer but checked himself out after the first month."

"Do you have any idea where he went?"

"Most of the men and women who pass through our doors have no idea where they might end up."

Jake expected that, but hope dies slowly. "Was he okay when he left? Did he seem all right to you?"

"The people we treat are homeless, and most come here to get help with their addictions. He was no different." She met his eyes briefly, then glanced away. "We've got quite a comprehensive program here, but it's based on an eight-week stay. We do our best to teach our clients life skills so they can reenter a community and start leading productive lives again."

"So you think he might be gainfully employed? Have a roof over his head?"

"I said we try. But in your friend's case, no, I don't think so."

"Why not?" Jake ran his hand through his hair, trying to hold on to his frustration. "If he was still suffering from withdrawals from whatever addiction he had, or showed signs of PTSD, how could you let him walk out of here?"

His tone made the woman's back stiffen. He could tell from the defensive expression on her too-old face.

"We can't force people to stay," she said. "Our doors are open for anyone seeking help. We offer education and counseling, but the person has to want to change. If not, we can't help him."

"Yes, that's true. I'm sorry. I know you're doing everything possible to help the homeless, and I admire you for that." A feeling of shame overwhelmed him. He was living in the lap of luxury while his brothers and sisters in arms were camping in bushes, living on the streets. Like Roy Foster, he wanted to make a difference. He'd always wanted to do something worthy with his life. That was his reason for choosing law, and the reason he'd signed up as a marine and fought for his country. But it was not enough. Not even close. "It's more than I'm doing."

A faint color painted her cheeks, and she seemed flustered by the compliment. "You have no reason to admire me, that's for sure." She gave a shaky laugh. "Been there, done that, and more."

"You were a client here," he guessed.

"Yes, I was." She smiled. "And I wanted to give back. This place saved my life."

"Well, I'm glad. I hope it also helped save Shane. He's not only a friend but a medic who was only trying to do some good in this world." Jake didn't know what else to say or what his next move would be. He nodded, grateful for the woman's time. "Thank you for your help."

"Anytime."

As he was leaving, he held the door open for a woman coming in. He watched her cross the lobby to the elevator, and the fine hairs on the back of his neck rose.

He returned to speak to Jan. "That woman standing at the elevator. Is she a patient here?"

"You mean Linda? She's a volunteer."

"Would I be able to speak to her? It's important."

The elevator opened, and the young woman stepped inside.

Jan studied him. "I could take your number and give it to her. It would be up to Linda if she wants to contact you."

"I understand. Please tell her that I only have a question or two, but I come as a friend. She reminds me of someone I knew a long time ago."

∽

Kari opened her front door to find Jake carrying a large Subway bag and sipping a Slurpee.

"What's the matter? You look like you're on the run. Is Monica tailing you?"

He smiled, but she could see he was nervous about something. "No, it's not Monica. I haven't eaten and brought enough for two."

"Thanks, but I had dinner right after I interviewed your friend Roy Foster. Which went very well, I'm pleased to say."

"Glad you two met. Hopefully he can put you in touch with the right people who can feed you good stories."

"I hope so too." She ran a tongue over her dry lips and asked, "Were you able to find out anything else for me on the Marshall story?"

"I've called dozens of people and left my number. Spoke to one guy, though, and he couldn't remember Marshall at all." Jake ran a hand through his hair. "It's not looking as promising as I'd thought. But I can't imagine being wrong about something like this."

"I'm sure it'll be fine, Jake. I have assistants working on it too."

"I'm also checking up on that Jamie Parsons story. I have a feeling that she lived and took the girl from the village back home with her."

"Really?" The night he'd told her the story, she'd gone home and researched it, not so she could report it, but for Jake, wanting to give him closure. She'd learned that the woman and child had died, so there was no happy ending. She hadn't wanted to tell him that, in case the negative memory did more harm than good.

Caught in a trap of her own doing, she looked away and said softly, "Well, that would make quite a story." Abruptly, she changed the subject. "So what's up with you? You look excited about something."

"I was at the Broward Outreach Center, and they told me Shane was a resident there. He left, but at least we have a trail and a place to start."

"That's great news." She took the Subway bag out of his hands and pulled him in. "Come join me for a glass of wine. I want to hear all about it."

He popped the cork out of the wine bottle while she got the glasses from the cupboard. She noticed how familiar they were in her apartment together. *Keep your guard up*, she reminded herself. *Don't let Jake slip under your skin.*

She got him a plate for his sandwich, and they sat at the kitchen table. He told her everything he knew, which wasn't much. When he was done, he continued eating in silence. Finally, he looked at her again, and she could see his eyes were troubled.

"What is it? You didn't come here just to tell me about Shane, did you?" she asked.

He swallowed and reached for his untouched glass of wine. "No, there's more."

"Jake. I'm not into guessing games." He was making her nervous, and she had no idea why.

He nodded. "Okay. I won't beat around the bush." He swirled the wine in his hand, then put the glass back down. "When I was leaving, a woman came in. She seemed familiar."

"You think you may know her?" At the look he gave her, Kari's heart began thundering. Surely, he didn't mean…

"I'm not sure," he said. "I'm even afraid to say it." He reached out and touched her hand.

Kari's hand flew to her mouth. A cacophony of sounds rang in her ears. Her stomach flipped around like a live fish was trapped inside, and when she reached for her glass, Jake had to steady her hands.

"Easy. I know this came as quite a shock."

"Not after all this time." She spoke calmly, although her entire body buzzed like it'd been lit with an electric wire.

Jake used his napkin to mop up the drops of spilled wine. "I shouldn't have said anything. You're probably right. I mean, what's the chance of it being her? Living this close."

"Then why did you say something?" Her voice was harsh, but she couldn't help it. She was angry, afraid. She'd clung to the dream of finding her sister for so long that she knew if it ever happened, the reality was bound to be a disappointment.

She breathed deeply, calming herself. Jake didn't deserve this. He probably thought he was delivering good news and that she'd be excited and eager to meet this stranger. Once, many years ago, she would have been. But how many times could you allow yourself to hope, only to be crushed again and again?

"What was it? What made you think she might be Alaina?"

"It was her eyes. Green eyes like yours are rare, and hers are green with a yellowish tinge. Cat's eyes. Quite unforgettable."

"I need more than that." She hugged her arms to ward off a chill. "Many people use colored contacts, so the woman you saw might have brown eyes, for all you know. Was there anything else?"

"I wouldn't say she was a dead ringer, but there was something about her."

"Well." She released a long breath. "I can't believe that if she's still alive, she's living only a few miles away. Doesn't seem possible."

"I know. You're probably right."

She was annoyed that he gave up so easily. She needed to be convinced. "Of course I'm right. She wouldn't just show up after all this time. We haven't had a lead in years. So long, I can't remember."

"But you still believe she's alive, don't you?"

She shrugged. "I'm not sure. I want to, but I know the reality. In my line of work, I see it every day."

"Look, I know you're thick-skinned and a touch cynical. As a journalist, you need to be. It's also perfectly reasonable that you don't want to get your hopes up again." He watched her closely. "But don't you want to see for yourself?"

"It's late." For emphasis, she glanced at her watch. "It's Friday tomorrow, and I have a lot of work to do. Got to get these stories up and running."

"If you don't want to go, that's fine with me."

She sighed heavily, not wanting to put herself through this again, yet knowing she had to. "I guess I could spare some time in the afternoon tomorrow." Her face felt as though it were carved in stone. "You know the odds are next to none."

Jake stood as well and took her by the arms. "I know, and I'm sorry if I'm wrong."

She relaxed against him. "I won't be able to take it again."

"Yes, you will. You're stronger than you think. And I'll be there with you. You won't be alone."

Against her better judgment, Kari allowed the possibility that this woman really was Alaina to slip into her consciousness. Immediately, fear coursed through her, and she looked up at Jake. "What if it is her? I might frighten her away. She could take off again, and then I'd never find her."

"I don't have any answers, Kari." He kissed the top of her head. "Maybe I should have kept my big mouth shut and done some investigating first. As you say, I only saw her for a moment."

"I guess I need to see her with my own eyes. I'll know." She stared into his face, hoping for confirmation. "Right? I'll know?"

"I hope so. The woman I saw looks older, and although she has the same green eyes that I remember, hers were empty." He frowned. "I really shouldn't have said anything."

"You're probably right. You shouldn't have." Instantly, she regretted her harsh words. "Sorry. I shouldn't have snapped at you." She pushed herself out of his arms and stepped away. "I'm exhausted. I'll see you tomorrow."

"I'm sorry, Kari. It's a lot to think about." He walked to the door. "Try to get some sleep."

She nodded. For the first time in her life, she was actually afraid that Alaina might come home.

# EPISODE FOUR
## CHAPTER EIGHTEEN

Jake woke up early, fueled by the knowledge that Shane was close. It was still dark when he left, but he wanted to check out the wooded areas around West Palm, where some of the homeless camped. As he drove the short distance, he thought about Kari and her mixed feelings regarding her sister. He understood her fear and that she preferred to believe Alaina was somewhere far away and happy, because he shared those thoughts. He didn't want to find Shane sleeping in a tent in the woods either. But if that was where he was, Jake would bring him home, just as Kari would bring back her broken sister.

Roy Foster had showed him where to look, and he followed a path through a heavily wooded area to find the encampment. He had picked up two dozen bagels and dispersed them to the men and few women there. No one knew Shane, but he spent an hour talking to the people, asking them why they didn't seek shelter. The answers surprised and appalled him. Some were housed in shelters, but most shelters had a time limit, and once they'd used up their time, they had been sent off to fend for themselves. Most of them had a dependency problem and were unable to get jobs, and their families and friends had turned their backs on them. As had the government.

The Department of Veterans Affairs, he had learned already, was drastically underfunded, and vet groups around the country were urging Congress to increase the budget. For vets, young and old, to live in such squalor was not acceptable, and whatever it cost him in time and money, he intended to take this fight all the way to the top.

Filled with righteousness, he went to his office and started writing letters, offering his services to the Disabled American Veterans and the Veterans of Foreign Wars.

By the time he finished, he had a roaring headache and the rising darkness was beginning to engulf him. He swallowed a couple of pills and closed his eyes, rubbing a spot between his brows. He breathed slowly. Staccato flashes ripped through his mind. Machine-gun fire, the sky lit up from an explosion, the sight and smell of burning flesh. As he sank deeper into the black hole, the images began to recede, and he couldn't hear, see, or feel anything at all.

A short time later, the meds took effect, and he was able to go back to his letter writing. He felt shaken but angry too. The battles he'd fought in Iraq were nothing compared with the one he intended to start right here at home.

∼

Kari called Jake from the station and left a message. "Call me when you get a chance. I need to speak to you as soon as possible."

She'd been working hours on the story of the medic, Lieutenant Marshall. His former commanding officer was back in Iraq but not available. The clerk she spoke to at the military base confirmed the incident on the date in question but didn't know anything about Marshall. By now, her stomach was roiling and she was popping Tums as if they were candy. Jake had warned her about his memory, but he'd been so sure about this story. So sure that she'd run it past Tom and George, and now to retract it would make her look bad. Which would make Jeremy look all that much better. She couldn't let that happen. This story had to be true. If it wasn't Marshall, maybe it was someone else.

Two assistants were working on setting up appointments for Operation Wolfhound and the Wounded Warrior Project, while Kari and her assistant Jennifer were still working the Marshall story, asking if it seemed familiar at all. "You got anything, Mary? Jim?"

Mary, a junior assistant, shook her head. Jim said he was on hold.

"I've been looking up injury reports, and I've tracked down the names of the marines from Jake's unit," Jennifer told her. "I've left callbacks for those who were there at the time of the alleged events."

"That's good. Keep on it."

As a preliminary, Kari had already taped herself introducing the story and had one of her assistants pull some Iraqi footage to add, only to put it aside. The story was looking more and more doubtful, and so was Jake's memory. He certainly didn't mean to mislead her, but whatever was in that head of his, it was not factual.

Around three in the afternoon, Jake called back. Kari skipped the niceties and cut to the chase. "The story you gave me on Marshall. My staff and I spent half a day yesterday and today talking to people from your previous unit. I'm sorry to say that no one remembers it the way you did."

She tried to keep her voice calm and nonaccusatory, but her bosses had been expecting the story and she had damn well better find something else, fast. "I was able to corroborate much of it: the truck with the explosives running through the wall and into the compound, killing forty-two servicemen, and wounding even more. But nothing on Marshall, or a sonogram."

"Well, I'm sure my imagination didn't make this up. I'll call a few buddies and see what I can find out too."

∼

Jake called several of his old friends whom he'd served with, hoping somebody could prove him right. He'd been so sure his memory was coming back and that the images were real. No way could his brain trick him like that.

Joe Barnes was the first man to call back. "Lieutenant Marshall?" the big man chuckled. "No friggin' way. He died just like everybody else. There was no sonogram. What are you making up stories like that for?"

"No. I remember it clearly."

"You're not remembering anything clearly, if you ask me."

An hour slipped by, and still he didn't hear from anyone else, so he tried to dig up information on Jamie Parsons and the girl from the village. If he remembered right, which was a big *if*, he thought Parsons had survived her tour, adopted the girl, and brought her back to America to live.

If the sonogram story fell through, he'd like to give Kari something else to use.

Jake called Kari back and said he'd see her at five. It was already half past four, so he hightailed it home.

"Anything positive?" she asked, the moment he arrived.

"Not yet." He tucked a lock of her hair behind her ear, and she turned her head. "I expect it will soon."

"I'm going to interview some of the men at the Stand Down House, and I also set up appointments with the Wounded Warriors."

"Good job, Kari. You're a fine journalist. The series will be a success. I'm sure of it."

"No more on the subject for now, okay? I've had a rough day, between that and thinking about my sister. Tell me something nice. Please?"

"You look beautiful."

She laughed for the first time that day. "I needed that."

She grabbed two cans of soda, and they sat down at the counter. He told her about his field trip into the woods. "You wouldn't believe how these vets live. It's shameful, it really is."

"You sound pretty worked up about this." She eyed him cautiously, wondering if he was mentally fit enough to explore this distressing world.

"I am worked up," he said. "Excited too. This is something I feel very strongly about, and it's great to be enthusiastic about something again." He told her about the letters he'd written, offering his services as a lawyer, free of charge, to the Department of Veterans Affairs and the National Coalition for Homeless Veterans. "I have to say, corporate law seems awfully dull compared with this."

"You're going to quit?"

"No. I still need a paycheck, but now I have something to care about, something worth fighting for."

"Aren't you tired of fighting?"

"I'm tired of fighting for the wrong reasons. Now, I'm fighting for the right ones."

"You always seem to know right from wrong. You have a clear definition of the two. Sometimes, to me, they get a little blurry." She leaned on the table, chin in her hand, gazing up at him.

He was always easy on the eyes, but tonight he looked so fired up she was drawn to him like a magnetic force. As hard as she might fight it, she couldn't stay immune to him. It was impossible. Whatever happened between them, past or present, she knew he was one of the good guys.

"Well, after I first came home, my truth was a little distorted. I must admit, I couldn't see what good I'd done over there."

"You did what you were trained to do."

"That's true. Now I'm going to use my expertise as a lawyer to make a few changes in Congress."

She saluted him with her can of soda. "Good luck with that."

"I may need it. Things move slowly in Congress, and I'm not the most patient man in the world. But I've got to start somewhere."

"Will your father help? He must have influential friends."

"I'm hoping he'll want to get involved. I'm going to write a plan and present it to him, so he knows I'm not running blind." He finished his soda and leaned toward her. "But enough about that. After we check out our green-eyed mystery woman, I'm going to buy you dinner. It's the least I can do for causing you so much worry."

Now that it was time to follow through on their plan, anxiety gripped her. "Did the woman from the shelter call you? Can we talk to her?"

"No call. But I have an idea."

Kari noticed the small tic in his cheek and knew he was worried that he'd fail her again.

"So, what are we going to do?" she asked, half hoping he'd call the whole thing off. She was too old to believe in fairy tales and happy endings.

"I think we should go back and talk to Jan, assuming she's working today—explain who you are and that we're looking for your sister." He eyed her carefully, a worried frown between his brows. "What do you think?"

"I guess it's worth a try." She was not going to get all worked up about this, she told herself. The woman might not even be there, and Kari was already preparing herself for what would happen if she wasn't Alaina. What were the chances?

"If we get to talk to her," Jake went on, "have you figured out what you'll say?"

She shrugged. "I'll just try to ease her into conversation, talk about the shelter or the weather, whatever. I'll start nice and easy. I don't want to scare her off."

He rubbed his jaw. "Look, Kari, I know she probably isn't your sister, but if she is, you'll frighten her away if she's not ready to see you." He put a hand over hers, and she left it there. "I don't think you should speak to her right away. Maybe you can have a look at her without her seeing you. If you believe it really is Alaina, then we can approach her."

"How will I know?"

He squeezed her hand. "I think you will."

"Okay." She nodded slowly. "You're probably right."

"Of course I'm right. I always am." He winked.

She laughed, but her laughter quickly died as she thought about what they were about to do. "Let's go," she said abruptly, "before I lose my nerve."

## CHAPTER NINETEEN

The receptionist, Jan, was at her desk when they arrived. When Kari explained why they were there, she was sympathetic but clearly unwilling to divulge personal information about the woman Jake had seen the day before.

"Sometimes she brings a guitar and sings to our clients," Jan said. "Did your sister play?"

"I don't know. Not when I knew her. She ran off at sixteen."

"Well, she has a lovely singing voice and the men enjoy listening to her."

Excitement bubbled inside Kari. That sounded like Alaina. She had always been pretty, and men had always liked her. Which had been half the problem.

"Do you think she'll come today?" Kari asked.

"She doesn't have a set schedule. Sometimes she shows up a few days in a row, but other times we don't see her for weeks."

"Perhaps it would be best if you don't say anything to her," Kari remarked, trying to remain calm. "If she is my sister, she may run again."

"If you see her from a safe distance, you may have your answer."

"Yes. I'm counting on that. Thanks so much for your help."

"Wish I could do more."

They left the building, heading for Jake's car. He suggested they give it a half hour, and if the woman didn't appear, they'd leave and try again the next night.

Ten minutes later, an old wreck of a car pulled into the parking lot. Half a fender missing, and it had enough dents and dings to be a retired New York City cab.

A woman got out and grabbed a guitar from the backseat.

"That's her," Jake whispered.

"She doesn't look like Alaina," Kari hissed. "Are you kidding me?"

"It's the eyes. You need to see her up close, but I have to warn you, nothing else resembles her." He raked a hand through his hair. "I never should have said anything."

"It's okay." She was disappointed but not devastated. Even from a distance, she could see the woman was a mess: extremely thin, probably anorexic, with long, stringy hair. As she walked toward the building, she seemed to be muttering to herself.

Kari shivered. She wanted her sister back, but her sister as she had been. Which was impossible. Whatever had happened to Alaina would have changed her, and not for the better.

She opened the car door and jumped out. "Alaina!" she called.

The woman's head whipped around.

"Oh my God," Kari whispered. "It is her."

She started toward the woman, Jake following. The woman stood motionless, warily watching their approach.

Jake spoke first. "Excuse me, miss, but I'm Jake Harrington. I left a card for you yesterday, with Jan." He cleared his throat. "I was hoping to speak to you. I'm looking for Shane Dawson, a vet who was here last year. Perhaps you know him."

"No, I don't think I do." The woman looked at the ground, scratching her arm frantically.

"We didn't mean to frighten you," Jake said softly.

Kari stepped closer. "Alaina? Is it you?"

The woman stared at Kari with frightened eyes. "Who are you? What do you want? My name is Linda." She clutched the guitar to her chest. "When I heard you shout, I thought you were shouting at me."

"I'm looking for my sister, and I thought it might be you." There was a slight similarity, Kari thought, now that she could see the woman up close, but this scared creature looked a decade older than Alaina would be, completely worn by life. Her sister had been bright and spunky, glowing with life and vitality.

The woman smiled, revealing badly neglected teeth. "Now, you tell me. Do I look at all like you?" She cracked up, doubling over with laughter, as if that were the funniest thing ever. When at last she could speak, she gave Kari the once-over. "I wish."

Kari stepped closer, peering into the woman's eyes. "Your eyes are the same." She caught her breath. "Please, tell me. Is it you?"

The woman said nothing. She didn't look away, didn't blink, didn't reveal anything at all. Her eyes were blank, lifeless, without emotion. Without any hopes or dreams.

Kari turned to Jake. "I can't tell. Oh, Jake, I can't tell."

The woman walked away, back toward her car.

"I'm sorry," Kari called after her, "but I searched and searched for my sister and never gave up hope. It's been sixteen years. I'm just not sure anymore."

"I'm not your sister." The woman got inside her car and drove away.

Kari didn't say anything for several minutes. Jake put an arm around her, and she was grateful for his support.

"I don't think so." She shook her head sadly. "I'm not sure."

"We knew this wouldn't be easy." He gave her a hug. "If your sister is alive and near, she doesn't want to be found."

"We could say the same for your friend Shane."

He closed his eyes and released a deep sigh. "This sucks." He stepped away to look at her.

Kari had no answer. This was not a reality she had prepared for. She wanted Alaina to still be lovely, perhaps a Vegas showgirl, or living an enchanted life in some exotic country. Not like this woman.

"If it is her, she knows where to find me and that I've never given up hope. But she'll have to convince me. After all, how do I know that she isn't just some woman from the streets simply looking for a handout?"

"Well, for one, we came to her, not the other way around," Jake answered solemnly.

She punched his arm. "Why do you have to be so practical? I want my real sister back."

"I know you do, but that's a dream that may never come true. Not the way you envision it, anyway."

"I know, but…"

"Enough 'buts' for one day. Let's digest this over dinner. Where would you like to eat?"

"My place? Why don't we just order in a pizza or something? It's been a rough day."

"Sounds good to me."

When they got back, Jake stopped at his apartment to grab a couple of beers. Seeing Kari in the doorway, Muffin started to growl.

She walked in and stooped to pet him, determined to win him over. "What's the matter with you? I'm not the one who wanted to off you."

He licked her hand, and she picked him up. "He's still got quite a scar from his surgery. Poor doggy. What was he doing on the road? I wonder."

"Probably running away from Tiffany, if he had any sense."

She laughed. Holding the small dog in the crook of her arm, she entered his bedroom to inspect the wall with the water damage. "You should probably not be staying here until the inspection is done."

"The handyman didn't think mold settled in. I'll be all right."

She nodded and walked around, noticing the mattress on the floor with nothing but a sheet and a cheap-looking pillow. Guy didn't even have proper bedding.

"Gosh, Jake. How can you sleep on this?"

He shrugged. "Compared with the conditions I'm used to, this is the height of luxury."

"I can lend you a comforter."

"Don't need it. I'll get stuff when the bedroom set arrives."

"What about TV? Are you hooked up yet? Our condo has basic cable, but you're going to need more than that."

"I don't watch much. Besides, when I do have spare time, I have a lot of case files from work that I'm catching up on."

He put some dog food out for Muffin and handed him a treat. "Only things I miss are certain sporting events. I don't know if it's worth a satellite dish."

"You can watch whatever you like on mine. One was already installed when I moved in."

He turned to leave, when she stopped him. "Let's bring Muffin. He must get awfully lonely here by himself."

"You don't mind?"

"Not at all." She grabbed his dog food. "Just bring whatever he needs, okay?"

Jake quickly packed a bag for Muffin, and they carried everything upstairs.

While Jake got Muffin settled, Kari called in the pizza and turned on the TV, finding him a baseball game to watch. The Atlanta Braves were playing the New York Mets, and the Mets were winning by three runs in the seventh inning. Jake popped the top on his beer, and she poured herself a glass of wine.

They sat together on her leather couch, and she watched as a bunch of grown men in tight pants wielding bats ran from base to base. It was so unlike anything that she and Sean would have done together. He had no interest in sports and preferred the news or a concert on PBS—occasionally a movie, sometimes a crime show or, when he was frisky, an adult movie. They spent many nights going for long walks and simply talking and holding hands. She missed that part.

"So, where are you going on your date tomorrow?" Kari inquired during a commercial.

"Renata's." He didn't take his eyes off the screen. "Tiffany made the dinner reservation. Guess it's one of her favorites."

"It's lovely. The outside terrace is so pretty at night. Very romantic," she couldn't help but add. "Every time I'm there, I see a local celebrity or two."

"I can hardly wait," he murmured. "I only hope I can get away early. You won't forget to call, will you?"

"I'll call around ten. That way you can finish dinner but not be obliged to spend the night. Although if Monica looks as good as her pictures, you're crazy to sleep on that mattress of yours alone."

"Have you seen her?"

"I looked her up online. Curiosity got the better of me." She felt her cheeks flame, and, not wanting him to see, she leaned forward to nab a slice of ultrathin pepperoni pizza.

"You looked her up? Why? She doesn't mean anything to me; why should she to you?"

"No particular reason." She wouldn't look at him, and he took hold of her chin.

"Then why are you blushing?"

"I'm not. Well, maybe a little. I was just wondering what she looked like, that's all."

"She's not as pretty as you. Not even close."

Kari held her breath, and the tension between them increased by about nine hundred degrees.

She bit her lip, her eyes on his. "If I invited you to spend the night here tomorrow, would you want to, or is that just something you'd say to Monica to get her to back off?"

His eyes left the TV screen, and he looked at her. "What do you think?"

"I'm not sure." Her stomach flip-flopped, and she knew she was in trouble. Spending time with Jake was stirring up feelings she didn't want to have. She could accept their being friends, but nothing more. She had hurt Sean, and she didn't want to add Jake to that list. He was much too fragile, and she had enough on her plate, between searching for her sister and keeping her job, to worry about his problems too.

"I want to stay." He glanced at his dog sitting next to her feet. "Look at Muffin. He doesn't even like you, but he wants to stay."

As if to prove it, Muffin lifted his head and woofed. Kari threw him one of his soft toys, and Muffin took off on a run.

Kari smiled. "I guess I can put up with the two of you. Even if I do think the whole situation is ridiculous."

"You haven't met Monica." He paused for a moment and then turned toward her. "Hey, why don't you come by tomorrow night and see for yourself?"

"You did two tours in Iraq and handled the enemy just fine, but you can't fight off one woman by yourself?" she said. "Big man like you."

He turned his head and grinned. "I'm afraid of her. I need protection."

"You've got a ferocious dog. What more do you need?"

His gaze flickered over her, and she knew she was playing with fire. Living one floor away from Jake was one thing; seeing him on a daily basis was another. They had mutually agreed to help each other, but how foolish it seemed now. Didn't she know better? She was the moth, and he was the flame.

She couldn't keep her emotional distance from him any more than she could fly.

"Jake?"

"Yeah?" His eyes remained glued to the TV. When she didn't respond, he looked at her.

"Watch the rest of the game. I have a little work to do." She scampered off to the bedroom and shut her door. She knew she was being cowardly, but away from him was the safest place to be.

## CHAPTER TWENTY

Jake knocked on her bedroom door. "You want me to leave?" he asked quietly.

She spoke through the closed door. "No, I want you to stay." She bit her lip. "This is a mistake, I know. We're seeing too much of each other, and it's making me uncomfortable."

"Why? I've done nothing wrong."

"I know, but we've gone down this road before, and I'm not real eager to try it again."

"I'll leave." She heard his footsteps and opened the door a crack.

"Jake, wait a minute."

He stopped walking. She came out of the room. "The inspection is tomorrow, right?"

"Right." He eyed her. "I'll stay at a hotel if I actually do have mold."

"They don't take dogs."

"Some do," he said. "I don't want you uncomfortable. That's the last thing I want."

"What exactly *do* you want?" Her heart thudded at the question, and she wasn't at all sure what she hoped the answer would be.

His gaze roamed over her face and lingered on her mouth. Then he met her gaze.

"The same as you." They stood in silence for a moment, then he cleared his throat. "I want to find Shane, and you want stories." He smiled, but the smile didn't quite reach his eyes.

"Why do you hang around me so much when you could find another woman to love?"

"I don't know. Why don't you ask yourself the same question?"

"I don't love women." She smiled. "Anyway, you're welcome to stay in the den until your inspection is done."

"No need. If Iraq didn't kill me, mold won't either."

"I don't want you taking that risk. Go downstairs, pack a bag, and come back here."

"Promise not to seduce me?" Jake waggled his eyebrows.

She slapped his arm.

"We're mature adults and we can handle this. Besides, it'll make me feel better knowing you're here. Mold can cause serious lung infections."

"I'm better off than thousands of homeless vets on the street."

"I know, but I can't let them all sleep here. Just you."

He glanced at Muffin, who'd settled into his dog bed. "I guess I could. But you've seen my nightmares, and they're not very pleasant."

"All the more reason you should stay."

His eyes held hers, and she felt a flutter of nerves as her insides began to heat. He nodded, then left. Fifteen minutes later, he was back with a small overnight bag in hand.

She led him to the den enclosed by French doors. "There's a small closet, but I don't have any drawers for you."

"That's okay. Don't need drawers. I'll be moving back downstairs Sunday morning."

He took his toiletries out of the bag. "Which bathroom should I use?"

"Not mine," she said quickly. She wouldn't be able to handle the image of him in her shower. She swallowed hard. "The guest bathroom has a shower, and you'll be more comfortable there."

"You're blushing."

She waved his comment away. "It's the wine."

"Uh-huh." He chuckled.

"Look, I let my guard down around you, and we've become friends. That's really something, considering how I felt about you only a few weeks ago." She smiled, shaking her head. "I really hated you, but I don't anymore. We can be friends, nothing more."

"That's fine by me. I don't want anything else either. You deserve someone much worthier than me."

Her stomach knotted, but she didn't answer.

"Well, if you hear me moving around at night, it's best if you ignore me. I'll be fine."

"Jake." She shook her head. "I can't do that."

"Sure you can. I can get pretty edgy, and I don't want to hurt you."

"You can't hurt me." His nightmares might take him to dangerous places, but not with her. She'd bet her life on that.

"I never intend to." Before she knew it, he hooked a hand around the back of her neck and his lips grazed her cheek. "Take that as an apology. I never meant to hurt you."

A sharp pang made her swallow hard. She needed to take a step back and shine up the armor. She'd need it with him around.

"Your apology is accepted. It was all so long ago." She stepped away. "Make yourself comfortable. I have work to do, so I'll see you in the morning."

Kari went into her bedroom and changed into her nightclothes, then settled on her bed with her laptop. She often worked this way on a report for the first morning newscast. It was always a challenge to make her news reports focused, lucid, and, above all, interesting. She had trouble focusing as thoughts of Jake kept intruding. The brief touch of his lips on her cheek had set her heart racing. How could it be? After all these years, how could her feelings still be so intense?

She forced herself to concentrate on her work and put Jake completely out of her head. He didn't belong in her head or in her heart, and she would have to keep reinforcing that if they were to remain friends.

Some time later, she heard Jake roaming around outside her door.

As she didn't hear the sounds of the TV, she figured he must be turning in for the night. She set her computer aside and slid off the bed, intending to see if he had everything he needed. Like sheets—she groaned, realizing she hadn't made up his bed.

"Jake?" she called as she walked down the hall to his door. "I'm sorry, I'm a terrible host." She tapped on the door. "Can I come in? I haven't given you any sheets or a blanket."

"Sure. But I'm good. No need to worry about me."

She peeked in and saw him lying on the sofa bed with his feet hanging over the side. He had a throw blanket over him, but it reached only to his knees. The air-conditioning made it cool in the house, and his legs weren't covered.

"Did I have the game on too loud?"

"No, not at all." Her work had been interrupted, but not by the TV—by the realization that the hate was gone. Her feelings had shifted without warning, and she had to be extremely careful. Jake was not a man she could love a little. He'd suck everything out of her.

"I'll grab the blanket and sheets," she said, "and we'll put your bed together in no time."

"Really, I'm fine. I've slept in a lot worse conditions."

"I'm sure you have. But not in my house."

When she returned with an armful of bedding, he was standing in his Jockey shorts, opening the bed. She walked into the room and stopped. She put a hand over her mouth to stifle her gasp, and the bedding fell onto the floor. She had seen the burns on his hands and his arms, but he'd never mentioned his shoulders and back.

"Jake?" Her heart beating fast, she walked slowly toward him. It took all her willpower not to wrap her arms around his waist and kiss the scars marring his back. His broad shoulders narrowed to a slim waist and hips, but right now, all she could see was raw, ravaged skin.

"You never told me how extensive your burns were."

"I thought you knew." He turned so he was half facing her but kept his gaze on the bed.

"How could I? I don't have X-ray vision."

"Look, it's no big deal. Not to me, anyway."

His face was still turned away, but she could see his jaw clenched. His entire body was rigid. "Thanks for the bedding," he said, picking it up off the floor.

"You're welcome." She grabbed the sheets out of his hands. "This will only take a second. Why don't you stand back and let me get to work?" She tried to calm herself, but the thought of the pain he must have suffered was almost unbearable.

"Knock it off," he said. "I'm quite capable of making a bed." He grabbed the sheets back, again refusing to look at her. "Think anyone else did it for me all these years?"

"Probably not." She watched him flap out the sheet to cover the thin mattress. She grabbed hold of one end and tucked it in. "You don't mind me helping, I hope?"

"Not if you do it correctly. You need to make the corner crease sharper. Like this." He tried to show her how to make the bed military-style, but after she flubbed up two corners, she threw up her hands.

"Forget it. I'm not going to learn that, no way."

"Why not? There are two ways to do something. The right way and the wrong way."

"Well, I like the wrong way better."

He laughed, looking at her poor attempt at a corner. "I can see that."

"Oh, stuff a sock in it. Why does a bed have to be wrinkle free when all you do is sleep in it and mess it up?"

"This won't get messed up." He folded his arms and kept his distance from her. "Not until I deserve a woman like you."

She released a deep sigh, feeling emotionally drained. "Sleep well, Jake."

# CHAPTER TWENTY-ONE

Kari was out the door the following morning before Jake awoke. When she arrived at the news station, she told her assistants to put the sonogram story on hold. "We need to set up something with the Wounded Warriors right away. I want personal stories, both from them and from the men at the Stand Down House. We will keep interviewing and digging until we get what we're looking for." She put her hands on her hips and sighed. "Let's get to work."

She gave her two morning news reports, then joined the hardworking assistants immediately afterward.

Jennifer glanced her way and handed her a printout. "Spoke to the Warrior group. A fellow by the name of Mike Fleming said you can come by anytime. They look forward to showing you around and said the publicity would do them good."

Kari glanced at her watch. "Do they have a Miami office? I could schedule it right now."

"No such luck. Jacksonville is the closest facility," Jennifer replied. "I took the liberty of setting up an appointment for Saturday afternoon. Does that work?"

"I'll make it work. Thanks, Jen."

"I'll come with you," Hugh, one of the cameramen, offered. "Jen, can you book us a flight?"

"On it as we speak." Jen turned to her computer and checked local flights. "Uh, guys, forget it. There's a two-stop connection, and it goes through the Bahamas." She laughed. "You can drive there in four hours."

Kari gave Hugh a high five and grinned. "Road trip." Then she sat at her desk. "Meanwhile, ladies and gentlemen, let's find out all that we can on the Wounded Warriors and get a preliminary tape rolling."

∽

Jake had had a sleepless night, for the most part, but he must have nodded off in the wee hours of the morning. Kari had already left for work by the time he stumbled out of bed.

He grabbed a coffee from the downstairs Starbucks, then went to his apartment to wait for the inspector. With a little time on his hands, he let his mind wander back to the previous evening and how much he enjoyed being with Kari. She was so comfortable to be with, not at all like being around Tiffany or her two girlfriends Maria and Monica. The M&M's. Maria had called him a few times, but he'd always made an excuse about why they couldn't get together. The last time he'd apologized, she'd called him a few choice names and hung up. He could only hope that Monica would do the same.

Kari was different. He liked being around her and knew she was mellowing too. He had no clue why she'd hated him so much, but he was grateful she didn't any longer and hoped to keep the good vibes going.

While the mold technicians did their work, he called a few guys he'd served with, hoping that by the time Kari got home, he'd have a worthy story for her from a reliable source. He'd served two tours, for God's sake. His buddies had to know something—their memories weren't all as fried as his.

Master Sergeant Todd Nichol laughed when he heard his predicament. "You shitting me, bro? What the fuck you telling her stories like that for? Happy endings—that's bullshit. You gotta be real, man. Tell it the way it is. People want the truth about what's happening over there. They get enough lies from our State Department. Damn politicians."

"I know, Todd. But I got things mixed up in my head. I didn't mean to mislead her, but now I have to make things right. Her boss wants feel-good stories, and wants them fast. She'll jump through hoops to get them."

"Seems like you're doing the jumping, not her," Todd said with a snort for a laugh.

"You've got that right. Well, let me know if you think of something."

"I'll do that. But don't hold your breath."

Jake moved to the next man on his list. And the next, and the next. They wanted him to speak up and tell it the way it was. Told him he was a Harvard lawyer, and with his father a general, people would listen to him. They might, he thought, but he wanted to get Congress on his side, not trying to bury him.

Jake put his head in his hands. She'd put her trust in him with that Marshall story, telling it to her boss and all. He'd fucked her up good.

After an hour, the mold inspectors completed their evaluation and reported his apartment was mold free. Now that the major scare was over, he needed to get the cosmetic work done before his furniture delivery. He sat down to call a water-damage specialist and set up an appointment to remove the drywall and restore the damaged wall and flooring to normal.

The work wouldn't be done until Monday morning, so Jake had the rest of the day free. He decided to take a drive out to his father's house, knowing that the general's sources were much farther-reaching than his were.

When he arrived, he found his father in his office.

"How you doing, son? You ready for that hot date tonight?"

"As ready as I'll ever be," he replied. "But I hate to say it: she's not really my type."

"You kidding me? That girl is everyone's type."

"I came to see you, sir, because I wanted to speak to you alone. You got a minute?"

"Sure. You want a coffee or a bottle of water?"

"Water's fine." They wandered into the kitchen, and his father handed him a cold bottle from the refrigerator.

"Tiffany's out shopping," his father said. "I swear she's going to put me in the poorhouse." He made a grand gesture with his coffee mug. "What could she possibly need? Every closet in the house is filled with her belongings."

"I don't know." He hadn't come to discuss Tiffany's buying habits. He had things more important on his mind. "I need to ask you a favor. Kari's replaced her runaway series with one about returning war heroes and needs some 'happy endings.'"

"Shouldn't be a problem with that."

"Well, she needs them fast. They air in two weeks."

"I'll call around and see what I can find out."

"Thanks, Dad." Jake took a slug of water, then wiped his mouth. "You heard from Brent? I spoke to him a couple of days ago, and he said he's leaving in a few weeks for his training."

"Yes, I know."

Jake was silent for a minute, uncomfortably aware of the anxiety churning in his stomach. He couldn't understand why his father would be happy to see his youngest son go off to war. He knew the risks. Unless a man was extremely skilled and extremely lucky, he would not come back uninjured, if he came back at all.

He kept his gaze on his chilled bottle as he spoke. "You think he's going to make a good military pilot?"

"We'll have to wait and see."

They sat in silence for a few minutes, then Jake told his father about Stand Down House, Roy Foster, and his need to participate in getting the homeless vets off the street.

"What do you want me to do?" his father asked, looking at him. "This is a growing problem, and it's not going to be an easy fix."

"Yes, sir. I agree with you, but you know people with political clout who can get things done. I'd appreciate if you could make some calls, help me get the ball rolling."

"I'll do my best. That's all I can promise."

Jake felt better having vented his concerns with his father. He knew he couldn't do a damn thing about all the lives lost in the fight for freedom, but he could do something for the vets who were lost right here.

∽

Kari returned home late in the afternoon, surprised that Jake was nowhere in sight. Needing to blow off steam, she decided to go for her five-mile run. She returned dripping wet, hair pasted to her skull, red in the face, but feeling great. Exercise always did that for her. No matter how bad she felt, a hard workout melted the tension away. She had started running after her sister disappeared, and it was the one constant in her life.

After her run, she found Jake in the kitchen, making more calls.

"How's the mold problem?" she asked.

"I got lucky. Just water damage." He rubbed his jaw. "Saw my father today. I told him about meeting Roy Foster and his housing project for homeless vets, and asked for his support." He glanced at her. "He's also checking for stories for you."

She grabbed a bottle of water from the fridge and gulped it down quickly. "That's great."

"You don't sound very enthusiastic."

"I'm just worried, that's all. I have a couple of great stories lined up, but they're going to take time, and that's not a luxury I have. I need something quick."

"I'm going to get you something. Don't worry, it'll work out."

"It better, or my series will be dead in the water." She remained where she was standing, wondering how much she dared push. "I never should have told Tom about that damn story until I'd done my homework and had it thoroughly checked out."

"Why did you?" he asked quietly. "You knew my memory wasn't solid."

"Jeremy was lurking in the wings. I had to take the leap of faith."

He began to pace the room. "Go take your shower. I helped create your mess; now I need to fix it."

"I need to cool down." She shook her head and sent perspiration flying.

He handed her a paper towel.

"Are you always such a pain in the butt?"

"You ain't seen nothing yet. I'm a stickler for cleanliness. I would have this place spotless if I had the time."

"It is spotless, but go right ahead. Knock yourself out." She wiped the sweat off her arms and chest and dropped the paper towel at his feet.

He picked it up with two fingers, looking as though he might get swine flu simply by touching it.

"You do that one more time, I might have to punish you," he said.

Noting the devilish twinkle in his eye, she played along. "Really? And just how would you do that?"

"Don't forget, I'm a highly skilled fighting machine and battle-hardened marine officer." He glanced at her. "I may have to take you over my knee."

"Spanking women is not a skill set." She laughed. "I think I'll go take that shower after all." Walking away, she tossed over her shoulder, "The fridge needs a good cleaning if you're restless."

She grabbed the bottom of her shirt and pulled it over her head, letting it fall to the floor. She wore a sports bra and snug athletic shorts, and knew exactly what she was doing.

He glanced at the shirt and walked toward her. "Don't expect me to pick that up."

"I'll get it when I'm done." She wondered why she was egging him on. Was she so worked up she needed a good fight?

"Pick it up." His gaze roamed over her, lingering here and there. Her body responded with instant heat. Maybe taking off her top had been an error in judgment. She was agitated, edgy, and angrier at herself than at him.

Frustrations had been building all day and needed a release.

"Go shower," he said, his voice sounding huskier than usual. "I still have calls to make."

"Phone sex with your model friend?" she teased.

"No. I'm going to find you a damn story. Now go."

He leaned toward her, and she held her breath. She half hoped he'd do something risky, like slip his hands around her waist and give her a meaningful kiss. Maybe that was what she needed to melt her tension. Hot kisses and mind-blowing sex.

Instead, he picked up her top and handed it to her. His gaze held hers.

## CHAPTER TWENTY-TWO

Kari finished her shower, dressed in a pair of shorts and a tee, and came out, ready to have a serious talk with Jake. She felt a little calmer than she had before, but she still had more questions than answers.

"Any luck?" she asked, plopping down on the sofa, tucking her feet under her.

"Not yet. I'm sorry." He had a defeated look on his face.

"It's all right. I'll get them."

"I had such high hopes that my memory was coming back, but I'm afraid it's not," he answered softly. "Nothing I said to you was true. Well, the events happened, but nothing ended the way you and I hoped. I even checked on that first story. Remember the young woman I told you about? Well, Jamie Parsons didn't make it out alive. I had the name mixed up. It was another female officer who adopted the Iraqi child and brought her home to America." He put his head in his hands and looked so woebegone that her heart softened for him.

"That's all right, Jake. I did my own research. The night you told me. I wanted to give you closure, help you so you'd know the ending and never have to wonder the way I do with my sister." She got up and found her notes. "See? I did this for you."

"You did this for me?" His face darkened. "Yet you never told me?"

"Once I found the truth, I decided not to burden you and hurt you. If it had a happy ending, I would have told you at once. I was afraid that instead of opening your mind, you might shut down again. I was worried for you."

His eyes were steady on hers. "You expect me to believe that?"

She jerked back. "It's the truth. Why else would I do it?"

He didn't say a word, and the realization of what he was thinking drained the blood from her face. She felt cold inside. Empty. "You think I would've used that story?"

He still didn't answer.

"I wasn't going to use it. Not without your permission."

"Kari. Your career is number one with you. Isn't that why you didn't want to marry Sean? Why you choose to live in this museum, without friends, photographs, or anything that might distract you from your goal?" He spoke in a low, broken voice. "You hold people at arm's length, not allowing yourself to care." He glanced away, and his shoulders dropped. "You would have used that story."

Kari opened her mouth to defend herself, and then shut it again. "That's right. I would have, and I've been using you too."

"I didn't say that."

"You didn't need to. And yes, if push came to shove, I would have aired that story. Maybe I still will if I can find the name of that real person. Why not?" She jumped up, eager to be away from him. "I have no intention of sitting still and letting Jeremy swoop in to steal my show. It's mine and I'm keeping it."

"I knew it, but at least I expected you to deny it."

She clasped her arms around her and tried to hold it all together, but inside, she was freaking out. "Why would I do that? I might be a user, but I'm not a liar."

"Kari…" He approached her and tried putting his arms around her, but she shoved him away.

"Don't touch me. I don't want you here. Please go."

He stared at her.

"You don't trust me, do you?" she whispered.

"I want to, but how can I?"

The words hung in the air.

Jake's jaw was set. "I'll sleep at my father's tonight."

"Yes." She walked toward her bedroom, not wanting to watch him leave.

∼

Jake packed his few belongings, picked up Muffin, and headed to the elevator. He didn't blame Kari entirely. It was her job to get stories, and that's what she'd done. But going behind his back…why? All she had to do was ask.

He'd tried to do the right thing by her. Actually, when he told her that first story, it wasn't for her series; it was purely for himself. He'd been excited that he could recall the flashbacks and had asked her to write it down, afraid that his memory wouldn't last until morning.

She'd recorded it and given him the tape. Then she'd gone home and researched the story. It was possible that she had told him the truth, but it was also possible that she would have used it anyway.

Hell if he knew. They both needed time to cool.

He knew how worried she was. If she didn't get her stories in time, her career would be in jeopardy. Even if he was good and pissed at her, he didn't want that to happen.

"Muffin, ole boy, we're in the doghouse together."

The dog licked his chin. "I know you liked it up there, but we've got our own place to stay. It's not as comfortable, but it's better than that doggy heaven you were headed for and nicer than my previous digs in Iraq."

"*Yip, yip,*" Muff answered.

He glanced at the dog's trusting dark eyes. "I wonder what Tiffany would do if I brought you along to our dinner tonight." He scratched behind the poodle's ear. "I have half a mind to take you to find out."

He opened the sliding glass door and put out a puppy pad, leaving Muffin to do his business. He took a shower, and when he returned, he could see that the wind had picked up, blowing in a full gale. Storm clouds were gathering, and heavy rain was imminent.

The last thing he wanted to do was go out tonight. They were supposed to dine under the stars. Fat chance of that. Taking his sweet time, he reluctantly put on a suit, straightened his tie, then walked over to the window to stare at the approaching storm. He was about to pour himself a single-malt scotch, when the phone rang. It was his father.

"The ladies have decided we should eat in."

"Uh, fine. Although I could take a rain check."

"Just come on over. Monica is anxious to see you."

Jake closed his eyes and shook his head. Didn't he have enough problems? "Can't imagine why. We don't have anything in common."

"She's a lot smarter than you think."

"Look, sorry if I'm a bit out of sorts, but I've had a rough day. Were you able to find any stories for Kari?"

"Not yet. This kind of thing takes time. But I started networking."

"Thanks, Dad."

"We'll see you shortly," his father answered. "And try to be pleasant."

"Yes, sir." Jake hung up and walked over to his makeshift bar. He poured himself a drink and tossed it back. He'd need a slight buzz if he had to spend an entire night with Tiffany and her friend.

What in hell would they talk about? The latest Milan fashions?

It was so damn easy with Kari. He could be anywhere with her and be comfortable. There was no pretense. It was the real deal. Or had been. Stinking stories. Should have seen that coming. The war had done more than screw up his memories. It had tainted his views on people and shaken his faith to the core.

∽

"Jake," Monica greeted him. "Let me take your jacket. You're soaking wet."

He shrugged off his coat, then ran a hand through his wet hair. "I'm parked in the drive and only walked a few steps." He shook his head, spraying water on the hallway floor, as well as on Monica. "I'll grab a towel." He ducked into the guest bathroom and dried off as best he could.

Monica waited for him. "I'm so sorry we didn't get to go out tonight," she gushed, taking his arm, "but this will be more intimate."

"Yes, well…"

"Hi, Jake," Tiffany sang out. "Come into the kitchen. I'm putting out appetizers, and your dad's pouring drinks."

Monica led Jake, and he forced a smile. It wasn't his father's fault that he kept such bad company; he'd always been a sucker for a pretty face.

"What are you having, son?"

"A glass of red?" He shook hands with his father and gave Tiffany a brief kiss on the cheek. "Steaks look good," he added, eyeing the platter on the counter.

"The finest porterhouse from Whole Foods," the general said proudly.

"And we have stone crab with mustard sauce for an appetizer," Tiffany squealed.

"Sounds better all the time." He picked up his wine and clinked glasses with Monica and the others. "Who needs to dine out when we have all this at home?"

They ate the cracked crab in the kitchen and, as expected, talked about nothing. When it was time to grill, Jake offered himself for the job.

"We can do it under the broiler," Tiffany said. "It's raining too hard to go outside."

"It's covered." His father picked up the platter. "We'll monitor the meat. You girls get the table set and whatever else you've got to go with it."

When the two men were outside, his father turned to him. "I've made a few calls, like you asked. Someone should be contacting Kari shortly. Also, the National Coalition for Homeless Vets called me back, and I told them about you and how you want to help. Gave them your number."

"Thanks, Dad. I appreciate that."

"How's the job going?"

"It's okay. Can't say I'm exactly enthused."

"Give it some time."

"I will. I'm sure that I'll get excited again once everything settles down."

"Good." He turned his attention to the slabs of meat. "You still like your steaks bloody?"

"Is there any other way?"

Monica poked out her head. "Baked potatoes are ready. Do you want asparagus or mushrooms?"

"Whatever's easier," Jake replied.

"How about both?" his father said. "We've got a young man here with a big appetite."

Monica's eyes raked over him. "I can see that. We don't want him to go without, now, do we?" She gave him a flirty smile, then swayed her hips as she walked away.

His father grinned and winked at him. "Hope you're hungry."

They took their time over dinner, and Jake listened to the women's lively conversation, letting his own mind wander. He was ticked at Kari, not so much about her researching the Parsons story, but for holding the information. Regardless of the outcome, she should have told him what she had learned. She must think him a real flake. Not mentally strong enough to handle unpleasant news.

He wanted her to be open with him, trust him, and have some damn respect, not treat him with kid gloves. Like Monica here. She didn't baby him.

She was sitting next to him, so he gave her a wink. "That was a heck of a dinner. You girls knocked yourself out." He patted his tummy. "Couldn't eat another thing."

Maybe the wink was misleading, because she bumped his shoulder and leaned in close. "Not every day do we get to serve one of our war heroes."

"Cut it out. I told you, I didn't do anything special."

"Don't believe you," she giggled, and it was obvious she was a bit tipsy.

Tiffany laughed. "Come on, everyone. Drink up. I'm going to make coffee and bring out the liqueurs."

Jake drank a couple cups of coffee but wouldn't touch anything else alcoholic. His head had started pounding right after dinner and was gearing up for a good one. "I'm not feeling so good. I'm afraid I should head home."

"Don't leave," Monica whispered. "We thought you'd stay the night."

"We have your bed made up for you," Tiffany told him. "If you're not feeling well, you can lie down here."

"Yes. There's no need to leave," his father spoke up. "Don't you have a mold problem?"

"No. The inspection proved otherwise. It's quite safe for me to sleep there." He glanced outdoors. "And the rain stopped."

His father smiled at Monica and gave Jake a meaningful look. "Take it easy, lad. Hang out for a while. We've got Tylenol or anything else you might need."

"Please?" Monica put her hand on the back of his neck and ran her fingers through his hair to massage his scalp.

Had they been Kari's fingers, he would have enjoyed it more.

"No, really. I'm bad company when these headaches come on." He knew he had to get away before he disgraced himself. "I'm sorry, everybody. It was a nice evening, and I'm sorry I have to spoil it."

"I'll take care of you." Monica's free hand squeezed his thigh, then slowly reached higher. "I promise."

He felt her hand touch his crotch, and he jumped. He knocked over his half-empty glass of wine. "Holy shit." He felt heat rise and flood his face.

He grabbed his napkin and attempted to blot the wine, not wanting to see the look of shock on everyone's face. No one got it. Just because he looked okay on the outside didn't mean a damn thing. He was damaged goods, not the hero they all wanted him to be. The sooner they realized it, the better.

"Time for me to leave. Thanks for dinner." He got up and walked out.

# CHAPTER TWENTY-THREE

On the drive home, Jake worried he'd pass out. Somehow, he managed to get himself back to the condo. He could feel himself sinking deeper and deeper into that dark hole of his, and instead of fighting, he welcomed it.

The flashbacks were vivid and swift, the faces he couldn't forget. The little boy and his mother. Alive one minute. Dead the next.

The phone rang several times, and he thought he heard Kari's voice, but in his mental state, the words were nothing more than jumbled noise. He tuned it out, just as he tried to tune out the sounds of heavy mortar fire and exploding grenades, and the piercing screams of his comrades falling around him.

He'd spoken to psychologists at Walter Reed, again at the burn unit in Tampa, and had seen one here too. He knew all about coping devices. He just had to use them.

Not bothering to get out of bed, he turned on the cheap clock radio next to him, setting the volume as high as it would go. The piercing noise grounded him and drove away the demons.

∼

Kari simmered for hours after Jake left. The fact that he had not believed her and had chosen instead to think the worst made her so angry she couldn't think straight. Oh, how she'd love to prove him wrong and shove it in his face. Make him feel like the complete idiot he was. After all they'd been through, how could he think so little of her?

If the story had the happy ending she'd been looking for, of course she'd have shared it with him and asked permission to use it, but since it didn't, she hadn't seen any reason to bring it up. She was protecting Jake, not using him.

Why had she let him get under her skin? Who cared what he thought? Let him think the worst of her. Good riddance. She didn't need him. She didn't need anybody. Hadn't she proven that over and over in the past ten years? The only thing she needed was her job, and now, thanks to him and his lousy stories, even that was no longer secure.

She cursed the day he had walked back into her life.

She poured a large glass of wine and sat down to think. She wanted to prove Jake wrong and make him eat his words, but what was the point? It was better for them both to simply go their separate ways and stop banging heads.

Without his so-called help, she already had three shows in the works—Roy Foster, Operation Wolfhound, and the Wounded Warriors would all make for excellent viewing. She had everything under control. Once the interviews were done, she could possibly have six weeks of fascinating stories.

She turned on the TV and watched a romantic comedy, but it didn't do anything to lighten her mood. Jake's distrust hurt her to the core, and until she got to the bottom of it, she wouldn't rest.

Kari was not the type of person to let things go. She'd fought hard to keep her sister's memory alive, to hang on to a thin thread of belief, and it was that same stubborn spirit that bugged her now. Picking up the phone, she called and left a curt message. An hour later, she tried again.

So he had gone out after all. Well, she damn well hoped he drowned in the rain. It was coming down in buckets. What kind of a fool would go out in weather like this?

She went to bed, and for a full hour, she tossed and turned. It was after eleven, and the more restless she became, the more she fumed. She couldn't sleep, and it was all Jake's fault. She needed to see Jake face-to-face and talk things through. Once she got this heavy load off her chest, she'd turn around and come back upstairs.

Minutes later, she was dressed and pounding on Jake's door. He didn't answer, but she could hear Muffin growling and making yipping sounds.

She knocked harder. "Jake! Open up. Let me in."

She heard his cursing, the loud mumblings, and a heartbreaking sob.

"Jake. Jake." She knocked again, not caring if she woke up the neighbors. "Open up. I need to talk to you."

The dog started to howl, and after several minutes, she heard someone fumbling with the lock. Then the door opened. Jake stood there, blinking as if he didn't quite know where he was. His hair stood on end, and his handsome, strong face looked tortured.

"What are you doing here?" he asked.

Muffin jumped around his feet, unusually agitated. He snarled at Kari.

"I...I wanted to tell you how mad I am. Are you all right?"

"No, I'm not." He made a move to close the door, but she pushed her way through. "What the hell!" he yelled. "What do you want from me, anyway?"

"You don't look very well."

"I don't need you or anyone else messing with me." He walked back to his bed on the floor and squatted. "I'm coping, all right?"

"What happened tonight?"

"Nothing. Just another headache."

"Can I help?"

"Go away, Kari." His eyes met hers briefly, then shifted away. "You were right to send me packing. I'm no good for anyone."

She took his arm and tried to force him to his feet. "Come on. You're coming with me so I can keep an eye on you."

"I'm not going anywhere."

"You're starting to piss me off." She glared at him. "If you won't come with me, then I'm staying here."

He put his head on the pillow and closed his eyes. "Get out, Kari."

She stood for a moment, undecided. Then she remembered standing outside his door and hearing the sound of his sob. She kicked off her sandals to lie beside him.

"What are you doing?"

"I guess I'm staying."

"Why are women so friggin' stubborn?" he growled. "Take your good intentions and fuck off."

"You can swear at me all you like, but I'm not budging."

"Go to hell."

She didn't say anything, just curled beside him without touching him. Jake tensed. Muffin found a spot next to their legs and rested his head on her.

She moved an inch closer, resisting the urge to touch him. She breathed his familiar scent and felt tears in her eyes.

"Why are you here?" he whispered some time later.

"You need me."

He looked over his shoulder at her. "If you don't leave now, I might do something really stupid."

Her heart raced. "Like what?"

Even in the darkened room, she could see the fire burning in his eyes. "You know what."

"No. I don't."

He turned fully toward her and pulled her roughly against him. Muffin yelped and hopped away. Even through her clothes, she could feel Jake hard for her. His mouth came crashing down on hers, and that was her last conscious thought.

She kissed him with all the hunger in her heart, not caring for one damn minute about the ultimate cost of her foolish actions.

"Take your shirt off," she gasped, undoing his buttons frantically. She needed to touch his flesh, taste his skin.

His hands were groping under her T-shirt, fiddling with the clasp on her bra, so she released the hook herself and tossed it aside.

Oh God, but it felt so good. She moaned and moved under him, wanting his hands, his mouth, everywhere at once. "More. Please, more."

He tossed her T-shirt over the side of the mattress and slid her shorts down her legs. His hands roamed over her breasts, tweaked her peaked nipples, slid over her tummy and down to the moist center that had been waiting for him to come back to her.

She bucked and cried out his name. His mouth clamped down on hers, and his fingers did things to her that only a man like Jake would know how to do.

A heat wave rolled over her, and a tightening in her belly warned her that if he didn't stop, she wouldn't last a second longer.

Her legs wrapped around him, but he didn't release the pressure; he continued touching and kissing her with equal fervor. She tried to pull away, but he held her fast.

The blood flowed to her sweet spot, and she shuddered and clung to him, crying his name as she came.

He wrapped his arms around her and pulled her on top of him. She lay with her head on his chest, gasping for air. She listened to the pounding of their chests, linking her fingers with his.

She knew she should be running to the hills, as far away and as fast as she could, but still she lingered, languishing in the warmth of his arms, in the feel of his body, in the taste and scent of him.

He kissed her brow and whispered, "Who needed who?"

She looked into his laughing eyes.

He flipped her over and kissed her shoulder. "That's all you're getting tonight."

"Jake. You can't..." she protested, but he rolled to his side, his back to her, and after a few minutes, she was listening to the sound of his snores.

She tapped him on the shoulder, but he didn't respond.

Muffin crawled up and laid his head next to her on the pillow.

After several minutes, Kari got up and walked around, fuming.

# CHAPTER TWENTY-FOUR

Jake heard Kari moving about but kept his eyes closed and made soft snoring sounds. He shouldn't have touched her the way he had.

If he wanted a woman in his life, it would be her, no question about that, but he had priorities and they didn't include romance. First, he had to find Shane. Second, he wanted to do something worthwhile with his life, and that meant getting homeless vets off the streets and into transitional housing—nationwide. Third, he had to heal emotionally and learn to live with his demons. Because they sure as hell weren't going anywhere.

Kari needed to find a man who was worthy. She was a beautiful, passionate woman, and even his limp dick got excited around her. He could only imagine sinking into her warm softness and holding her forever in his arms, a dream he didn't dare dream. He didn't deserve that kind of happiness. Not after the things he'd done. Maybe he'd find that kind of forgiveness in heaven, but he sure couldn't find it down here.

He must have dozed off, because when he woke, Kari had curled beside him. She had her hand under his pillow, and her sweet face was inches away from his. Something big burst inside him, and he felt like a huge marshmallow. He put up a finger to caress her cheek and stopped just in time. He didn't want to wake her. Not yet. How many mornings would he have to look at her like this and breathe her scent? He wanted to kiss her soft lips trembling just an inch from his. Her shoulder was bare, so he shifted the thin blanket to fill his eyes as well as his senses. She'd removed her clothes but kept her panties on.

Her breasts were plump and rosy, and he longed to touch, to hold, to put one of her delicate rosebuds in his mouth. God, he was so hard looking at her. She was so tiny and lean, and he wanted to stroke her flat stomach, maybe slide his hand to her inner thigh. The urge to take and to possess grew by the second.

If he couldn't have her, the least he could do was save her.

He pushed the blanket off to slide out of bed, when he felt a hand on his shirt, tugging him back. "Where are you going?"

"I have phone calls to make."

"At this hour? Who will be up?"

He bent over and kissed her mouth. He needed to shut her up for one damn minute.

She responded warmly by putting her arms around his neck and letting the blanket slip. Her naked breasts were an inviting feast. He cupped both and slid down to take them in his mouth.

She held his head as he suckled her nipples erect. One hand slipped into his shirt and roamed over his chest and his shoulders, then to his stomach.

He sucked in a breath and moaned with pleasure. Her hands and mouth couldn't pleasure him enough. He was bursting for fulfillment but hadn't earned it yet, and maybe never would. A man like him didn't deserve love. If she knew the things he'd done…After several hungry, deep-throated kisses, he pushed away and stood.

Her face registered disappointment, but he knew it wouldn't for long. Not if he could get her stories.

"Kari, get dressed. Go upstairs and make us some coffee. We have a lot of work to do."

"What do you mean?"

"Your stories, Kari. I'm getting them for you. It's the least I can do."

"It's not your job, Jake. It's mine. My problem, my mess."

He smiled and cupped her chin. "I'm going to make this right if it's the last thing I do. You might forgive me, but I can't."

She sat up, seemingly unaware that she was half naked. "You mean that?"

"I do." He tossed her clothes to her. "Give me half an hour."

She jumped up and kissed him. "The coffee will be waiting."

He waited until the door closed behind her, then jumped in the shower. He forced himself not to panic. He'd already called half a dozen guys this week, but he had plenty more on his list. He would call every damn last marine he'd ever served with and more, if it meant making Kari happy.

Once he was dressed, he packed up Muffin and headed upstairs.

He helped himself to a coffee and told her to take her time with breakfast.

"Okay. I'm going to run to the market and pick up some fresh croissants. We'll have those and an omelet, and strawberries for dessert."

"Sounds good." Already, he was dialing numbers.

A couple of the men had passed on to a better life; some had their numbers disconnected or didn't pick up. Others wanted to chat about old times and get together for a drink but had nothing to offer in the way of good stories. Finally, he spoke to an Army captain he'd been hospitalized with at the burn unit in Tampa. They'd spent several months in rehab together, and there was no stronger bond than two men who'd gone through the same hell.

"Yeah, Jake," Lou Brady said in his soft Southern drawl. "I'm pretty sure I know a good story or two. And I agree with your lady friend. The world needs something to lift us up. With no peace in sight and this darn economy, we've got enough to worry about." He chuckled. "Let me think on it a while, and I'll call you back."

"I'd be mighty grateful if you could do that." Jake was already smiling. Lou was the most laid-back man he'd ever met. He'd gone through excruciating pain and cracked jokes the whole time.

"Give me an hour or two, and I'll have something for you."

Kari walked in, a bag of groceries in her hand. "Anything?" she asked.

Before he had a chance to answer, the phone rang. It was Lou calling back.

"Okay, I'm not sure if this is what you want or not, but I remember something. There was a firefight, and we had a lot of newbies in battle, blasting away like kids at a fair. We were fighting a bunch of insurgents, and grenades were exploding, shrapnel was flying, the place was smoking. Suddenly, from out of nowhere, a young boy seemed to rise from the dust, riding through the combat zone on his bike. The firing stopped at once. Everybody put their weapons down and watched the boy until he got to safety. No more shots were fired that day."

"Anybody know who the kid was?"

"He was an orphan, deaf and mentally challenged, and he became something of a mascot for our unit. We'd ride him around in the jeeps, parading him like a hero. He was our good-luck charm."

"Thanks, Lou. I appreciate this." Jake lowered his voice. "I think my girl's going to love it."

"Uh-huh. And now she's 'your girl,' is she?"

"One thing I know for sure: she won't be if I can't get the stories. I owe you, Lou."

"I'll call if I think of another," Lou said. "You take care, now."

Kari came out of the kitchen. "Did you get one?" she asked in an excited voice, sounding much like a kid. He wouldn't be surprised if she started jumping up and down.

"You give me breakfast, then I might tell."

She ran over and jumped on him. "Tell me, tell me, tell me."

Instead, he pulled her head toward him and gave her a thorough kiss.

"I'm starved. Let's eat, and I'll tell you what you want to hear."

He set the table, and Kari served the cheese omelet with warm croissants laden with butter and strawberry preserves. Then she took a seat next to him. "Eat and talk at the same time."

He laughed. "Okay. You've been patient long enough."

Between bites, he gave her the story, and Kari's eyes grew big. "Oh my gosh," she said. "This is great."

"I'm glad I could help." He took a bite of croissant, then wiped his mouth. "I figured Lou Brady would come through, and he did. He's going to check around for more stories too."

"That's so great. I can't thank you enough." She smiled, and he thought she'd never looked prettier. "Of course, I'll need the boy's name and will have to interview some of the men who knew him."

"You'll get it, Kari. When do you need it by?"

"Yesterday."

He didn't laugh. "I'll try to have it to you by noon tomorrow."

"I appreciate this, Jake. It'll be an excellent follow-up to the Roy Foster interview." She ate her last bite, then pushed her plate away. "This will certainly make my bosses happy and keep my series running, for a little while, at least."

He picked up the plates and carried them into the kitchen. He rinsed them, and Kari put them into the dishwasher.

"What do you have planned for today?" he asked.

"I've been thinking a lot about that woman Linda. I may try seeing her again."

"You're still not convinced, are you?"

"No, I'm not. The way she said 'I'm not your sister' didn't ring true. It was as if she was trying to convince me of that. I could imagine Alaina saying that, meaning she wasn't the same person she used to be."

He poured them both more coffee. When he put her mug in front of her, he placed his hands on her nape and massaged the back of her head and shoulders. She rotated her neck, working out kinks.

"Do you ever do anything besides work?"

"Not often. Why don't you get out of my hair and go look for Shane?" She stood on tiptoe and gave him a quick kiss. "You'll stay here tonight, won't you?"

"I might, if you'll have me."

"I still owe you."

He didn't ask what for.

# EPISODE FIVE
## CHAPTER TWENTY-FIVE

Kari spent an hour working on her interview, and once finished, she became increasingly restless. Talking about Linda had given her more questions than answers, and she needed to put her mind at ease.

She drove to the Broward Outreach Center and positioned herself near the entrance of the building, keeping her back to the parking lot. She was dressed in jeans and sneakers and had on a Nike cap pulled down low. No one would recognize her as the morning anchorwoman, and that was just the way she wanted it. She certainly didn't want Linda recognizing her and running back to her car.

After a half-hour wait, the car appeared. Linda grabbed her guitar from the backseat, slung it over her shoulder, and began walking to the building.

Kari kept her head low until she heard Linda's footsteps, then slowly turned. "Hello, Linda." She kept her voice soft and serene, her body motionless, as if she were trying to befriend a wild animal. "I was hoping to see you again. It's me, Kari Winslow, and I wondered if I could take you for coffee."

"You? You're that woman who accosted me a few days ago. Get lost. I've got nothing to say to you."

"Please, let me explain," Kari said. "I'm sorry if my friend and I frightened you the other evening. That was certainly not my intent."

"What do you want with me? I told you, I'm not your sister. I can't help you."

"I know you're not. I realized that once I spoke to you, and I'm sorry about that too. I've waited a long, long time to see my sister again, and it's hard to keep believing."

Linda had a hand on the door, but she hesitated and seemed to listen. She nodded. "I can imagine. Why do you think she's still alive?"

Kari gave her a weak smile. "Why don't you?" She wet her lips. "I have had no evidence confirming that she's deceased, so I prefer to think she is living somewhere, happy, or at least safe."

"Then why wouldn't she just come home?"

"I don't know, and I wondered if you could spare ten minutes, have coffee with me, and help me understand what might have happened to her, and why she'd willingly stay away."

"What makes you think I have answers?" Linda pulled the door open a few inches but didn't go inside.

"I don't know why. I'm almost as confused as you are as to why I'm here. I just want to try to figure out what happened to Alaina." Kari's voice nearly broke. "What would make a young girl run away? She wasn't mistreated at home, but she did have a drug habit she couldn't kick. Or didn't want to. Why? Why would she choose a life on the street instead of getting the help my parents offered her? And if she is still alive, why would she never contact me?"

Kari sniffled and wiped away a tear. She couldn't remember the last time she'd cried, and she wasn't going to do it now. She needed answers, and if she fell apart, she'd never get them.

Linda dropped her hand and turned to face Kari. "I don't know what you expect me to say, but I can see that you're in pain, and if I can help, why not?" She shrugged and glanced at her cheap watch. "I can spare ten minutes. We can get coffee inside."

"Thank you, Linda. I appreciate it."

Jan was at the reception desk again. She greeted Linda and looked at Kari suspiciously, but didn't question them. Linda led the way to a small coffee shop on the main floor.

They sat at a corner table, and Linda vigorously stirred sugar and cream into her coffee.

"Okay," she said. "What do you want to know? Since I've never met your sister, I can only guess at her motives."

"That's good enough. I've been doing that for years." Kari added cream to her coffee and tried not to grimace at the bitter taste. No wonder Linda added so much sugar.

"Alaina was sixteen years old when she left," she began. "She was very pretty and very popular but ran with the fast crowd at school. She started experimenting with drugs, marijuana at first, then pills, and then cocaine. I don't know what all she tried."

"Did she get in trouble at school? With the cops?"

"The school called my parents in—they were disturbed by her changes in behavior, the poor grades. They asked for her to be drug tested, and my parents had no choice but to comply."

"And they found a whole bunch of drugs in her system, right?"

"That's right." Kari sipped her coffee again, then shuddered and pushed the cup away. "My parents got her to see a counselor a couple days a week, but it didn't help. She started skipping school, and finally they suspended her. The school counselor suggested a rehab program."

Kari looked down at the table, remembering how frightened they had all been when they'd taken Alaina to the rehab clinic, how lost they had felt just leaving her there.

"She did okay, got clean, was out in four weeks and back at school. But then she fell right back into her old ways. Hanging out with the same kids, doing the same old stuff."

Kari stopped, remembering how things had only gotten worse. At least before rehab there had been some hope that they could reach her and save her. "After rehab, she didn't seem to care about anything except scoring her next high. Mom and Dad were beside themselves. They tried all the strategies the counselors at the rehab program suggested, but none worked. Finally, everyone agreed that Alaina would have to go back to rehab, and for longer this time."

"She didn't go?"

"No." Kari looked at Linda. "That morning when my parents got up to take her, she was gone. We haven't seen her since. That was nearly fifteen years ago."

Sympathy softened the hard look in Linda's eyes. "I don't know how I can help. If you haven't been able to find her, she must have covered her trail pretty good."

"What would make a young girl do something like that?"

"Did anyone go with her? A boyfriend? Someone she knew? A pimp? A dealer?"

"Not that I know of, but then, we didn't know the people selling her this shit. She never gave Mom or Dad names, and they didn't press, because she was so crazy then, they were afraid to push her too hard."

"I wouldn't be surprised if she had a boyfriend who got her hooked, then pimped her out. Happens every day."

"So you think she ended up on the street, turning tricks, and either is still at it or came to a bad end?" She shivered in spite of herself.

"Let's just say it wouldn't surprise me. Why else would she have never called, never come home?"

Kari knew it was true. Her happy dreams of finding Alaina alive and content in some other life were just fanciful dreams, not based on any reality.

Her shoulders slumped. "I don't want to believe that," she whispered.

"No one ever does." Linda covered her hand with her own, and it was that act of kindness that was Kari's undoing.

She let out a sob that wracked her whole body and frightened the heck out of her. "Oh my gosh. I'm so sorry. Please forgive me," she mumbled as tears flooded her eyes. She felt them slide unchecked down her cheeks—wet, sloppy tears that kept coming. It was as if a floodgate opened, releasing all the hope she still carried inside.

"That's okay," Linda said. "Let it out. Sometimes it's good just to cry." She continued patting Kari's hand. "I have a feeling that if your sister is still alive, she'd want you to believe. Don't give up on her."

Kari looked at Linda, though the tears still filling her eyes blurred the woman's face. "Thank you, Linda. I really do wish you were my sister."

She smiled shyly. "So do I."

They briefly hugged, and Kari walked away, glad that she'd come. By the time she got home, her emotions were on overload. She changed into her running shorts and took off on a five-mile hike. When she returned, she felt at ease with the world once again. She turned on the shower and stripped out of her wet clothes, wondering if she should lock the bathroom door or leave it slightly ajar.

Locking would be the sensible, prudent thing to do, but leaving it open would be a hell of a lot more fun. She knew she shouldn't be so gung-ho with Jake and should take a lesson from the past. But it was new and exciting, and in some ways even greater than before. They were both mature and had suffered terrible losses, which made finding each other again that much sweeter.

He deserved some good loving. Funny thing was, when he'd been young, he'd felt entitled to anything or anyone who came his way. Now, his spirit was wounded and he didn't feel worthy of either.

She didn't know what had happened over there, but one thing was for sure: whatever he had done had been for a very good reason.

Tonight, she wanted to release him from his bondage and free him as a man.

When she heard a key in the door, her pulse raced. Without thinking, she ran a hand through her short hair, fluffing it.

He entered, carrying a large bag of rotisserie chicken, a pint of potato salad, a bakery box, and a bottle of wine. "I didn't want to come back empty-handed. I feel like I'm freeloading off you."

"Don't be silly." She laid out the food and peeked into the box. "Carrot cake. My favorite."

"I knew."

"Thank you." She was touched that he remembered after all this time. "So, how did your day go?"

"I don't have much to tell."

"I do have things to tell."

"Let's sit down and have a drink."

"I have a bottle of white open."

He headed for the fridge, and she followed him. "What happened?" He grabbed the bottle and poured two glasses of wine. "Did you get some work done?"

"Even better." She toasted glasses with him and took a sip. "I saw Linda, and I'm certain she's not my sister, but we had a nice long talk and she made me feel better."

"I'm glad. You need closure." He gave her a small hug. "Put that chapter behind you."

She smiled at him, feeling way more than she should. She couldn't help thinking that maybe another chapter was about to begin.

## CHAPTER TWENTY-SIX

They took their wine out to the balcony to enjoy the late-afternoon sun. The courtyard was humming with activity, and a small band had set up to play. She asked him about his day.

"Interesting, to say the least." He rubbed a hand over his jaw, as if trying to recall. "I took Muffin for a walk on the beach, and he got a big kick out of it. Ran into the water, rolled in the sand. Made a big mess of himself." He shot her a look. "Wouldn't believe who I ran into."

"Oh, no. Don't tell me."

"Yes. I took him to Carlin Park, and there were Tiffany and Monica, strolling the beach in their teeny bikinis. Tiffany spotted Muffin and let out a bloodcurdling scream."

Kari sputtered, nearly choking on her wine. "Oh my gosh! She thought he'd been put down."

"True, but she pretended to be overjoyed to see him alive. Didn't fool me a bit." He chuckled. "Muffin took a good nip out of her when she tried to pick him up. He's a smart dog, I tell you."

"Where is Muffin?" She gave him a worried look.

"I had to wash him, and he's home drying. If you want, I can get him later."

"Please do. We don't want him all alone, gnawing on that wound of his. Why does he do that?"

"The surgery scar is still healing, so I guess it bothers him."

"Poor baby. Hope he bit her good."

Jake nodded. "She thanked me for saving him and said she'd made a mistake and wanted him back."

She gave him a questioning look. "What did you say to that?"

"No fucking way." He grinned. "I think those were my exact words."

"So, was Monica pissed because you didn't stay last night?"

"I'd say so. She hardly said a word and gave me frosty looks."

"Maybe she got the hint."

"It was as subtle as a brick."

Kari toyed with the stem of her wineglass, feeling somewhat smug. After all, she'd shared the same bed with Jake last evening, and he wasn't running away scared.

"Jake, what are you doing for your headaches?"

"I've been prescribed an antidepressant, but I don't like depending on a drug." He explained further, "I use relaxation techniques—positive self-talk, imagery rehearsal therapy, all that crap. It works."

"I'm glad you have methods that help you cope." She touched his hand. "I don't like to think of you downstairs, alone. I'm glad you'll be here tonight."

"Ignore me if I have one of my nightmares." He got up to refill their wine.

"Like hell I will." She followed him. "I'll warm up the chicken, and we can eat early. I have a little more work to do this evening and a promise to fulfill." She was standing very close to him, close enough that he could slip his arm around her waist and pull her toward him if he wished.

His eyes darkened, and he looked at her lips. She knew he wanted to, but he held back.

"Why don't you kiss me?"

"I don't deserve you yet." He looked away. "I did things at war, things I'm not proud of. I have to do something right to make up for the wrong."

"Will that take long?" she asked with a smile.

"I hope not." He still didn't look at her. "Meanwhile, you should be seeing other guys, not wasting your time on me."

"Don't have the time or the energy. My job sucks a lot out of me."

"That's too bad. A woman like you should have to beat men off with a stick."

She laughed. "Not interested. Now, I can either pop your meal in the oven for five minutes or zap it in the microwave. How would you like it?"

"Are we still talking about food?" His eyes roamed over her.

"Don't flirt with me unless you're ready to finish what you start."

"Aw, shucks." He laughed. "You're no fun."

"Like last night. Why?"

"Why not?"

"Because it's just wrong. Sex shouldn't be one-sided."

"You saying you didn't enjoy it?"

"I'm saying I could enjoy it more."

He sat on the stool and watched her get the food ready. "You dated Sean for two years. You must have loved the guy. I still don't understand why you didn't say yes."

"I don't want to get married. The whole idea of being stuck with someone forever...well, quite frankly, it frightens me. Besides that, if he was around all the time, he'd have gotten on my nerves."

"What about me?" Jake asked. "Think I'll get on your nerves?"

"You planning to hang around all the time?"

"I might. If you'll let me."

"Then probably yes." Hiding her grin, she put his plate of food in the oven.

He came up behind her and placed his hands on her hips.

"I think you're lying," he said, his breath warm on her cheek.

"Don't count on anything." She turned and faced him. "Especially me." Her heart sped up, and she breathed deeply, trying to steady it. Damn heart. It wasn't safe anywhere near this man.

"Why's that?" He dropped his hands but remained very near.

"Because when somebody gets too close, I push them away."

"I'm close right now and you're not pushing."

She gave him a playful shove. "Go sit down. I'll bring your food when it's ready."

He grinned. "Now you sound like a wife."

"That's something I'll never be." She spoke convincingly, for his benefit as much as for hers.

He took his seat at the dining table. "It's different with me, because I'm so fucked up and feel like I have to do something right to make up for all the wrongs. But you…you're different. You're beautiful, smart, and you should have someone to come home to at night. Someone who adores you and makes you laugh, and holds you when you cry."

"I don't need anyone. I'm perfectly happy." She didn't like the direction this conversation was going. The last thing she wanted was for him to mention children, because she refused to think about the fact that she might be sterile. She didn't want to know. And if she never wanted a family, she wouldn't have to find out. She had her own coping device, which worked perfectly fine, as long as people didn't pry.

She smiled brightly, forcing negative thoughts out of her head. "Eventually, I want to move to New York and work for one of the big networks." She brought him his food and sat next to him. "After college, I moved around a lot. Took low-level journalism jobs all around the country, learning everything I could. Never stayed in one place for more than a year or two, and each move was a step up." She fiddled with the salt and pepper shakers. "I've always been ambitious. Too much so for the average guy."

Jake sliced off a piece of chicken. "You don't deserve an average guy. You deserve someone special, and he will come along one day and change your priorities."

"I'll kick his ass every which way to Sunday if he dares try."

Jake sputtered and choked, he was laughing so hard.

She gave him a fond look. "Okay, now that marriage is off the table, how about sex? No reason why we can't enjoy each other once in a while, is there?"

"Kari, you don't want me. I'm a mess. You've seen that yourself." He stroked her cheek. "Hell, if I was my old self, you wouldn't be able to get rid of me."

∼

After dinner, Kari left Jake to watch TV and went into her bedroom to work. A couple of hours later, she came back into the living room and found him napping on the couch. She left him there and returned to her room to prepare for bed. She put on a black silk nightie and slipped under the covers. Her emotions were all over the place, and she figured she might have a hard time sleeping, but within a few minutes, she drifted off.

An anguished scream woke her.

She lifted her head, and then she heard it again.

*Jake!* She got up, panic building inside her. He'd said not to come if he was having a nightmare, but she couldn't leave him alone.

As she stepped into the hall, she heard moans and thrashing coming from the guest room. She entered quickly and quietly and stood next to his bed.

"Jake," she whispered. "Jake, wake up. You're all right. You're safe."

He flipped over in the bed, flailing his arms and yelling. Even in the dim light from the hall, she could see sweat covering his face and body. When he screamed again, she knew he was in pain.

She touched his arm, trying to wake him. "Jake? Jake, please wake up. You're not hurt. You're fine now."

He flung her hand off him, shouting as if her touch worsened his pain. She sat at the edge of the bed, prepared to dodge his thrashing limbs.

She shook his shoulder and spoke louder. "Jake. I want you to wake up now."

"Get away!" he yelled. "Can't you feel it? Fuck. The heat…Oh my God." He moaned. "Oh, God, it hurts."

"No, it doesn't." She touched his cheek. "It doesn't hurt, Jake. You're better now."

He grabbed her hand, and slowly his eyes opened.

His expression was wild, and for a second she thought he might do her bodily harm. He wouldn't do it intentionally, but he was in the grip of a fearsome nightmare. Perhaps reliving the explosion, the fire that killed his comrades and nearly consumed him.

"Kari?" He struggled to sit up. "Did I do anything? I didn't hurt you, did I?"

"No. I'm fine." She smoothed the hair from his damp forehead. "Just another nightmare."

He took her hand and put it on his bare chest. "I'm burning up. Can you feel it?"

She smiled. "You're warm but not that warm." Leaning over, she kissed him lightly on the mouth. "I don't want you to suffer anymore."

"It's all right." He pulled her down next to him. "It's all right now."

She maneuvered onto her side and put her head on his chest. She snuggled into him, feeling the warmth and dampness of his skin, and her nose twitched at the male scent of him.

He kissed the top of her head and wrapped an arm around her. "I like having you next to me."

She did too. Being in Jake's arms was like coming home, which should have frightened her but didn't. She was the one in control. "I could stay if you want."

"I want you to. Go back to sleep if you can. You have a big day tomorrow."

She nodded and swallowed a lump in her throat. She knew she had to tell him about the baby eventually, but for now, she just wanted to leave things alone. Everything was so fresh and sweet between them, she didn't want to stir up the ugly past.

Within minutes, she felt the rise and fall of his chest, heard his steady breathing, and knew he was out cold. But sleep eluded her. Memories of being with Jake, making love in the backseat of his car, behind a sand dune, in his room when his family was out, she relived them all. Even now, she wanted him physically. Even after the hurt he'd caused her. Even knowing she'd loved him more than he'd loved her.

Her cheek rested on his chest, and she listened to the sound of his breathing, reveling in the warmth of his body, the steady beating of his heart. She had such an intense yearning that it was almost a physical ache.

Kari shifted her weight, wanting to slip out of his arms and escape to her own safe bed, but he moaned and tightened his grip. She rested her head back down and lay still, afraid if he woke up, she might not leave at all.

## CHAPTER TWENTY-SEVEN

Kari woke up early the next morning, still cradled in Jake's arms. Lifting her head, she gazed at the sleeping man beside her, his face furrowed into the pillow, mouth slightly open as he softly snored. She watched the rise and fall of his chest, tempted to run her fingers through the patch of dark, curly hair. Her stomach churned again, but this time, she recognized the feeling. She ached. She wanted. She needed.

That ache came exactly at the right moment, reminding her not to be foolish. How could she let herself get so comfortable with Jake that she'd sleep with him? Had she not learned a thing in the past fifteen years? There was way too much sexual energy between them, and it was going to be hard enough to remain friends. Because that's what they were. She had never thought it possible that she and Jake could get to that point, but they had and she was glad. He had not been responsible for the loss of the baby. She should have spoken to him instead of driving off when she was so distraught, but at the time it had been easier to blame him instead of herself.

She slipped out of bed, careful not to wake him, and went to shower. It was only 4:00 a.m., but she wanted an early start. She didn't have a moment to waste if she wanted her series up and running on time, and with Jake around it was good to keep herself occupied.

When she came out of the bedroom, showered and wearing her robe, Jake was in the kitchen, dressed only in Jockey shorts and making coffee. "Morning. Did you sleep well?"

"Yeah, I slept okay," she answered grumpily. What was he doing up?

"You upset about something?" he asked. "I didn't do anything I shouldn't have, did I?"

"I'm just rushing out, that's all." She brushed her wet hair off her face. "Got a lot to do this morning."

"No problem. I won't get in your way. Want some coffee?"

"Uh—yes." She took the offered cup. "Thanks."

"How about a piece of toast?"

"No. I'll just grab a yogurt."

He took it from the fridge. "Here it is."

She glared at him. "Do you have to be so nice at four in the morning? Why don't you go back to bed? I'm not a morning person, and I like my quiet."

"I won't say a word. I'll just sit here quiet as a mouse." He smiled, which really irked her. "And just as cute, I hope."

She should have laughed, because he was being funny and she was being a bitch. But she didn't laugh. For more years than she could remember, a large hole had existed inside her, but lately, it had become bigger, making her feel emptier than ever. She was so afraid, so afraid that the only way she could ever be whole was to give everything of herself, the way she had when she was young. That would make her vulnerable, something she never wanted to be.

"Suit yourself." She went in to dress, and when she came back into the kitchen, Jake had put on a pair of jeans.

"Did I offend you somehow?" he asked, walking up to her and standing much too close.

"No, Jake, you didn't do anything wrong. I'm just not sure about us getting so close. It would be easy to love you again, but I need to focus on my career and you need time to heal."

He stepped back and stuck his hands in his pockets. "I don't want to drag you or anyone else down. I won't let that happen."

∼

After her early-morning show, Kari sat in a small boardroom with Tom and George. She called the meeting to explain that they couldn't use the story of Lieutenant Marshall and the sonogram, but she was working on something better.

"He didn't make it out alive? What kind of feel-good story is that?" George asked. He prowled around the room like a hungry jungle cat. "I'm worried about you, Kari. It's not like you to use an unreliable source."

Perspiration trickled down inside her bra, and she resisted the urge to squirm. "Look, I know I've thrown a curveball at you, but we will get things straightened out in time. I promise."

"How are you going to do that?" George yelled. "We're airing in three days."

"I want to do a show on Operation Wolfhound, about companion dogs for veterans coping with PTSD. I already have a preliminary tape made, and I'm getting the interviews this week. I'm also driving to Jacksonville on Saturday to meet with the Wounded Warriors and interview a few of the men. This is all good stuff, but it just needs a little time."

"How much time?"

"Well, we're launching the series with the Roy Foster story, which buys us another week. I should easily have the Wolfhound story up and running for the second week."

"We don't need promises. We need guarantees."

"If you're not comfortable with that, I still have several taped episodes of my runaway series, and if we used them to delay the hero stories, it would give us all some breathing room." She straightened her shoulders, sucked in a breath, and went for broke. "This new series is going to be great, but in the best interest of the station and our viewers, we don't want to be too hasty."

"Too hasty?" George glowered at her as he wiped a hand over his shiny head. "If you did your job right, there wouldn't be a problem."

She put her shoulders back and gave each man a measuring look. "I'm only suggesting we hold off for a couple of weeks so I can nail these stories. I have one about a boy who rode a bicycle through a hailstorm of gunfire and came out unscathed. There's a young woman, a marine, who saved an Iraqi child when a village burned, and adopted that child." She was thinking quickly on her feet. "A medic who was captured and tortured, and his miraculous rescue..."

"That sounds interesting."

"Yes, well, the thing is, there are many incredible stories to tell, but we want to do this right." She probably should stop talking, but if she cowered and didn't hold her ground, she'd be eaten alive and spat out.

"You have a scheduled date," Tom told her. "We've already spent time and money on advertising this new series. If you can't do this, tell me now."

"I can and I will. And that's a guarantee." Quickly, she gave him the details of the Lucky Charm story. "My source promised me that he's working on it and will get back to me sometime today. I trust him."

"Your source," George scoffed, "sounds like an ass. Not the least bit reliable."

"He's a United States Marines officer, and his word is his honor."

"You willing to bet your job and reputation on that?" Tom asked.

She gulped. It was a difficult choice, but she had to make it now. "Yes." She had to trust Jake. She didn't have any other option, except to hand in her resignation. "I expect to have this corroborated by noon."

"Well, Jeremy can have the spot if this doesn't pan out. You've really disappointed me. I went out on a limb for you, figuring I owed you that much, since I gave Jeremy the nightly news."

"Is it a done deal?" Disappointment hit her like a smack in the face.

"We came to a decision late last night." Tom's voice softened. "This is best for our station, Kari. He is the more experienced man for the job."

"*Man* is correct. He's not as experienced in local news as I am. I know this town; I understand the people and what gets them excited."

"Good. Now knock 'em dead with this series."

"I intend to."

Her hopes for the nightly anchor job had just been shot to hell, and Tom was throwing her a bone, acting as if he was doing her a big favor. She'd paid her dues, worked hard, and earned every bit of her modest success. She had a faithful viewing audience who turned on her shows each morning and watched her special Friday-night series. But this was business, and in a lot of ways, it was still a man's world.

Kari walked out of the office and sat down at her desk, busying herself with the noon report. She had calls to make and a last-minute editing job, but really, it took no time at all. She was waiting for Jake, and she could not concentrate on anything else. Her goose was cooked if he bailed on her now.

He had not called by the time she was on the air at noon. Knowing that Tom and Jeremy were both watching her—Tom overtly and Jeremy covertly—she did her professional best to remain cool. But the minute she finished, she headed straight to the receptionist and asked if Jake Harrington had called.

"A minute ago. He left a number."

"I have it. Thanks." She went to her cubicle and sat down, swiveling her seat so her back was to Tom's office. Still, she could feel his eyes on her.

"Jake? You got it?"

"I do. The story checks out. You got a pen? I can give you the name of the kid and a few of the troops who called him Lucky Charm."

She let out a deep sigh of relief. "Thanks, Jake. My boss really put me through the wringer this morning."

"Why was that?"

"He was not happy when I told him the Marshall story didn't check out. Said he'd gone out on a limb for me."

"You should tell him to take a flying leap."

"Not if I want to keep my job."

"I'm sorry. I know how important it is to you."

"Don't be sorry. You've saved the day." Smiling, she added, "My hero."

"You get working on this story, and I'll see what I can do to find you another. I'll see you tonight."

Rolling her seat around, she saw Tom staring at her through his open office door. She gave him a thumbs-up, and he grinned.

# CHAPTER TWENTY-EIGHT

When Jake arrived at Kari's apartment that night, Kari had to cool her jets. She was so damn grateful that he'd come through with the Lucky Charm story and single-handedly saved her career that she felt like jumping all over him.

As wickedly handsome as he looked tonight, she needed to try—somehow—to keep her emotional distance.

"Hi, Jake." She frowned. "Didn't you bring Muffin?"

"No. He's sleeping, and I had a better idea. Instead of you cooking, I should take you for dinner."

She looked at the salmon fillets on the counter and figured they could wait another night. "Sure. Sounds nice. It's been a rough few days." It would also get them out of her apartment and away from the temptation to show him her gratitude by removing his clothes and getting naked with him.

Jake took her to Spoto's Oyster Bar, and over dinner she told him about her visit to Stand Down House and how she'd questioned several of the residents but hadn't come away with anything usable. "I had such high hopes too. Figured once they opened up, I'd have a constant lifeline of beautiful stories to tell."

"You're under a lot of pressure to come up with stories quick. This isn't fair to you or to your audience. Or to the men you interview, for that matter."

"You're right, but I can't let Jeremy get this show. He's taken enough from me."

His eyes met hers. "You're also talking to vets who are still struggling with their own problems and trying to come to terms with their experiences over there. The men and women who have been back longer and have strong family and friend connections, or support groups, they're in much better shape. I'll help you get your stories. It'll be easier for me."

"I don't see how—"

"Some people are close-mouthed, especially when it comes to the media. And they especially don't want to talk to you about things you have no experience with, or even an inkling of. I'm one of them. Let's leave it at that."

"Thank you, Jake." She sighed, then lifted her glass of wine and took a sip. "Can we put work aside for an hour or two? Let's enjoy our meal."

Since her favorite subject was off the table, Kari amused him with local gossip about a few of the more high-profile residents of Palm Beach, and that carried them through dinner. When their plates were cleared and they'd finished the last of their bottle of wine, she asked him how his work was going.

"I'm getting back into the swing of things," he answered, leaning back in his chair and looking very content. "I'm up to date on all our major accounts, and a couple of partners have pulled me in on some big deals under negotiation."

"That's excellent, Jake." She leaned forward, folding her hands on the table. "So what does a corporate lawyer do in a typical day?"

"Let's see." He smiled. "You got an hour or two?"

"Sure. Shoot. I want to know how you justify your money."

"Okay. Remember, you asked." He told her that the firm counseled its clients on mergers and acquisitions, purchasing and selling businesses, employment and severance agreements, tax exemptions for nonprofit companies, and contractual disputes. "And that's just for starters."

She had to laugh. "Okay, enough. How are you going to fit in time to volunteer your legal services to the organizations you contacted?"

He shrugged. "I'll make it happen." He leaned forward, his gaze suddenly intense. "Our problems are going to get a whole lot bigger. The number of homeless vets will increase as more and more come back from Iraq and Afghanistan. We need to take action now, not ten years from now."

"You'd think the government would want to help," Kari said.

"The government's doing a lot, but it's not nearly enough, and there simply isn't enough money. Bottom line, we need more funding."

"What about private donations? Is that a way out?"

"Perhaps short-term, but we need a much longer approach than that. Except to people like Roy Foster, homeless vets are invisible. We need to raise their visibility, and we need to convince the politicians in Washington and the ordinary person on the street that these people deserve whatever help we can give them."

"I admit I'd never considered what they're going through before. And seeing your passion about this, I'm ashamed of that. Maybe there's some way I can get people to open up their pockets, once this new series of mine is a go."

"That's a good idea." He spoke quietly. "I'm determined that ten years from now, no more vets will be falling through the cracks and ending up untreated, on the streets."

The depth of his commitment was evident in the set of his jaw and the fire in his eyes. He had never looked more attractive than at that moment, and her heart swelled with pride.

"I'm going to see Roy again tonight," he said abruptly. "He's taking me on his nightly sojourn. We'll be roaming the woods and parking lots until the wee hours of the morning. He keeps trying to convince the men and women out there that help is available, and that all they have to do is reach out a hand."

Regardless of what medals might or might not decorate Jake's uniform, Kari thought, he was truly a hero.

∽

When dinner was over and she was back in her apartment alone, Kari's entire body was humming. Jake might be far from perfect, but he was still the most appealing man she'd ever met. She needed to put the brakes on and proceed with caution. The less time they spent together in private spaces, the better. If the simple touch of his hand on her back as they'd left the restaurant was enough to quicken her breathing and heart rate and send arousing heat through her body, sitting alone with him on her couch would be about as wise as throwing a lit match into a can of gasoline.

It was fortunate that he'd decided to leave tonight and was out searching the woods. If he'd stayed, who knew what might have happened? Now, she could get back to work, occupy her mind with something other than Jake and how very much she wanted him in her bed.

She made coffee and spent the next few hours prepping for her next day's reports and going over the Lucky Charm story. She rewrote it several times, until it had just the right impact and emotional punch, then finally went to bed.

At 2:00 a.m., she woke to a banging on the door.

Sleepy-eyed, she kept the chain on as she opened the door a crack. "Jake," she muttered, "what's happened?"

"I found him. I found him, Kari."

"Come in." She'd get no more sleep tonight, but she didn't care. This was too important, and she wanted to share his happy news.

"I can't believe it," he said as he walked in. Dark circles of exhaustion marred his eyes, yet his voice filled with energy and hope. "I found Shane. He was sleeping in his car in a Walmart parking lot."

"Jake, I'm so glad." She gave him a warm hug and kissed his cheek. "Is he okay? Where is he now?"

"Roy took him to Stand Down House and found him a bed. He's in good hands right now, and I'm going to check on him in the morning."

"How'd he look?"

"A little worse for wear. He was always a handsome kid, and he still is, but those bastards who captured him…" Jake hesitated, and Kari braced herself. "I found his prosthesis in the trunk of the car. Don't know why he wasn't wearing it." His voice cracked, and he stopped for a moment. "How did they expect him to treat their wounded men with only one hand?"

She shook her head in response and steered Jake to her sofa. "Sit. Let me get you some water or coffee."

"Water's fine."

She came back with a chilled bottle, and he downed it all. She sat beside him, not saying anything for a moment or two. Finally, she asked, "What was his mood like? Did he want rescuing?"

"Not sure. He wasn't real pleasant." He ran a hand over his face. "I took him to Denny's for a meal and asked him why he was here instead of back in California, where he had friends and a job. He swore at me and asked how he was supposed to be a firefighter with one hand."

"Did you tell him that Brent's in the army now and doing flight training?"

"No, I didn't want to go into that tonight. He's too close to a dangerous edge." Watching Jake, Kari could see that his anxiety was eating him up inside. "At least he had a car and decent clothes."

"What about drugs? Is he using?"

"Roy doesn't think so," Jake said as he walked into the kitchen and tossed his empty bottle in the bin. Kari followed him, and he continued. "Shane has to get a physical tomorrow—well, later today—and that includes a urine and blood sample. Substance abuse is not tolerated at the Stand Down House, but if he's willing to stay, he'll get straightened out."

Kari knew from her interview with Mr. Foster that along with free housing and nutritious meals, the vets received physical and mental health care, counseling, and job training. The rest was up to them.

"Jake, you found him." Suddenly misty-eyed, she batted back tears. "I'm so proud of you."

He lifted a hand to her cheek. "You have no idea how good that sounds." His eyes seemed to plead with her. She sensed how needy he was, how emotionally overwrought.

She smiled at him as he cupped the back of her neck and pulled her close. "Am I forgiven?" he asked softly, his breath warm on her cheek.

She didn't know if he was referring to breaking her heart or his misguided memory. But she didn't pull away.

"I'd like to make it up to you." His hands slid down her back, and he pulled her against him. "I need you to forgive me."

The words touched her deeply. If ever there was a moment when he needed absolution from all that he carried inside, this was it. "How exactly would you do that?" Her voice was husky, but she hoped he wouldn't notice.

"Do you want me to tell you or show you?" His lips moved against her ear, and she tingled all over.

"Show or tell, show or tell? Uh…let me think." She tilted her head back, wanting his lips on her throat.

He obliged at once. He tasted her skin, offering her soft kisses and little nips of pleasure. She held back a moan, not wanting him to see how much his mouth aroused her.

His hands slid down to her backside, tilting her pelvis forward. He stood with his back to the kitchen counter, with her against him. She could feel the hard length of him through his jeans. Want raced through her, making her wet with excitement.

His tongue plundered her mouth, and she could barely breathe, but it didn't matter. He was in control, and she liked that. She always had.

She pressed against him and kissed him back, her mouth open, hungry, demanding. Holding his face in her hands, she let her mouth explore his jaw and neck. She pushed his shirt aside so she could taste the warm flesh of his shoulder, making him shiver, fueling her desire.

Half carrying her, he led them into the living room and toppled her onto the sofa, landing on top of her.

Putting one leg around his, she slithered up his firm body until they were chest to chest, her needy center in touch with his manhood, only clothing separating them. She kissed him again, unable to stop her moans of pleasure. He pushed his hips into her hips, and the fire inside her flared wildly.

"Jake?" She hugged him tightly, her hands holding his hips against her. "I forgive you. But if you leave me again…"

He looked her in the eye. "Won't happen. I promise."

They kissed and explored each other until she was dancing out of her skin. At some point, he rolled them over so he was underneath her. She could hardly stand another moment of this. She wanted sex so badly, she pushed aside her fear. She was mature, experienced—more in touch with her emotions. She could handle a little lovemaking and still keep a piece of her heart intact.

She undid a couple of buttons on his shirt and slipped her hand inside. He sucked in a breath at her touch. The warm, hard flesh under her fingers felt so good, she wanted to rip his shirt off and lick every inch of him.

His breathing was ragged.

She unbuttoned his shirt slowly, one hungry kiss at a time. She licked his damp skin, letting her fingers and mouth do the talking.

When she reached the waistband of his jeans, he groaned. She smiled, unzipping his fly.

His hands cupping her head, he urged her to look at him. "Do you know how long it's been since I wanted a woman?"

"Shush. Enjoy." She ran her tongue over his belly.

She released him from his pants and took him in her mouth. She let her tongue slide up and down the length of him, loving the feel of him in her hands, the taste of him in her mouth.

"Stop it, Kari." He shifted his weight and dragged her body up his so she was lying on top of him again. "I want to do this properly. In your bed."

She slid off him and took his hand, pulling him off the couch. It was almost a dream, she thought as they walked into the bedroom, being with Jake again. She knew him so well, and yet this man who'd come back from the war was almost a stranger. A stranger she wanted very much to make love with.

She pulled back the covers of the bed, and he embraced her from behind, kissing the back of her neck. She turned around to face him. He crooked a finger under one thin strap of her tank top, pulling it down and exposing her breast.

He bent his head and sucked on her nipple, and she thought she'd collapse right there. This had to be the most delicious feeling in the world. He unzipped her shorts and tugged them down to her ankles and over her feet. He took a second to admire her firm breasts, and then he kissed them as if they were precious offerings.

Before she could stop him, he knelt to the floor. She held her breath in anticipation. His warm mouth nuzzled her lacy panties. She caressed his head, her hands tangling in his hair as her hips thrust gently against his mouth. She whispered his name as flickers of desire built inside her, demanding release.

Pushing the lace aside, he explored her moist heat, first with his fingers and then with his tongue, finding and playing with her most delicate spot. Her knees were weak as she clung to him.

"No, not like this," she told him between gasps of delight. "Do it right."

He chuckled and stood, lifting her onto the bed. She watched him as he quickly undressed, kicking off his shoes, jeans, shirt, and then boxer shorts.

Jake was, burns and all, still the most glorious man she'd ever known. She admired his beautiful, broad chest, narrow waist and hard-packed abs, and something else swollen, erect, and ready to pleasure her. "Do you have anything? Protection?" he asked.

"In my drawer," she whispered.

He found it quickly enough, ripped the packet open with his teeth, and slipped it on. He crawled onto the bed, easing his way between her legs. She took him in her hand and guided him where he wanted to be. He teased her for a moment, slipping the tip of his penis in and out, making sure she was ready to take him. Arching her hips, she rose to take more, and when she couldn't stand another second, he thrust himself to the hilt.

His strokes were strong, confident, his kisses thorough. She wrapped her legs around his back, meeting him thrust for thrust. She'd always enjoyed sex, but this was Jake, and it had been so long since he'd loved her. So many years that her body had remembered him while her mind tried to forget.

Calling his name, she bit softly into his shoulder and she nearly wept. When the explosion came, she couldn't stop, feeling wave after wave. Jake used his arms to push himself off her chest, pumping into her with fast and furious strokes; then he shuddered and gave her everything he had.

She held him for several minutes, enjoying the weight of him, loving how good he felt still inside her. She stroked his back, and a lump formed in her throat as her palms felt the rough edges of his scars.

"You okay?" he asked softly, rolling them to their sides.

"Better than okay." She kissed his mouth. "It's strange being with you again. Familiar but better than before."

"I couldn't agree more." He stroked her cheek and kissed both her eyes. "No more talking. You need to sleep. Anything that needs saying can wait until tomorrow."

"Jake?"

"Yes?"

"Welcome back."

## CHAPTER TWENTY-NINE

Jake was sleeping when Kari slipped out of bed a short time later. She could hear his soft snore as she turned on the shower. Stepping into the warm spray, she tilted her face upward, hoping the shower would revive her energy. She felt zapped. Sex with Jake was beyond good. It was spectacular.

She turned around, and there he stood—a bar of soap in his hand. "Hi, beautiful," he said as he began soaping her down. "You smiling because of me?"

He leaned down to wash her legs, and she indulged him for a moment. His soapy hands slipped between her thighs, and when she pushed them away, he laughed and moved to her breasts. As much as she enjoyed his touch, she didn't have the time to spare.

"Jake, I have to go to work."

"I know you do, and I'm here to help get you out of here on time."

He took the bottle of shampoo and squeezed some onto her hair. His long fingers massaged her scalp, and it felt so wonderful, she let him continue. Men had never spoiled her, mainly because she never allowed it, but she could get used to this. In another minute, she'd be purring if she wasn't careful.

When she was clean from head to toe, she turned off the water and gave him a kiss. "I'd stay and do you, but I've got to fly."

He grinned. "Have a good day at work."

Reluctantly, she left him to dress, surprised that Jake quickly showered and dressed too.

"Little early for you, isn't it?" she said.

"I'm going to put in a few hours at the office so I can head out later this morning to check on Shane. Can we get together tonight?"

"I'm attending an opening at an art gallery. You interested?"

"I'll pass. I need to spend time with Shane anyway."

"Yes, you do." She ran a hand up his arm. "Thanks for the shampoo. Too bad you can't stick around for the blow job."

"You're damn cheeky, you know that?"

She laughed and kissed him good-bye.

When she arrived at the station, she was still smiling.

Tom approached her. "I hope that grin on your face means good news for me."

She nodded and refrained from giggling. "Sure does. We're going to get our stories. Once they start, I'm sure they will keep coming."

"They better," he replied. "You ready to go with that Wolfhound story?" At her nod, he questioned again. "And Lucky Charm?"

"Wrote the piece last night. We've already pulled video coverage of the area."

"Have you got interviews to go along with the video footage?"

"I'm working on them. A few of the men are still on active duty. Interviews with them are not easy to get, but they'll be done."

"See that they are."

"Will do, boss."

She reported her two early shows, then took off for an hour to do chores. She was back at the station well before her noon report.

Jeremy was waiting for her.

She congratulated him on his new official title as anchor for the nightly news, even though it galled her to do so.

His smile was unpleasant. "Tom and I were talking about this hero series of yours. He told me you had some trouble corroborating one of your stories. Mind if I help?"

"I do, actually."

"Come on, we're all on the same team here."

"I'd like to think so." She had a few nastier comments on the tip of her tongue but wisely kept them to herself. She had to play the game, even if it gagged her.

"You're not upset with me, are you, just because I signed the five-year contract?" His smile turned even more unpleasant. "It was never going to be offered to you."

"Says you." She cringed as she spoke the words, thinking how she was slipping fast. Soon she'd be sticking out her tongue and making faces behind his back.

"Ask Tom if you don't believe me. He wanted a man in that time slot." He stuck his chin out and preened. "I've been told that I'm better-looking than Brian Williams. And I'm younger too."

"Younger, maybe. Better-looking, hardly. And I don't see how you can even compare yourself to Brian Williams."

"I could charm the pants off a nun." He raised his eyebrows a couple of times and gave her a devilish smile.

She rolled her eyes. "Charming."

He laughed. "Look, let's bury the hatchet, shall we?" He held out his hand. "Come on, give it a shake. We got off on the wrong foot, but we can still be friends."

"I'd rather shake hands with a snake."

Jeremy's eyes narrowed, and he exhaled an angry breath. "I've tried everything to get along with you, to no avail. You're only making it worse for yourself. If push comes to shove, who do you think Tom or George will listen to?"

Jeremy was right, dammit. But she couldn't seem to stop butting heads with him. He brought out the worst in her.

"Okay. You win. I'll bury the attitude." She nodded in acquiescence, knowing she'd only hurt herself if she continued offending him. "We need to get along. It's in the best interest of everyone in the newsroom."

"Now you're talking." He gave her his best TV smile. "I want this series of yours to succeed as much as you do. If our ratings go up, it means better exposure for me, as well as everyone at PB News." He gave her a measured look. "I can help, if you'll let me."

"Help me how?" She still didn't trust him. She never would fully.

"Your story about the female marine in Iraq. The village burned, and Susan Fields snuck in during all the chaos and bloodshed and rescued a child. Later, she adopted that child. It's a heart-wrenching story."

"What are you talking about?" Kari's nerves stood on alert. This was Jake's story, but she hadn't discovered the name of the marine who'd survived. Jake had said he'd gotten the names mixed up, but he'd been so angry when she'd told him about researching the story that she had never questioned him further. So how had Jeremy come up with this?

"Tom ran your stories past me, and I knew they were good. I've already talked to Fields. She was stationed in Baquba, where she befriended a young girl whom she then adopted and brought back to the States. I have her number. Give her a call."

"And you can corroborate her story? You have statements from other sources?"

"Of course. I'm not stupid." Jeremy's eyes narrowed, and he crossed his arms over his chest.

She was excited but annoyed that Jeremy had discovered this Fields person before Jake. It was his story, only not the person he remembered.

"I'd like to speak to the woman myself." She kept her voice level, not wanting him to see how eager she was to get this rolling. "Once I talk to her, I'll schedule a meeting."

"No problem. I'll forward everything I've got. This is your story. I was only trying to help."

"Thank you." She gave him a brief smile, although she still had doubts.

Why would he go to so much trouble when they weren't friends? Was this his peace offering for stealing the nightly news position from under her nose? As he had clearly stated, it was in his own best interest for the station to succeed. The higher the ratings for the news programs, the more highly regarded the station and its news staff would be.

It *did* make sense, and yet…

# EPISODE SIX
## CHAPTER THIRTY

The moment Kari got home, she called Jake's cell. He told her he was at the VA hospital with Shane. Shane had a bad cough and was undernourished, and the doctors suspected he had a bronchial infection.

"I called Brent," he went on, "and gave him the news. He's excited I found Shane, but he's also pissed that because of his training he can't get away."

"That's too bad," Kari said. "It would do them both good to see each other. I'm sure Brent could help straighten him out better than anyone."

"I couldn't agree more." He sighed. "How'd your day go?"

"Broadcasts went well, and the Lucky Charm story is pretty much ready to go. I had an assistant get a few more testimonies today, but, Jake, I have to ask you something." She took a deep breath. "Jeremy came to me and said your story about the woman who befriended the young girl in Iraq checked out. Said her name was Susan Fields. Do you remember her?"

"No, I don't think so. But, remember, my memory is shaky at best." He gave her a funny look. "How did he know about the story? You weren't going to use it."

"Not at first. You'd told me it wasn't Jamie Parsons, and I had already done my own research and knew that. Then you said it was someone else who adopted the girl, so I knew the story was still out there to tell."

"Why didn't you ask me?" He sounded disappointed.

"You were already annoyed with me over this story, and I figured I wouldn't need it. Thought I'd have plenty to choose from. I may have dangled the story line in front of Tom when he was hounding me about what I had, but I hadn't researched it further and didn't know the woman's name. Seems like he ran my ideas past Jeremy, and Jeremy took it upon himself to investigate."

"I wonder why he would do that."

"I have no idea. I don't trust him, but if the story is accurate, I can't see the harm in using it."

"You should," he agreed. "It's a great story."

"Hmmm." She rubbed a finger between her brows. She was getting a headache over this. "I guess I'm reluctant to accept this because it's coming from Jeremy."

"His reputation is also on the line, don't forget. He couldn't very well feed you wrong information and not expect it to bite him in the ass."

"Good point. You're right." She released a big sigh of relief. "That would totally discredit him, and he's too smart to do something that stupid."

"Good. I'm glad you agree. Maybe you need to give him the benefit of the doubt. He might actually be on your side."

"It's possible, I suppose." She tried to shake her negative thoughts. "I don't have any concrete reason to distrust him."

"Then don't. Put your mind at rest." After a beat of silence, Jake asked, "Still going to that art exhibit tonight?"

"Yes, I have to be there at eight." She sighed. "I have more important things to do, and details to work out, but I'm obligated to go."

"Can't you cancel?"

"No. Unfortunately, this job entails more than just reporting the news."

∽

Susan Fields's story checked out. After her noon broadcast the next day, Kari called the woman in Chicago and had a long talk with her. She agreed to let Kari interview her, and Kari made plane reservations for herself and Hugh, her favorite cameraman, to fly to Chicago. She was thrilled and excited, and so was Jake when she told him.

They caught a four o'clock flight and arrived a few hours later. They rented a car and drove to Rolling Meadows, northwest of Chicago, where Susan lived with her husband, Mike, and her two children. She had a ten-year-old daughter, Tamara, and the adopted child, Sarai, who was six.

Kari expected the interview to be emotional, but Susan's heart-wrenching account of her time in the desert and the subsequent bombing of the village that left Sarai an orphan was, journalistically speaking, too good to be real.

"I was recruited right out of high school," she told Kari. "My parents tried to dissuade me, but they didn't have much money and it seemed an easy answer to getting a free education."

"So, joining the Marine Corps was a means to an end?" Kari asked.

"Not really. I was eighteen when I enlisted, and America was at peace. I never figured that one day I'd be halfway around the world in an active war zone, but then, I never expected 9/11 to happen either. When those suicide bombers hit the World Trade Center, I wanted to fight back. They couldn't do that to us without some kind of retaliation."

"You were a marine reserve, is that correct?"

"Yes. I didn't intend to make a career out of the military, but I wasn't opposed to the idea either. Even as a reserve, I had to complete twelve weeks of basic training."

"Had the war in Iraq started by the time you finished your basic training?"

"No. The war started in March of 2003, and I was through the basics and had already completed my four-year college degree. I was working on my master's when I got the call I was shipping out." She squeezed her husband's hand and spoke with pride. "Marines can be deployed within twenty-four hours, anywhere in the world, and usually are the first ones in."

"They're the first military unit on the battleground?" Kari asked.

"Yes. We're a special branch of the Navy. They drop us off; we go in."

"Were you married at the time of your deployment? Did you have Tamara?"

"Yes. Mike and I married in 2001 and had Tamara two years later. It wasn't until 2005 that I deployed to Iraq. I was only there for six months and then sent home. One tour of duty was a small price to pay."

Kari had eased Susan into the interview, and now that she was comfortable, it was time to ask more probing questions.

"Can you tell us how it felt to be away from your family for six months and how you made it through this most difficult time? What kept you alive?"

"Well, physically and mentally I was a trained marine, and I knew from the get-go what I signed up for and what to expect. But of course, the reality is far worse than anything you could imagine. Emotionally, I was not prepared. I missed Mike and Tammi terribly. It was torturous being away from them, and I was so afraid I'd never see them again and that Tammi would never get to know me."

"Well, I'm not a mother, but I'm sure that if I were, I'd feel the same. And if your girls wanted to join the military, what would you say to them?"

"I might try to discourage them, but if they truly had the calling, I would be proud and supportive of their decision."

"Could you tell us what the adoption process was like, and did you encounter opposition from any family members or any of Sarai's relatives in Iraq?"

"I waited until I was back at home to start the adoption procedure. Mike and Tammi were both very supportive—that was a great help. By the time I met Sarai, she had already lost most of her family, with only her mother remaining, but then she died in the explosion as well, and no one came forward with any claim of kinship. The sad truth is that there are hundreds of thousands of orphans in Iraq, many of them needing medical attention, not to mention a good home. So I had little opposition."

"May I ask how you intend to raise Sarai? Will you allow her to practice the Muslim faith?"

Susan and her husband exchanged looks. "We've talked a lot about this," Susan said, "and we've decided it will be entirely up to her."

Kari concluded the interview not long afterward. She knew she had more than enough for a single show. Hugh took a few group photos of the family, then he and Kari thanked Susan and Mike for their cooperation and drove their rented car back to the airport. Both were tired but elated at what they had accomplished.

When Kari got home late that night, she fell into bed, too tired to do more than undress. Four a.m. would arrive all too soon.

∽

The following morning, Kari was back at the station before five, sipping a cup of coffee and editing her first report. She left a Post-it note on Jeremy's desk, thanking him for finding Susan Fields and letting him know the interview had gone well.

She spoke with Tom before her noon report. He'd seen the video of the interview and praised her for her excellent job.

"Do you want to use this on Friday," he asked, "or stick with the Lucky Charm story?"

"I thought we'd do the Wolfhound story next, but it can wait."

"So which one?"

"Lucky Charm is pretty much ready to go. Maybe a little more tweaking, but I think it's great."

"Fine. See that it is."

She gave him a mock salute. "I'll have it on your desk first thing tomorrow, and you can see for yourself."

She was at the door when she turned around. "Tom, one more thing. Hugh and I are driving to Jacksonville to speak with a representative from the Wounded Warrior program. We just learned that this month, several warriors are starting a monthlong trip from coast to coast on their specially built bikes. Men without limbs, one without sight, proving they can do anything they put their minds to, and that for them, life's not over, not by a long shot. They will cross four states, which includes an uphill climb through mountainous terrain. This is going to be an incredible story and should be good for follow-ups too."

"Good job, Kari." He nodded with satisfaction. "I'm also pleased to see that you're making an effort with Jeremy. George and I were talking, and if this new series works out, we might have you coanchor with him."

Kari's jaw dropped, and she damn near trembled with excitement. "You mean that?"

"I sure do. Make me proud."

She walked out of Tom's office wrapped in a warm glow of happiness. Everything she had always wanted was so close, almost within her grasp.

## CHAPTER THIRTY-ONE

Kari was in the mood to celebrate. On her way home, she called Jake to see if they could get together once he finished work.

"I'd love to," he answered right away. "I'll stop and see Shane first, but I should be able to make it by eight."

"Wonderful. Tonight is my treat." She couldn't contain her enthusiasm. "I have so much to tell you. Tom practically said—"

"Whoa, hold it." He laughed. "Don't spoil the surprise. I want to see your face when you tell me."

"Oh, Jake. I can't tell you how happy I am. You did this for me."

"No, I didn't. This whole thing was your idea, and you've come up with some great material. I didn't get either story right, and it was my buddy who came up with Lucky Charm."

"Don't be so modest. You've helped me so much." She knew she was talking fast and if she didn't slow down, she'd trip over her tongue. "I'm going to show you my appreciation in so many ways you won't be able to stand it."

Once home, Kari quickly changed into athletic gear and went for her five-mile run. Some days were more difficult than others were, but today her feet matched her mood and she practically flew. After the run, she took a long, leisurely shower and primped for the night ahead.

Jake deserved good sex tonight, and he was going to get it. Their relationship was changing, but under control. Friends first, lovers second.

It had been like that with Sean too. Strange that she barely missed him. At the beginning of their romance, she thought of him all the time and couldn't wait to be with him, but naturally the passion waned over the passing months and years. She had found him intelligent and interesting and enjoyed his company, but, as fond as her memories were, she certainly didn't want him back, marriage or no marriage.

She wanted her life exactly as it was. Her job and Jake. Pure and simple.

A familiar ache began low in her belly. She could identify it now. That burning hunger never quite went away. When she'd been younger she'd hungered for love, she'd hungered for Jake, and then for someone who could replace the emptiness inside her. She'd met a few men who'd done that for a year or two, but, as with Sean, the emptiness had returned and the hunger had not been appeased.

Jake's companionship didn't do it either. Instead of sating her appetite, it teased her into wanting more. What would it take to make this feeling go away? She'd tried to satisfy it with work, and at times that seemed to help, but now, when her dreams were within reach, her belly was still not content.

By eight o'clock, Kari was starving and couldn't sit still. After her shower, she fielded several calls from the station and worked her Lucky Charm story to death. Finally, she put it aside before she did more damage than good. When she'd been less experienced and unsure of herself, she'd had a tendency to overwork a story and edit the life out of it. Now she knew when to quit.

At last the doorbell rang, and she ran to answer it.

"Jake." She grinned and pulled him inside, immediately wrapping her arms around his neck and giving him a big, welcoming kiss.

"You look happy," he said.

"I am. Very." She looked at him and her smile faded. "What's wrong?"

He stuck his hands in his pockets and stared at the floor. "Shane. He doesn't want to stay in the hospital or at Stand Down House. He says he's fine and just wants to be left alone."

"What are you going to do?"

"I'm not sure what can be done. He's free to leave. No one can make him stay or force him into a treatment program." He ran a hand through his hair, and his expression was grim. "Kid's like a brother to me. I want to smack some sense into him."

She smiled briefly. "What's his addiction?"

"Booze, among other things. He had a bottle of cheap rum in the car when I found him. Weed too. I don't think he uses anything else, but hell, what do I know?"

"I'm sorry. I know how hard this is for you."

"The kid's depressed. It's the damn prosthesis. He says he looks like a freak and refuses to wear it. He does everything with his right hand."

"Have you seen the prosthesis? Is it that bad?"

"It's all right. Not the most attractive thing in the world, but better than nothing." Jake scratched his jaw. "He told me the hook was better, but he didn't want that either. The guy's stubborn."

"And foolish."

"Agreed. Anyway, I ended up telling him that Brent was heading to Afghanistan to try to put an end to this war, but he clammed up and wouldn't talk." Jake swore, and wiped his mouth. "He didn't even ask anything about Brent. His best friend."

"He will when he's ready." She didn't know anything about Shane, his depression, or what it would take to snap him out of it. She was simply trying to ease Jake's fears. He was her number-one concern. Not Shane, not Brent.

He glanced around and saw the bottle of champagne sitting on ice. "You're right." Lifting the bottle from the ice bucket, he gave her a weak smile. "Let's forget Shane for tonight. I know you have something to tell me and we have celebrating to do."

She shrugged. "We don't have to." She wanted to give him a chance to back out if he was no longer in the mood. "We could do this another night. The champagne will keep, and so will I."

In answer, he removed the foil from the bottle of Cristal and used his thumbs to work the cork. It flew across the room, making them both laugh. She grabbed the glasses, and he quickly poured.

"I'm sure." He bent to kiss her. "I promise not to be a downer."

She gave him a wicked smile. "If you're going to be down, there's only one place I want you to go."

He hugged her. "You know something? That's what I like about you. You always make me feel good."

"You make me feel good too."

They sipped champagne, their eyes on each other.

"I have beluga caviar and crackers to enjoy with the bubbly," she told him. "Then I'm taking you downstairs for dinner. Someplace close so we don't need to drive."

"You've got it all figured out." He sat on a barstool as Kari took the plate of caviar from the fridge. She added chopped onions and egg as condiments, along with a small wicker bowl filled with various crackers.

Then she sat next to him. "You ready for my big news?" She grinned and squeezed his arm. "Tom said if this series works out, he might make me coanchor."

"You mean the night job you want so much?"

"Yes!" She squealed and hugged him. "What do you think? Isn't it exciting?"

"With Jeremy?" he replied in a deadpan voice. "You'll be working with him?"

"Uh-huh. But I've been thinking that you're right. I should give him the benefit of the doubt. After all, he found Susan Fields's real name."

"I'm happy he came through for you, and I'm sorry I didn't."

"You seem angry that Jeremy helped me. You shouldn't be. I would never have her story if you hadn't told it to me first."

He piled caviar onto a cracker and popped it in his mouth, then took a sip of champagne. "So, you'll be working nights if this all works out."

"Yes. Not every night. I'll have my weekends off." She could see he wasn't as enthusiastic about her good news as she had expected him to be, and it sucked the joy out of her. His approval mattered. It shouldn't, but it did.

When he didn't say anything, she snapped, "Now what's your problem?"

"I don't have a problem. Look, just drink, okay?" He poured more champagne, then toasted glasses with her. "To the night shift."

"Jeez. Can you sound a little more excited?"

"I'm trying, but it's not working." He gave her a weak smile. "I know how much you want it, but have you considered the hours you'll keep and how it'll affect your life? You'll work until midnight, get home exhausted. By the time you get out of bed and get rolling the next day, it'll be time to head back to the studio to get ready for the six o'clock broadcast. What kind of life will that be?"

She felt sucker-punched. She expected him to be delighted for her. A friend should be supportive of another friend's goals and dreams and rejoice in her accomplishments. Not complain and want to hold her back. How could she have been so wrong about him?

"The life I've always dreamed of," she said. "Can't you see that? And be happy for me?"

They looked at each other, and Kari's shoulders slumped. He was certainly a killjoy, and he was wrong about the job. Wrong about everything. Maybe she'd been wrong about him. She thought he'd be in her corner, her number-one supporter, the guy who had her back. Instead, he was letting her down again.

"Yes, I know." She lifted her chin. "I want this job, and until a second ago, I wanted you. Us. The way we are, right now."

"I'm sorry, Kari." He put a hand over hers. He leaned over and kissed her cheek. "You may have noticed me around here a lot." He nuzzled her ear. "I like being with you. You've helped me come out of my cave."

She pulled away, still upset.

"I'm just thinking that if I work days and you work nights, we won't see much of each other."

She bit her bottom lip, feeling anxious and unsure of herself. She didn't want to lose this bond between them, but she needed to know she had his full support.

"So what?" she said. It was better for her to remain cynical. Less hurtful that way. "If you cared about me at all, it would make our time together that much more special."

"I care about you, all right. But I see your career will always be number one. You really do like your relationships casual, don't you? You sent Sean packing because he wanted more."

"It wasn't more of me," she sniped. "He wanted the whole kit and caboodle. Marriage, kids, the whole frickin' nine yards." She thought about the baby she'd lost, and it was on the tip of her tongue to tell him, but how? How could she tell him now? He was struggling with so much, and whatever they had together was still so fresh and new. Nothing but sadness would come of it, and it wouldn't bring their baby back.

"You know, it doesn't have to be a bad thing."

She bit her lip and fought back tears. "I didn't say it was a bad thing. But it's just not for me." She took a swallow of champagne. "He didn't fill my emptiness inside."

"Do you even know what you're searching for?"

"Do you?" She glared at him. "You're what, thirty-four? I don't see you married."

He glared right back. "I was fighting a war."

They kept staring at each other, until finally Kari looked away. "Why are we fighting? I had such high hopes for this evening."

He twirled her bar seat around. "What am I really to you? A friend? Someone to go to bed with? What?"

"Why are you asking?"

"I'm asking because you drive me crazy. I want you so bad it hurts."

# CHAPTER THIRTY-TWO

Jake tucked a hand behind her neck and pulled her in for a serious kiss. He gave her exactly what she wanted, slow kisses, deep tongue, and sucked the breath and the fight right out of her. Then he took her by the hand and led her to the bedroom. There, he unzipped her dress and made her sit on the bed, then sank to his knees in front of her.

This was his fantasy girl, all right, and he'd show her exactly what she'd be missing if she worked nights.

He removed her pink high heels, kissing the hollow of each foot, sucking on her toes.

"What are you doing?" she asked.

"Shut up and enjoy it." His tongue took a slow journey up her lower leg to her thigh, and he hooked his thumbs in the waistband of her panties, sliding his hands under her buttocks to tilt her pelvis toward his face. His tongue slid into her moist, sweet opening and found her pleasure spot. He licked relentlessly until she moaned and bucked. He released her, but only for a moment, then went right back to what he'd been doing.

Her thighs wrapped around his back, and her hands were in his hair, her long nails raking his scalp. He took his time, licking and sucking, driving her over the edge. His cock was ready to burst out of his pants, but it would have to wait, because he wasn't through with her yet. Not anywhere near.

She thought she could take him or leave him, did she? Well, he thought not. By the time he got through making love to her, she'd be a whimpering mess, begging him to give it to her again and again. He'd always been a good lover, and even if he was somewhat out of practice, he could remember a trick or two.

His tongue flickered in and out, teasing, tasting, making her squirm. He slipped a finger in to play with the delicate nub and listened to her moan.

Damn her attitude. She was more like a man than a woman when it came to sex. Didn't want anyone to tie her down.

Well, he'd damn well see about that.

He stripped off his shirt and climbed on top of her. Using one shirtsleeve, he tied her hands together. He tied the other sleeve around the nearest bedpost.

"What are you doing?" She laughed, pretending to fight him. Her bucking underneath him made him hurt for her more.

"What does it look like?" he said, caressing her beautiful breasts. "I'm going to have my way with you. Any objections?"

"Uh. No." She laughed softly. "I think I might like that."

"I promise you, you will."

He took one breast in his mouth and sucked on the erect nipple. It hardened into a tight pebble, and he licked it while one hand moved back to her clit.

She stopped squirming and sucked in her breath. He touched her again and again, moving his thumb against the hard, warm nub until she gasped his name.

He bent and took her in his mouth, kissing the essence of her.

She pulled at his hair, making him raise his head. "Jake. Not like this. Please. I want you inside me. I want to make you happy too."

Blood heated his veins, and his heart thundered in his chest. Happy? Was he worthy of happiness? He remembered being a killing machine, and flashes of the desert, smoke, fire, and sniper attacks took hold of his brain. He closed his eyes, took a deep breath, and forced them out. *Not now. Fuck, not now.*

He unzipped his fly and pulled his pants down. Grabbed a condom out of the drawer and quickly slid it on. She was still tied up when he entered her.

Her eyes widened. She licked her lips and watched his face. "Do it, Jake. Now." She lifted her hips off the bed to meet him halfway. "I want to feel you all the way to my bones."

The moment he entered her, he nearly exploded. He needed release, but he wouldn't give in, not yet, not until she peaked again. His cock filled her, slipping in and out, hard and furious, pounding her, driving so deep he was lost in her.

She cried out and shuddered, and finally he poured himself inside her, giving her everything he had. Collapsing on her, he lay spent, too exhausted to move a muscle, then remembered Kari had her hands tied.

"You okay?" he asked as he freed her.

"Couldn't be better," she answered with a grin.

They held each other for a long time. They didn't speak, partly because they didn't have any breath left, and partly because words were redundant. Their bodies had spoken for them.

∼

That Friday night, the first episode of Kari's hero series aired. It was the interview with Roy Foster and the story of Stand Down House, an easy way to jump-start the new show. Mr. Foster was by every definition a most worthy hero.

As with her runaway series, she opened the last ten minutes of the thirty-minute show for viewers to call in, and she took their questions live. Most of the questions were directed at Mr. Foster, with people asking how they could help.

Later, George and Tom both came by to congratulate her. They'd received a healthy number of calls, a good sign the show had pulled in a respectable number of viewers. She went home feeling elated but edgy. She knew she had some good stories lined up, but not nearly enough. Once the series got under way, she was sure people would contact her with their stories, but until then, she still needed Jake's help.

As much as she liked the excuse to see Jake, she hated to rely on anyone but herself.

∼

Jake called when she was already curled up in bed. It had been a long week, and she was looking forward to sleeping in the next morning.

"Did I wake you?" Jake asked.

"Yes." She yawned. "I know, I'm lame, but early mornings are killers. Welcome to my life."

"You stayed up pretty late last night," he said, sounding pleased with himself.

"Yes, well, I had a very good reason. I was all tied up."

He chuckled. "Yes, you were."

"So what's up? Is it Shane? Did something happen?"

"Nothing bad, but he is a mess. He doesn't want to stay at Stand Down House, so I booked him a room for a month at a Days Inn. It's not fancy, but it beats living out of his car."

"That was a wonderful thing to do. But why doesn't he stay with you until he gets on his feet again?"

"I thought about that, but I don't want him around if he's using drugs. The man I knew wouldn't go near that shit, but after what happened to him, he'll never be the same again."

"You're strong and smart and have good judgment. Whatever you do with Shane, I'm sure it'll be the right thing."

"Thanks." He cleared his throat. "I'm still looking for more stories. My father has feelers out too."

"Great. You're my best buddy."

"Just what I've always wanted to be." He laughed and hung up.

∼

The following evening, Jake called, asking if she'd like to grab a pizza and go with him to meet Shane.

"I'd love to. It's been another rough day, and I don't feel like working." She added, "Tom's happy with the tape we did for the Wounded Warriors, and I have to admit, it's pretty damn good."

"You deserve a night off."

"I do. My shoulders and back are aching, I skipped lunch, and I'm starving. Are you ready to go?"

"I'll be up to get you in ten minutes."

True to his word, he knocked on her door right on time. She gave him a quick kiss. "I'm so excited to meet Shane. Thanks for asking."

"I figured you would like that, and I know you're working too hard." He slid his hand behind her neck and began massaging the tight muscles in her neck and shoulders. "You need a good rubdown."

"Oh, that does feel good," she purred, allowing him to spoil her for a few precious minutes. She took his hand and kissed his fingers. "Much better. Thank you."

He kissed her lips. "Anytime, sweetheart. You ready to go?"

She grabbed her handbag and keys. "Lead on." She slipped her hand under his arm as they walked to the elevator, and leaned against him, enjoying his masculine warmth. When they reached his car, he opened the door and she slipped in, wishing the Jag's seat didn't keep her away from him.

"Remember the old days when cars had only one seat instead of two?" She grinned. "It was so much better for making out."

He laughed. "The backseat was put to good use."

"Too bad we don't have one here."

He winked at her and put a hand between her legs. "You need another workout?"

"Mmm, it would help me relax." She sat up straighter and put his hand on the wheel. "First, I need food."

They drove to a small Italian restaurant, and over their pizza she asked him again about the rescue mission. "Do you think he'd let me tell his story?"

Jake shook his head. "He's fragile, Kari. I'm not sure if that's a good idea."

"I'll hold off until he's ready, but can you tell me how he escaped?"

"I can, if you promise not to use it."

"I won't. Not without his permission."

"Okay, this is what I know." Jake leaned back in the booth and rested his hands on the checkered tablecloth. "He told me a SEAL team crept into the enemy camp, found him, cut him loose, and smuggled him out before anyone knew what was happening."

"Like a movie," she whispered.

"Only it was real life. Anyway, he was so malnourished he was unable to walk, and one of the marines threw him over his shoulder and carried him to the chopper. Before they made it, they were spotted and the extremists came after them, firing their weapons.

"The SEAL who was carrying Shane got hit in the leg, but he kept going, got Shane to that chopper. A SEAL's creed is that if knocked down, he will get up. He'll use every ounce of strength he has to protect his teammates and defeat his enemy. He will not fail." Jake's voice filled with pride. "They live and die with honor, like medieval knights."

"What a wonderful story. I can't wait to meet him." She was eager to meet Shane for many reasons, most importantly because he was a close friend of Jake's brother. Second to that, he was a man who had fought for his country and been captured and tortured. She knew how to get a person to tell her things, even when he didn't mean to. It was a secret all good journalists shared.

And she would delicately weave that magic with Shane.

## CHAPTER THIRTY-THREE

A half hour later, Jake and Kari pulled up to the Days Inn and knocked on Shane's door. They could hear the sounds of the TV, and a dim light was visible through the pulled drapes.

Shane didn't answer, so Jake knocked again, louder this time. "Shane, it's me. Open the door."

The TV grew louder.

Jake pounded on the door and shouted. Kari looked around at the other units, wondering if someone might call the police. They were definitely causing a disturbance.

"Shane, open up, or I'll kick the door in."

Kari glanced at Jake's face and realized he was telling the truth. She had never seen him look so fierce and had an inkling of what he'd been like in battle.

He hit the door with his fist again, and finally, the door inched open.

"I'm busy," Shane said. He started to close the door, but Jake shoved it open.

"Don't ever do that to me again," he said as he strode into the room.

"Go away," Shane answered, and lay down on the bed, staring at the TV.

Kari followed Jake into the room. It was sparsely furnished and could benefit from new paint and a nicer bedspread, but it was better than living on the street. Too bad Shane didn't see it that way.

Shane was tall and terribly thin, with long, stringy hair. He looked dirty and unkempt, the type of person she'd have done her best to ignore a few months ago. But, knowing everything she did now, she felt her sympathies aroused.

An open bottle of scotch and a glass stood on the nightstand. He wore only jeans, and his feet were bare. Scars marred his chest: small, round ones, like cigarette burns; and long, thin ones, as if he'd been whipped. And his left hand was gone. To her inexpert eyes, it looked as though the wound had healed well. She wondered if, as she'd heard happened with amputees, the missing hand still hurt.

He sat up enough to pour himself another drink, and Kari glanced at Jake. His jaw was tight with tension, and that muscle twitched in his left cheek. He was fuming, but she was sure his anger was directed not at Shane but at the terrible things Shane had endured. He also clearly didn't know what to do about Shane.

Kari touched his arm, then stepped forward, stopping at the edge of the bed. She simply stood until Shane finally looked up.

"What do you want?" he snarled.

"Just to talk. I'm a longtime friend of Jake's and Brent's, just like you."

"How come I don't know you, then?" Shane tossed back his shot of whiskey.

"We met a few times. Since I hung out with Jake, we probably just didn't pay attention to each other, I guess."

"Oh, I think I'd have paid attention to you." His gaze slid up and down the length of her.

"Shane, I'm a reporter with a local news station. Jake told me about your rescue, and I wondered if I could get your permission to tell your story."

Jake took a step toward her, his eyes flashing. She shot him a glance, silently telling him to trust her. She knew what she was doing.

"Now, why would I do that?" Shane said. He was staring at the TV again.

"Because it's newsworthy. But more importantly, the American people want to hear about a successful rescue mission. They want to hear about men like you who served their country and did it with honor. We need to hear these stories, Shane. There are too many bad ones getting all the press. Sometimes good things happen too."

"Nothing good happened over there," Shane said to the TV. "Now, if you don't mind, I'm not in the mood to entertain guests." He picked up the remote and turned the volume to high. "You two can see yourselves out."

"Shane," Jake said. "What can I do for you? Tell me." His voice was full of anguish. "You know I'd do anything."

Shane turned to Jake. "You mean that?" His gaze flickered to Kari. "Helluva guy, isn't he? Well, Jake, why don't you pour me another goddamn drink? Better yet, go out and buy me a new bottle."

Jake lifted the bottle of scotch and looked as if he would throw it, but thought better of it. He splashed some into Shane's glass. "There you go. Drink yourself to death. That's what you want, right? You don't give a shit that a dozen Navy SEALs put their lives on the line to rescue you."

He looked at Shane with disgust. "They didn't quit, and failure was not an option. Not like you. So have another drink. Who cares? If you want to feel sorry for yourself, then go right ahead. But I'm not going to stand here and watch you."

He marched toward the door. "You coming, Kari?"

She glanced at Shane, wanting to say something to help. But she had no answers to his problems.

She nodded and walked to the door. Shane kept drinking, never looking up.

"Why did you do that?" Jake asked as soon as they were back in his car and driving away from the motel. "Why did you tell him you worked for the local news station and that you wanted a story?"

"Well, it's the truth, and I think he needed to hear it. Besides, I knew what I was doing."

"Yeah, well, that went over real big."

"Don't turn ugly on me just because Shane is in trouble." Kari said gently, knowing Jake was hurting. "He needs to come to terms with what happened to him. He needs counseling, and you are going to see that he gets it."

"Oh, I am, am I?" he said through gritted teeth.

"Yes, you are, because that's what loyal, caring friends do for each other."

Jake had no retort for that.

"And you need to let Brent know what's going on." She glanced at Jake. The harsh lines of his face looked chiseled from stone. "Maybe he can get out here before he goes overseas."

"I'm sorry, Kari."

"I know you are." She smiled and patted his knee.

He brought her hand to his mouth and kissed it. "I could use your loving tonight. Or are you too tired?"

"I'm not too tired, but no marathons. I don't want an all-nighter, just something to help us both sleep." She gazed at him, thinking how dear he was and how much her feelings had changed. She still needed to be careful, but she wasn't as frightened as she used to be.

"I think I can do that."

"I know you can."

∽

The next morning, Jake stayed in bed for an hour after Kari went to work. He enjoyed a long waking-up period, when his mind could wander all over the place.

The pillow next to him still smelled of Kari, and he snuggled with it, reliving last night's lovemaking session. He would have enjoyed taking his time and prolonging the pleasure, but she'd had other plans. Taking control, she'd led him to the bed and used that sexy mouth of hers until it had driven him damn near crazy. Then she'd climbed on top of him and ridden him hard. She'd arched her back, driving him in deeper, and he'd filled his hands with her sweet breasts. His orgasm had come swift and strong, and she had followed a few moments later.

Making love to her was so damn good. Problem was, he wasn't good for her. Not good for anybody. He knew the bad stuff that had happened overseas hadn't been his fault—he'd done what was expected of him—and it was war. He knew that, but that didn't make up for the fact that he'd killed a lot of people—terrorists and insurgents, mostly, but there had been innocent people too. They'd been in the wrong place at the wrong time. Still, how did anyone justify that?

He punched the pillow and flipped onto his back. No good thinking about it. The only way he could make amends with himself was by doing good here, getting vets off the streets, making sure that the men and women who had fought for their country were treated right at home.

∼

Jake had a busy day at work. First on his agenda was to assist a new client with the legal issues of a recent acquisition. After that were two meetings with partners, and then he had to finish a court filing. Kari and Shane were put aside, and it was nearly four when he remembered his promise to get Kari another story. He called Lou Brady. Maybe he had something new.

"Did you see the story on Roy Foster and the homeless vets last Friday night?" he asked Lou.

"I sure did," Lou said in his low, thick-as-molasses voice. "Damn good job."

"Lucky Charm's going to be on tomorrow night. Thought you'd be interested."

"That's real nice to hear."

"Kari needs a story a week to keep the series alive. She interviewed some vets at Stand Down House, but their memories are not exactly upbeat. I really want to help her out."

"Yeah, I saw this lady of yours. I'm not surprised. I'd like to please her myself."

Jake laughed, although he didn't think it was particularly funny. "Keep those thoughts to yourself, big man. We're just friends. Old friends from way back."

"I'll bet." Lou chuckled. "I'm sure I can come up with a story or two. Of course, I might have to meet Kari myself and deliver it personally."

"Not a chance."

Lou laughed, a deep, rumbling laugh, and Jake had to smile.

A few hours later, Lou called back to say he had heard about a group of American marines at a base in Iraq who had healed more than a thousand Iraqi kids. They were volunteers helping burn victims recover, and most of the men had no medical training until they joined the army.

"They treat the kids with tenderness and Tylenol," Lou said, "and rely on donated supplies."

"That might work. Let me run it past Kari and see what she says."

"You're sure you don't want me running it past her?"

"Why don't you just take care of that pretty wife of yours?" Jake said a little testily.

"I got enough lovin' for two," Lou answered.

"I'll get back to you." Jake hung up, more chafed than pleased.

Really, his feelings for Kari were getting out of hand. He had damn well better not let her see how much she meant to him, or he'd be kicked out on his ass.

Telling her stories was one thing. Making love to her each night was another. She didn't want anything to come between her and her career, and he had too many demons to fight. Staying away from Kari shouldn't be too difficult, and he had a solid excuse. Shane needed him more.

Tonight, he intended to talk sense into that thick head of Shane's.

Jake told Shane he'd take him to Duffy's for burgers and beers but he wasn't allowed in the Jag unless he showered and shaved. Shane grumbled a lot, but he did clean himself up.

Now, with his clean hair pulled into a ponytail, and wearing jeans and a tight black T-shirt under a collared shirt, not only did he look respectable, but some young women at the bar were giving him the eye.

"See that?" Jake said with a laugh. "You're still a stud."

"I don't wanna be a stud," he answered, staring at his beer. "I wanna be left alone."

"Then why are you here? You could be sitting alone in the depressing motel, facing four plain walls. Instead, you're at a fine-dining establishment with me, watching a Marlins game on a big-screen TV and ignoring a couple of pretty gals who would like to know you better."

Shane glanced around. "Nobody's looking at me. And if they were, it wouldn't be a good-looking girl."

"You're wrong about that. See the three women sitting at the bar? The one on the left keeps glancing your way."

"The one who's stacked?"

"That's her."

Shane swallowed some beer. "I'm not interested."

"Guess you're sicker than I thought."

Shane glowered at him. "What's that supposed to mean?"

"Well, most men, if they're young and single and straight, they look back when an attractive, well-endowed lady gives them the eye."

"How do you know she's looking at me? Could be you she's after."

"Uh-uh." Jake smirked. "The one in the center has her sights on me."

"You got that all figured out?" Shane's eyes darted to the women, then quickly returned to the big-screen.

"Yeah. Took me all of a second."

"She's probably thinking what a freak I am," Shane said, holding up his missing hand.

"You going to cry in your beer all night?" Jake asked.

"Look, I appreciate you buying me food and beer, but I don't need to sit here and put up with your bullshit." Shane made a move to get up, but when Jake didn't do anything to stop him, he sat back down again.

"I'm not bullshitting you," Jake said. "You're a smart, good-looking kid, and if you could get your head back on straight, you'd do fine." He leaned forward. "Now, I know you're not going to want to hear this, but you need counseling. You can't go on the way you've been. Remember what your life used to be like? You and Brent enjoying the surf, dating pretty girls, fighting fires. All that good stuff?"

"That life's over." Shane swallowed the rest of his beer.

"Not for all the men who still work at CAL FIRE, and it doesn't have to be over for you. Sure, your work options are limited now, but you won't know what you can do unless you try." Jake spoke firmly. "You've got to get better. And that's an order."

"I've talked to enough military quacks." Shane shrugged. "They all say the same things."

"And did you listen?"

"It makes no difference. All the stuff in my brain, it's not going anywhere. It's gonna stay there until I die. Might as well get it over with, 'cause I sure as hell don't want to live with those memories." Shane's gaze was glued to the Marlins game, but Jake would bet it wasn't a baseball game he was seeing.

"I saw some bad stuff too," he said. "I still have nightmares. Go off the deep end once in a while. How about if we both do this together? All for one and one for all." Jake grinned. "Maybe we can get a group therapy discount."

"You're a whack job." Shane finally looked at Jake; then he shrugged and signaled the waitress. When she walked over, he said, "Could we have another round? And we want to buy those three girls a drink."

# CHAPTER THIRTY-FOUR

The following night, the second installment of Kari's new show aired. Wearing an off-white Escada suit, Kari was smiling and confident as she related the story of the boy who became known as Lucky Charm.

"Here with us tonight is Sergeant Jeff Langdon, who witnessed the miracle of the boy who rode a bicycle through the middle of a gun battle and came out unscathed." She faced the sergeant. "Tell us what was going on around you when Jamai first appeared."

"We were in a neighborhood of Baghdad where a lot of extremists were hiding out. My unit had orders to clear them out, but the extremists were not going quietly. The scene was total chaos. Heavy machine-gun fire, grenades exploding, men screaming as they were hit. It was the worst firefight I'd ever been in, and then out of the smoke and dust came this little boy on a bike, riding like the wind as shots flew around him. One by one, men on both sides stopped shooting. Weapons lowered, and everyone watched the kid ride to safety. The battle just stopped. Not another shot was fired that day."

"Is it true the boy became a mascot for the American troops?"

"Yes. He was an orphan, and he'd been born deaf. Our infantry sort of adopted him, and Jamai loved to ride around with us." Langdon smiled at the memory. "He became a hero to the people living in that neighborhood, and Iraqi kids would follow him around and want to touch him for good luck. That's why we started calling him Lucky Charm."

They talked for several more minutes while the background screen displayed shots of Lucky Charm and his neighborhood. The video contained clips taken weeks after the event—when the streets were unnaturally quiet and empty, some of the buildings partially damaged, others completely destroyed—and in the present day, with people and cars filling the streets, a lively marketplace, a café filled with diners.

Kari had been able to obtain old tapes of the boy and had pieced together a moving tribute, including a picture of the boy sitting on the hood of a Humvee and waving the American flag. He was grinning ear to ear as children gathered around the vehicle, alternately cheering and trying to entice the smiling American marines into a game of soccer.

Kari urged viewers to call, and as the picture faded and they broke for a commercial, she breathed a sigh of relief. That had been great. Langdon's story had even brought a tear to her eye, and she was about as unemotional as it got.

The calls from viewers came fast and furious. She fielded some, and Sergeant Langdon took the rest. As always, when calls came live, there were some unpleasant people who had to be handled delicately or, in some cases, cut off, but for the most part, the viewers were wildly receptive.

After Langdon left the set, Kari took her time divesting herself of her microphone and gathering her notes, hoping to get feedback from others in the newsroom. She had just stood when George Collins joined her.

"Nice show, Kari. Keep up the good work."

*Big praise indeed,* she thought, *from the big man himself.*

When Jake called her the next day, she was delighted to hear from him. When he told her he had another story for her, her happiness meter went off the charts.

"That's awesome, Jake. If it's good, I might have to have hot monkey sex with you for a week."

"I'll hold you to that," he said, and then went on to tell her about his evening with Shane. "So now I've agreed to go into therapy. You wouldn't know of anyone, would you?"

"Why? You think I need it?"

"That's not what I meant, but considering your insistence on not committing to a relationship, it might not be a bad idea."

"Don't be ridiculous." She didn't mean to snap, but he might have scored a home run on that remark. She knew she had issues, but she preferred to deal with them privately.

"I'm not. I'm thinking about the huge discount we could get for a threesome."

"Intriguing idea, but I think I'll pass."

"What about the other kind of threesome? You ever considered one of those?"

"You're already more than I can handle."

"You're no fun."

She melted a little. "Yes I am. And if you come over later, I'll prove it."

"Is that all you want? Hot sex?" He said it jokingly, but considering the earlier comment, she wasn't sure if he was teasing or not.

"Hot sex and stories," she said. "What could be better?" It was getting more difficult every day to keep her feelings in check. Jake had wormed his way back into her heart, whether she wanted him there or not.

∽

When Jake arrived, he carried a bag filled with takeout from a local Chinese restaurant—Singapore noodles, beef broccoli, and Szechuan shrimp, her favorites.

"So, what do you want first?" he asked as they sat at the table. "Sex or story?"

"Story, please." She gave him a sweet smile. "I have to know how hot to make the sex."

He shook his head, but he was grinning. "You're a brat, you know that?"

"So you keep telling me." She leaned over and gave him a quick kiss. "I love the fact that you're going into therapy with Shane. You make me proud, Jake."

He put a hand over hers on the table. "You make me want to be better than I am."

She swallowed a sudden lump in her throat and batted back tears. "Jake, that's one of the nicest things anyone has ever said to me."

"It's true." His beautiful blue eyes were dark with emotion.

She felt that need inside her again. "Jake..." She squeezed his hand, then looked away, quickly changing the subject before she showed him how much she cared. "Now, about that story."

He told her what he knew about the servicemen caring for injured Iraqi children. Kari set up her laptop and immediately started researching the unit. If she could get interviews, it would make an incredible story.

Kari dug into the Chinese food, and once her plate was empty, she went over her schedule. "So, let's see. I have the Wounded Warrior story this week, next the Fields story, then Operation Wolfhound if I can pull it together, and now this. That would take care of four weeks, and then I need more, and more, and more." She closed her eyes. "What did I get myself into?"

"It'll work out, Kari. Just you wait and see." He stood and moved behind her chair, resting his hands on her shoulders. "Relax and let me give you a back massage."

"I've got a better idea." She turned to look up at him. "Let's take our clothes off and you can massage me all over."

"I like your idea best."

He found lotion and a scented candle in the bathroom. They both undressed, then he told Kari to lie on her stomach on the bed. He straddled her and began massaging her back with firm, even strokes.

Kari lay there, enjoying every second. His strong hands were doing wonders for her tight muscles, although just his presence was therapeutic. She felt relaxed, dreamy, in a state of bliss. Everything in her life was perfect at the moment. Her career was on the rise, Linda had helped her accept the loss of her sister, and Jake…

Dear Jake. She had loved him deeply once, a joyous, exciting sensation. What she felt now was almost frightening in its intensity. Emotions swirled around her, and she seemed to be blossoming on the inside, like a tightly closed rosebud finally opening, releasing every negative thought that had ever haunted her, and filling her with love.

"You're awfully quiet," he whispered. "You haven't fallen asleep on me, have you?"

"No. It feels so good I might cry."

His hands stilled. "Why?"

"Because I'm afraid," she mumbled into the pillow. "My life is almost too good right now, and I'm so scared something will happen and take it all away."

Jake kissed her back, tiny kisses that were as arousing as his massage had been soothing. "You worry too much," he whispered. "Nothing bad is going to happen. I won't let it."

"Jake?" She turned her head. "Stop. I need to talk."

He didn't answer, and his mouth was moving lower and lower on her back, angling toward her bare butt.

"I mean it," she said, squirming from under him and flipping onto her back.

He took her hands, holding them above her head. He kissed her softly on the mouth. "We can talk later."

"No, I want you to know how I feel."

"I know how you feel. Creamy, soft skin, sexy curves, delectable ass, and edible breasts." His mouth fastened on one of her nipples, and his tongue teased it until it hardened.

"That's not what I meant."

"Will you stop talking? I'm not in the mood."

"But I was going to tell you something. It's important."

He poised himself above her and slid a condom on but did not move. "Can it wait?"

She arched her back, and he slipped inside her. "I want you, Jake. Damn, but I want you."

He bit her neck and slammed into her harder. "No more words. Just enjoy."

He thrust into her again and again, and she cried out with pleasure, wanting something so badly, she felt slightly unhinged. There was a hunger in her soul that she'd never known before, and nothing, not even Jake inside her, filling her, could appease it.

He rolled off her. He kissed her shoulder.

Tears filled her eyes when she turned to him. "Jake, I've never felt such hunger before. It frightens me."

"Didn't you get enough food?" He kissed her cheek and pushed back her hair. "Come on, sweetheart. Don't cry. I think I know what you want, but until you know, there's nothing I can say. You need to figure it out."

"No! Tell me what you think. Dammit, Jake, tell me."

He took her hands in his. "What do you think, Kari? What do you feel inside?"

"Fragile," she admitted. "Lost. Afraid."

"Anything else?"

"I feel like I did when you left me, when I was eighteen. All stirred up inside. I have a longing that is so great, it doesn't feel like it will ever be satisfied."

He cradled her head against his shoulder.

She didn't pull away. It felt so good, so right, that she stayed where she was. His warm body wrapped around her, and eventually she drifted off to sleep, no longer afraid.

∽

That Friday night, the Fields story aired. Susan, her husband, and their two daughters were there. When Kari and her editor had dissected the video Hugh had shot, as good as it was, they decided it needed more energy. Kari had called Susan and asked her if she and her family could be on the show. Susan had told her that her kids would love to be live on TV. PB News had flown them to Palm Beach International, and a limousine had brought them to the station.

The family appeared during the middle part of the show. Tamara was so excited she could barely sit still, but Sarai was shy and quiet. Kari coaxed her out of her shyness, and she answered questions about leaving Iraq and moving to the United States with her adopted family. It was a heartwarming story and made for excellent television.

During the last ten-minute segment, calls flooded in. Most people wanted to wish the family well, while others asked about the adoption process. A few callers voiced how happy they were with the new show.

Jake was waiting for her when she walked out of the studio, and he insisted they go out to celebrate. He took her to the Breakers, the most luxurious hotel in Palm Beach. They dined at the Seafood Bar, sitting at a table near the window so they could enjoy the glorious views of the Atlantic. Jake ordered a bottle of champagne, and Kari figured that she could get used to this. Having a man around. Being treated like someone special by someone who thought she was.

"It's not Jamie's story," Jake said as he toasted her with his champagne glass, "but I'm glad Susan had her happy ending. I just wonder how Jeremy found her."

"I don't know, but I'm thankful he did." She glanced around the room, enjoying its casual ambience, vaulted, open-beam ceilings, white plantation shutters, and expanse of windows facing the ocean. It was a lovely setting in which to celebrate…anything.

"I can't figure Jeremy out," she continued, "but I must admit, he's been pretty wonderful recently. I'm changing my opinion of him day by day."

"He's got nothing to gain by hurting you."

"You're right." She leaned forward and held his hand. "But I don't want to talk about him. I'd much rather talk about you. How's the therapy going?"

He shrugged. "What can I say? This old guy talks to Shane, then it's my turn. After he's listened to us individually, we meet together. We just talk about the war." He moved around his place setting, avoiding her direct gaze. "Can't see what good talking about it does, but I guess it's better than leaving it inside to fester."

"How's Shane doing?"

"Better. Baby steps, but he's opening up a little. Doesn't want to talk about his captivity, though." Jake glanced at the view. Although it was too late to see the ocean, tiki torches lit the beach, and they could watch the waves break along the shore.

Kari curled her fingers around his. "He's going to need to talk about it if he wants to get better. And so will you."

"Rome wasn't built in a day."

She grinned. "Nice cliché. Anyway, I'm glad the two of you found someone, and if you persevere long enough, I'm sure it'll help."

He lifted their joined hands and brushed his lips against her knuckles. "Personally, I think being with you has helped more than anything."

"That's nice to hear." She added in a teasing voice, "I think you're kind of swell too."

The next few weeks flew by for Kari. When she wasn't working on her daily broadcasts, every waking hour was filled with finding stories, corroborating the people, places, and events, interviewing marines, and assembling video. But she loved every minute of it. Not only did it honor the men and women in the service, the show made for great television.

On top of all that, she tried to make time at night for Jake. It was a good thing she required very little sleep, because there simply weren't enough hours in a day. But she'd never been happier.

The first four episodes of her hero series went well. The studio received a constant stream of phone calls and e-mails, many of which simply complimented the station on the new show, but some offering her new leads. Her sixth show was airing that night, and it was the story of the volunteer soldiers in the burn unit. It was not going to be pleasant to watch at home, but the enlisted men deserved honoring too.

"Good evening, everyone." She was sitting at her desk in front of the cameras, wearing a light blue St. John suit. "This is Kari Winslow with a very special segment of *Returning Heroes*." She kept her eyes on the teleprompter, although she knew the words by heart, having written them herself. She was relaxed, confident, and excited about this particular show. It was gritty, it was real, and, above all, it was heroic.

"Our story tonight is about servicemen still in Iraq, special men and women doing miraculous work in a burn unit at a military base outside of Baghdad. More than a thousand Iraqi children have been helped with only volunteers and donated medical supplies in primitive conditions. You will meet two of these miracle workers, men who had no medical training before they joined the Army, but who have made such a difference in these children's lives."

She sat back to watch the footage. But instead of seeing the burn unit, she was watching herself on tape, telling the story of a young medic and an explosion at a military base. While she spoke, stock footage of combat zones filled the screen behind her. It was Jake's story of Lieutenant Marshall, the medic who claimed his life was saved by his unborn child's sonogram. But she'd never finished that segment, because the story had not been true. The young lieutenant had died. What the hell was going on?

Color drained from her cheeks, and she pushed herself out of the chair. How in the hell had that tape gotten into the hands of the production team? Why was it airing instead of the prepared story?

She had to stop this now. They couldn't show this to the world. The story was a lie.

# EPISODE SEVEN
## CHAPTER THIRTY-FIVE

The cameramen stared as she stormed past them and shoved open the door to the control room. She had to get them to switch the tape, even though she knew it was too late. The damage was already done.

"Arnie! Pull it. It's the wrong tape!"

He stared at her, confused and shocked.

"The wrong friggin' tape," she whispered. "It's supposed to be about a burn unit." She looked around as if she might see the correct tape just lying around, perfectly visible. Her hands were shaking; her legs trembled so badly, she nearly sank. An acerbic taste filled her mouth.

"We have to shut it down. Shut it down!" she yelled.

On the control-room monitor, she heard herself saying, "But Lieutenant Gary Marshall wouldn't die this day…"

"We'll go to commercial," Arnie said. He turned to an assistant and told him to queue the next segment of ads. "Kari, get back to your chair. You'll be back on in sixty seconds."

On the monitor her taped image said, "In his pocket was the sonogram of his unborn son that saved—"

Her image vanished, replaced by an ad for City Mattress.

Kari straightened her jacket, putting her shoulders back. She ran her fingers through her hair, took a deep breath, and released it slowly. "Thanks, Arnie." He'd almost stopped the tape in time.

Arnie gave her two thumbs up. "You can salvage this." His voice was steely, trying to instill in her the confidence she badly needed. "I know you can."

She strode back to the set and took her seat. The cameraman signaled her, counting down the seconds until they'd be live. The red light came on, and she was back on air. She'd had no time to consider what she was going to say. She'd have to wing it.

"My apologies to our audience," she spoke to the camera. "There was an unfortunate mix-up, and the wrong tape aired. I assure you that we will find the correct story and you'll have a chance to meet the men and women of the burn unit who deserve to be honored."

She took a quick breath and forced a smile. "What you saw just now, the story about Lieutenant Gary Marshall, is, unfortunately, not true. It's a beautiful story, and I wish it happened as reported, but there was no happy ending for Lieutenant Marshall. There was no sonogram that saved his life." She waited a second to let that sink in. "Someone who served with Lieutenant Marshall told me the story of his remarkable bravery, but he also told me that he did not survive that lethal attack on the base. I suppose we all want happy endings. I taped this segment before I learned the truth. Again, I apologize for airing an inaccurate story such as this."

She stopped, still staring at the camera, wondering what the hell to do now. She still had eleven minutes of airtime to fill and absolutely nothing to say.

A long thirty seconds slid by, and she could see the cameraman rolling his hands, telling her to say something. She opened her mouth and said the only words that came to mind.

"It seems as if we are unable to find the tape that we had for you, so I would like to let you know about some of the other stories we have lined up." She licked her lips nervously and clasped her damp hands. "Next week we have a heartwarming story about the Wounded Warriors, who will be testing themselves once again. A group of men, some without limbs, another without sight, will ride their bikes through four states and mountainous terrain in a one-month heroic battle of wills."

She smiled and took a calming breath. "There is another incredible tale, about a young medic captured and tortured in Iraq, and the Navy SEALs' mission to rescue him. Shane Dawson is a local hero, and he was saved not only by the SEALs, but also by another hero, a man who searched for his missing friend and didn't give up. He found his friend homeless, helpless, in a parking lot. He…"

The camera suddenly swiveled to her left, and, looking in that direction, she saw Jeremy step onto the set. He sat in the other chair, where interviewees normally sat, greeted her, and then faced the camera.

"We are ready to take your calls," he said in his normal, easygoing way, as if nothing had happened.

Kari stared at him, hoping the camera was still on him and not on her. She was sure her expression revealed her confusion and anxiety. She was grateful he'd smoothly segued to the caller portion of the show, and yet would the callers bombard her with accusations of incompetence and fraudulence?

"We have a caller from Wellington," Jeremy said. "Go ahead, please."

A woman's voice came over the studio speakers. "My son's been in Iraq for the past year. His name is Anthony Lorenzo, and his first baby was born three months ago. He carried his baby's sonogram with him everywhere he went. He swore it saved his life on several occasions."

Jeremy answered, "Thank you for calling. It is true stories like this that we need to hear. Please keep them coming."

Another one came through. The woman said her son had been a medic. He'd been caught in an ambush and had saved a dozen men before being shot. She asked Kari to dedicate the show to his memory.

For the next eleven minutes, Kari and Jeremy fielded calls from viewers, and by the end of the thirty-minute show, she was limp with exhaustion. The cameras turned off, and she faced Jeremy. "What just happened? Was the story a hit, or am I going to be fired?"

Jeremy drummed his fingers on the arm of his chair, looking relaxed and perfectly at ease. Her world had tilted on its axis, and he was acting as if it were business as usual.

"I can't say for sure what'll happen now." He whipped around, his nonchalance abruptly vanishing. "But how the hell did you let the wrong tape get into the control room? What were you thinking?" He glared at her as though she had personally put that segment about Gary Marshall in the lineup. He could accuse her of anything—but not stupidity!

She knew the protocol. All the videotapes that were supposed to run on any given news show were queued in advance. Tonight's lineup should have been on a schedule and timed exactly. The only way the production crew could have played the wrong tape was if someone had slipped it into the queue. She could think of only one person who might want to do that.

"I didn't give that tape to production," she said, sucking in a breath. "I never even showed it to George or Tom because I never corroborated the story." The fight left her, and her shoulders drooped. Let Jeremy think what he wanted. She had bigger worries on her mind. "I wouldn't make a mistake like that."

"I wouldn't think so, but you're going to have to come up with some sort of explanation."

She rubbed a finger between her eyebrows, stroking the tension away as she thought hard. When had she seen that tape last? "I thought I'd tossed it in the recycle bin. That's where it should have ended up. I had no reason to save it. I couldn't use it."

"Well, somehow it got out of the recycle bin and into tonight's queue. You got any enemies you can think of? Anyone who wants your job?"

"No, of course not. I wanted the night anchor spot, but far as I know, nobody wants mine. How many people want to get up at four each morning? Who wants that?"

"I'm guessing someone does."

"Jeremy, I don't have any enemies that I know of." She eyed him, trying to figure out how far she could push. "You wouldn't hate me that much, would you? I know we had our problems initially, but…" She swallowed hard. "But I can't imagine you doing something like this."

"It wasn't me, Kari," he said, and if he was lying, he hid it extremely well.

"All right," she said. "And thanks for coming to my rescue tonight. I appreciate it." She stood slowly. "I guess I'd better go talk to George. Wish me luck."

He nodded. "You're going to need it."

"Thanks for the vote of confidence." She tried to smile, but it was too painful. She knew Jeremy was watching her as she walked away, and she hoped she didn't look as pathetic as she felt.

George waited for her at the doorway to his office, and the look on his face was grim. Well, she expected to be fired, so it wouldn't be a big surprise. She deserved it too. She'd done the network a disservice. Not intentionally, but still, it had happened.

Her feet were heavy, and her spirits were about as low as they could be. With every step, she felt more defeated. She loved her job and wanted to keep it. People liked her, they respected her, and she had a following of loyal viewers. Even the new series was off to a good start.

The walk from the studio set to George's office was a short one, but it seemed to take forever. George stepped aside when she reached him, and she entered his office as if it were an execution chamber.

He closed the door behind her. "Sit down."

She did. "I can explain—"

"I hope to hell you can, because there is a lot of explaining to do." Sitting behind his desk, arms crossed, he regarded her with eyes like a serpent.

If she'd been wearing boots, she would have quaked in them. Instead, she kept her gaze on his and told her side of the story as well as she could.

"So, you're telling me you dumped the tape in the recycle bin and it somehow mysteriously ended up in tonight's program?" George tilted his seat back, gazing at the ceiling as if looking for answers.

"That's as much as I know. Jeremy insinuated that perhaps someone has it in for me and may have found the tape and used it to hurt me."

"And why would anyone want to do that?"

"I have no idea," she answered quietly.

"Neither do I." The chair righted itself with a thud, and George turned his gaze back to her. "Have you had a run-in with anyone lately?"

"No one. Well, besides Jeremy. We never got along, but lately he's been very helpful."

"He has no reason to discredit you. It serves no purpose."

"That's true, but someone did."

"You know we have to let you go, don't you?" His tone was gentle now, which made it even worse. "I don't want to. You've been an asset to PB News, and I'm sorry things turned out this way, but we can't tolerate a screwup of this magnitude. Airing the wrong tape containing inaccurate information is unacceptable. We're in the worst decline I've ever seen, along with a lot of other small stations." He ran a hand over his bald head. "Our ratings are continually slipping, and we've lost approximately twenty-five percent of our viewers in prime time."

"I understand." She licked her lips but didn't move. Maybe if she continued to sit long enough, he'd change his mind.

"Advertisers are cutting back on their commercials, and we don't expect to see that revenue coming back."

"I'm sorry to hear that, sir."

"The Internet is killing us, just like it's destroying print media."

"I agree. It's a frightening time, that's for sure."

"We're trying to generate revenue through local advertisers, but it can't begin to compare to what we've lost."

"That's true. But people like this new series." She forced strength into her voice. "They like these feel-good stories. They want more. I know I can fix this, make things right. Did you hear some of the feedback from callers? They supported us, mistake and all."

"I'm sorry, Kari. I wish you the best of luck, but I need you to clear your desk. I'll have security come by to help."

"That won't be necessary."

"I know, but it's the way things are done."

She stood up and offered her hand. "It's been a pleasure working here, and I'm going to miss it. I'm so sorry I let you down."

"I'm sorry too."

She walked out, closed his office door behind her, and headed for her desk. Most newspeople were gone, but she knew the few who were left were watching her. She didn't want to see the embarrassment or pity on their faces, so she stared straight ahead and sucked back the threat of tears. No way would she cry now. She would have plenty of time to wallow in tears, but not in front of her colleagues. Her ex-colleagues.

She reached down and picked her handbag up off the floor. She opened a desk drawer and stared at the junk piled inside it. A retractable umbrella, breath mints, one bottle of Midol and another of Advil, a package of tampons, lipstick, a hairbrush, and a purse-size bottle of Chloé. What was she supposed to do with her stuff? Dump it into the wastebasket to take home?

More importantly, what was she supposed to do about her career? It was over in Palm Beach, but she didn't want to move. She might be able to anchor news in some hick town somewhere, but it would mean leaving Jake, and she just couldn't. He needed her, and right now, she needed him more than ever. He was the only solid, good thing she had. But if she stayed, what would she do? She wasn't trained to do anything other than journalism. She didn't want to do anything else! She wanted Tom, or Jeremy, or someone, to come running in and take responsibility for this fiasco and save her. But sometimes wishes weren't enough.

She tossed her useless belongings in the bin and headed toward the door, stopping when she heard her phone ring. She glanced at the phone, feeling a strong pull to answer it yet knowing it was no longer hers to answer. Straightening her shoulders, she lifted her chin in the air, determined to exit the building with as much dignity as possible.

Halfway down the hall, she stopped and turned. The phone in her cubicle was still ringing, calling out to her. Prickles tickled her skin, and she shivered. She turned and ran back to the phone, holding on with unsteady hands. "Ms. Winslow speaking."

"I think you've been searching for me."

Her heart thudded and her knees gave way. She sank into the chair. "Alaina? Is that you?"

## CHAPTER THIRTY-SIX

After a long hesitation, a soft voice answered, "Yes, this is me. I've been watching your shows, watching you for years. I wanted you to know."

"Alaina—where are you? Can we meet?"

"No. But I wanted to say I'm sorry."

The line went dead.

Kari dropped the phone and ran to the reception desk. "I need to trace the last call," she shouted to the young woman.

"I'm sorry, Ms. Winslow, but you need to leave."

"I'm not leaving. I have to know the number of the last caller. We were disconnected."

"I know. I disconnected your line. You can't take any more calls. I'm sorry, but it's company policy."

"You've got to be kidding me." Kari moved within inches of the woman. "Megan Travers, give me that number. Now."

A security guard moved quickly. "Ms. Winslow, may I escort you from the building?"

"No, dammit. No! I need that number. It was my sister."

She started to cry, and she didn't care if the entire world witnessed her breakdown. "Please, just give me that number. Megan, please…

"I'm so sorry," the receptionist whispered.

The security guard opened the door. "Ms. Winslow. Don't make trouble. We don't want that."

Her feet were having difficulty moving. Her entire body felt sucker-punched, and every instinct urged her to fight back. She took a few steps, then stopped at the door. Her eyes met Megan's, and she could see compassion in the young woman's eyes. "Please find me that number. Please? I'm begging you."

Megan nodded but didn't answer.

The fight went out of Kari, and her shoulders slumped as she left the building. The security guard stayed with her until she reached her car. "Good luck, Ms. Winslow," he said. "I'm sorry. Will you be okay to drive?"

Her throat constricted, and she was unable to speak. She gave him a curt nod.

Her thoughts whirled around like a cyclone in her head. Her sister was alive. She was somewhere out there, but just as far away as before. Emptiness filled her soul, and images of Alaina tormented her mind.

She drove home on automatic pilot, with no memory of the drive. Once inside, she turned on only one small lamp and headed straight for her bedroom to change into her robe. She poured herself a large glass of wine and was heading for her balcony, when she heard someone pounding on her door.

She knew it was Jake, but she didn't want to see him. Not right now. Not until she'd wrapped her head around all that had happened and could think things through.

"Kari," he shouted, "let me in. I know you're in there."

"No." She walked over to the door to talk through it. "I can't face you or anybody right now." She leaned her forehead against the door and closed her eyes. "I need to be alone," she whispered.

"Open the door."

"Go away." Her voice broke. "Please?"

"Open or else." His voice was gruff, but she knew he was only concerned.

"Not tonight, Jake. If you care about me, let me be." A tear fell from her eye.

"I'm warning you. If you don't open this in the next five seconds, I'm going to bust it down."

She knew it was probably not an idle threat. Still, she didn't want him to see how truly broken she was.

She opened the door a crack. "Alaina's alive. I found her, but only for a second, and now she's gone again."

"What are you talking about?"

"She called as I was leaving my desk. I spoke to her, then we were disconnected."

"Did you call her back?"

A sob ripped out of her. "They wouldn't give me her number," she gasped. "The receptionist told me I had to leave, and the security guard led me away." Her voice trembled. "They threw me out and wouldn't even let me speak to my sister."

"Oh, Kari. Sweetheart. Let me in."

She opened the door and fell into his arms. "I don't want you to see me like this. I'm a mess. I can't stop crying."

"That's all right, baby. I'm right here. I'll take care of you."

"No. Not tonight. All I can think of is Alaina. Now that I know she's alive, I have to find her."

"I'll help you. Let me help you." He tried to comfort her, but she pushed away from him.

"Please go away, Jake. I can't do this right now."

"Dammit!" He grabbed her shoulders and looked into her blurry eyes. "I'm not leaving you like this. I saw the program. What happened?"

"I don't know." Her voice broke. "I should have shredded the tape."

"How did it end up at the studio? Did that asshole Jeremy slip it in somehow?"

"I'm not sure. Maybe."

"It's my fault for telling you a story when I knew my memory was shit."

She had no answer for that.

"Kari, I know how upset you were, but why did you talk about Shane and me?" She could see distress in his eyes, and it broke her heart. "I asked you not to."

"I had to say something, and I didn't know what to say."

"It's okay, Kari. I understand, I think. You were in crisis mode, fighting for your survival."

Her chin went up. She couldn't stand his sympathy; it was cracking her up inside. And, as always, when people got too close, she pushed them away.

"Jake, I wasn't in a war zone. I crumbled under pressure and sold you out. I would have said anything to save my career. You know how it is. It's more important to me than people."

"That's not true."

"It is true. You heard me. I betrayed your trust, and I would do it again in a heartbeat."

He didn't answer. He just looked at her, his eyes full of sorrow.

"Why are you saying this? I know you're hurting, and maybe you're blaming me. If I hadn't fed you this story, none of this would have happened."

"That's not it," she answered quietly. "I don't want your comfort right now. Tomorrow, maybe. But I need time to figure some stuff out."

"I see." He sounded weary. Defeated. "I'll leave you, then."

She sucked in a breath as a sharp pain hit her. "Jake. I'm sorry." She'd make it up to him tomorrow, but right now it might be too easy to say things to each other that they'd regret. She didn't want to risk the chance.

"So am I. More sorry than you'll ever know."

All she had to do was wrap her arms around him, and he'd know exactly how to make her feel better. But, as usual, she had to handle this alone.

She had Alaina to think about now, and career decisions to make. Being with Jake would cloud her judgment. If she stayed here to be with him, her career would be over. Could she live with that? Would she eventually resent him if she did?

She had no answers. Everything was happening so fast.

She let him leave and took her still-full glass of wine outside. Although she didn't want to think about anything, her mind scattered all over the place. Shoving aside thoughts of her future, she indulged in memories of her youth—when her sister was still with them and they'd been a normal family. Her mother had given piano lessons at the house, so when she and Alaina came home from school, they had to be quiet until she was done. They would go to their bedrooms and do their homework, or play outside until their mother came for them, greeting them with smiles, hugs, and plenty of kisses. Then she would prepare dinner and their father would come home from work. Dad had loved his children, but more than anything, he'd adored his wife.

Even as young children, Kari and Alaina had been aware that their parents had an unusually strong bond. They'd hug and kiss frequently, much more than parents of their childhood friends. Their love for each other never waned and seemed to only grow stronger with the years.

What would it be like to have a love like that? she wondered.

∽

Jake returned downstairs, knowing he didn't deserve the right to hold and comfort Kari. If it hadn't been for him, she'd never have made such a terrible error that could possibly cost her her career. Then, to save herself, she'd betrayed his trust.

His gut knotted just thinking about it, and his head pounded.

She didn't want anything to do with him right now. She loved her career more than she could ever love him. Not that he could blame her. He'd fucked up by telling her stories. She'd probably lose the only thing that truly mattered to her. She'd never advance her career, if she even kept her current job at all. His fault. Entirely his fault.

He slammed his fist on the table and didn't even wince when it hurt. Kari was so smart. sweet, and caring, and he'd never met anyone who made him feel the way she did. She was the best thing that had ever happened to him, and he'd managed to dump on her twice.

He couldn't get the image out of his mind of how scared she'd looked tonight on TV. When that damn tape of her talking about Gary Marshall had come up, he'd known it was the wrong tape. They'd stopped the tape midsentence, and when she'd come back on the air, she had obviously been upset, and her voice had trembled as she apologized to her audience.

She'd sat there stunned for several minutes, unable to say a word, then started talking about upcoming shows. Then she'd started talking about Shane and him. Had she been planning to use that story all along?

He knew what reporters were like. They'd hunt down stories and ruthlessly expose a person's darkest secret for the simple reason that it made good press.

Still, he'd take ten years off his life if he could hold her right now and kiss away her tears. But that wasn't going to happen. He grabbed his keys and headed out the door. He thought of calling Shane, but he wasn't in the mood to deal with him tonight. When he got into his car, he sat with the keys in the ignition. He had no idea where he wanted to go. No one he wanted to see. Suddenly, with no warning whatsoever, sobs ripped him apart.

# CHAPTER THIRTY-SEVEN

Kari sat outside on her balcony, staring at all the activity in the plaza below yet not seeing a thing. Her mind was numb and her thoughts unfocused, like bits of paper caught up in the wind, blowing every which way, never settling in one place for long.

After a long while, she went inside, crawled into bed, and burrowed under the covers, wanting to drift off into oblivion and not have to face reality. Unfortunately, her wishes didn't come true. Within minutes, her phone rang, and, thinking it might be Alaina, she jumped up to check caller ID.

Her answering machine clicked on, and she heard Lisa's voice. "Kari. I know you're there. It's Lisa. Remember me? I haven't talked to you this week. Come on. Pick up the phone. Please?"

Kari couldn't. Just hearing the concern in her friend's voice brought tears to her eyes. She struggled out of bed, trudged to the living room, and found she had six messages. Hitting play, she listened to her friends and coworkers express their opinions about tonight's fiasco. She deleted one after another, then stopped when she heard Jeremy's voice.

"Hey, Kari. Heard what happened in George's office, and I wanted to say that I'm really sorry. I think he jumped the gun and should have given you a chance to redeem yourself, but that's show business. One screwup, and adios."

Well, wasn't that sweet of him? The arrogant prick. He was probably gloating right now. Hell, he might have pulled the switch himself. He was the only person who had anything to gain. Her time slot. Her show.

Still, she had no legitimate reason to accuse him, or proof of any kind. Now that she'd been fired and escorted out of the building, she would never get any answers. The only good thing that could come out of all this would be for Alaina to come home. That would be the silver lining. Hopefully Megan would call in the morning and have a number where she could be reached.

She crawled back into bed and punched her pillow. She should have known that disaster was about to strike. Whenever her life was floating along beautifully, something came along and snatched her happiness away.

The first time had been when she was eighteen and in love with Jake. She'd planned to leave for college in the fall, but then her sister had disappeared. The second setback came many years later. No sooner had she moved back to Palm Beach after being hired by PB News than her mother had been diagnosed with cancer.

Personal happiness seemed to elude her, and for a long while, her career had sustained her. Now she had a chance to make a switch. Would she be willing to forget the career and see if she could work things out with Jake? Maybe this had been her fate all along. That hunger in her soul—perhaps it was love after all.

As she turned off the light and snuggled under the blanket, she felt less unsure of her future. She wanted to be with Jake. Why had she sent him away?

∼

Jake woke up with a brilliant idea. Since it was the weekend, he didn't need to hang around. It was too close to Kari, and he needed to give her some space; they both had things to sort out. He'd understood her babbling, saying the first things that came to mind, but he still couldn't shake the feeling of betrayal. A little distance would do them both good.

He called Shane and asked if he'd like to fly out to Alabama to see Brent. Then he booked them a flight for later that afternoon and made boarding arrangements for Muffin.

When they arrived at the Dotham Regional Airport, a half hour away from the Fort Rucker flight training center, Brent was there to greet them. He'd finished his first phase of preflight instruction and was about to enter phase two, ten weeks and sixty flight hours in the TH-67 Creek training. The program took thirty-two weeks in all, but he was on the fast track due to his ten years of flight experience and being combat ready.

The three men hugged awkwardly, patting one another on the back, then started talking at once.

"Shane, hot damn. It's good to see you, bro," Brent said, giving his friend's shoulder a light punch. "What were you doing in Florida instead of California, where you belong?"

"The weather's better. And we don't get the dry Santa Ana winds and all those crazy bushfires." Shane grinned, and Brent laughed.

"Yeah, well, that's what kept us in business all those years." Brent scratched his head. He had a military buzz cut now and looked leaner, harder, tougher than before. "You need to come back to L.A. and hold down the fort."

"Nothing to come back to," Shane answered.

"That's not true," Brent replied. "While I was driving here, I got to thinking. I need somebody to take care of my apartment, and you don't have a place to live. Besides, it'll be nice to have someone to come back to."

"You two a couple now?" Jake cocked an eyebrow and looked at them suspiciously. "Never thought I'd see the day. Does Dad know?" Jake was about to continue the brotherly teasing, when Shane interrupted.

"Hey, I haven't eaten since three time zones ago. Let's grab some grub and beer."

"I know just the spot," Brent said, leading the way.

The three men climbed into Brent's jeep and drove into town, stopping when they spotted a Houligans. After a few beers and a massive stack of ribs, the conversation flowed as if they'd never been apart.

"So what exactly are you doing here?" Brent asked Jake. "I mean, don't you lawyer types work eight days a week?"

"Only if you want to make partner, but I'm not all that interested anymore," Jake replied. "Besides, I needed to get out of town for a few days, and so here we are."

"Glad you brought Shane with you. Now all I have to do is convince him to come back to L.A. and take care of my apartment."

"And leave my room at the Days Inn?" Shane guffawed. "You must be crazy, man." He pushed his empty plate away. "Not to mention, I've signed up for therapy sessions, and I sure wouldn't want to miss out on that."

"We've got shrinks there too. And pretty girls. I remember one who was awfully fond of you. I think she's still available." Brent pulled out his cell phone. "Should I give her a ring and ask her?"

Shane grabbed the phone. "You got my old girlfriend's number keyed into your cell?"

Brent laughed. "Are you still interested?"

"No. I just figured she could do better. That's all."

Brent ordered another round of drinks, and Jake told them what had happened with Kari, keeping her later comments to himself. He didn't want Shane to know anything about it, and since she was probably going to lose her job, it didn't matter now.

She'd betrayed them both, and it was all for nothing.

Brent whistled and rolled his eyes. "You fucked up, man. You can kiss that relationship good-bye."

Shane shook his head. "Damn. She was hot."

"Don't remind me." Jake finished his drink in one long gulp.

"Best way to get over a broken heart is to bed the first beautiful woman you see," Brent said. "Works like a charm every time."

"You're all talk," Jake answered. "You still haven't gotten over Nicole. You dated for, what, two years, and you kept saying it was too soon for you to make a commitment. But I bet if she walked in right now, you'd be all over her."

"She's six months pregnant."

Jake's eyebrows rose. "How did that happen?"

"The usual way, I suppose," Brent said dryly. "But it's not mine."

"Hell," Shane said. "I can't believe it. If I'd known you weren't the one for Nicole, I'd have made a play for her myself."

"Shut the hell up," Brent snapped. "You know how I felt about her."

"She have anything to do with you joining the army?"

"Not really. But a little distance won't hurt. The last thing I want is to run into her and see her baby bump."

"There's plenty more fish in the sea," Shane answered.

"Hope this teaches you a lesson," Jake said. "You don't let the good ones swim away."

"Isn't that what you're doing with Kari?" Shane asked.

## CHAPTER THIRTY-EIGHT

Thoughts of Alaina and the need for caffeine drove Kari out of bed. She couldn't remember the last time she'd slept in past eight. She wondered where her sister was right now. She hadn't spoken to her long enough to know if it had been a local call or from the other side of the world. She could be anywhere.

She put on the coffee and waited for it to brew. If she could be reunited with Alaina, nothing else would matter. Her deflated spirits jumped at the thought. Alaina could live with her, right here, in her second bedroom. She had enough savings to last a few months, and she could always find something to do. She knew a lot of people. She wouldn't be a lady of leisure for long.

After finishing a bowl of cereal, she went for her five-mile run, came home, and showered. She checked her messages and was disappointed that no one had called. She wanted to speak to Megan, but the receptionist had the afternoon shift and wouldn't be in until two.

Where was Jake? Waiting for her to make the first move? Well, she had thrown him out and said some unkind things. She'd told him she'd do anything to save her career, even if it meant betraying his trust. In a moment of panic, she'd done just that, but her intention had never been to hurt him. Hopefully he would understand that, and her need to suffer alone.

She called his cell phone and left a message, then decided she'd better speak to Lisa. Her friend picked up right away. "Are you all right? I've been worried about you."

"I'm sorry I didn't call sooner, but I didn't want to talk about it." She still didn't, but Lisa was her best friend, and she couldn't put this conversation off forever. "So, before we get into my dreary story, tell me how you are. Everything okay with you and David?"

"Couldn't be better," Lisa said. "Especially the sex."

"That's good to hear," Kari said with a laugh. "You did the right thing by taking him back."

"I know I did. One mistake was not worth destroying our marriage, but if it ever happens again…"

"I'm sure it won't." Kari spoke the comforting words her friend wanted to hear.

"Okay, so stop stalling," Lisa said. "What happened last night?"

Kari told Lisa, ending with the call from her sister.

"That's amazing. Your sister is alive," Lisa exclaimed. "I'm so thrilled for you."

"We were disconnected, and now I'm afraid that she might not call again."

"Oh, I'm sure she will. Why wouldn't she? After all, she reached out to you."

"Yes, yes, she did. I can't wait to talk to her, to see her, to have her back with me."

"I know, honey. You've never given up on her. And this takes some of the sting out of what happened last night."

"Oh, yeah. Forgot to mention it. They fired me."

"Can they do that?" Lisa asked. "Don't you have a contract or something?"

"Yes, but they can get rid of me if they have just cause, and unfortunately, they do."

"But you came back on the air and admitted the mistake. You didn't try to hide it, and from what I could see, the viewers didn't seem to care."

"True," Kari said, "but it introduces an element of doubt, of mistrust. People might be out there right now saying, 'Just proves what I always knew: these newscasters just make this stuff up.' I can't have people doubting my credibility with every news report I make."

"Oh, Kari, that really sucks."

"You're telling me. I don't know what I'm going to do or where I'm going to go. I won't get another job in this town, that's for sure."

"But you're well known and respected in the business. Surely someone will hire you."

"My credibility has just been shot to hell." Kari sucked in a deep breath, surprised at the pain it caused.

"But what about the calls from the viewers?" Lisa wasn't giving up. "They seemed to be on your side."

"Doesn't make any difference. The news director already let me go."

"Well, we can't stand by and let that happen. I'm going to call the station myself and demand they return you and the show."

"Thanks for the thought, sweetie, but it's going to take a miracle for them to offer me my job back."

"I believe in miracles," Lisa said.

"Good. If I get Alaina back, I will too."

∼

Kari waited until ten past two; then she called the station, knowing that Megan would answer the phone.

"Megan. It's me. Kari. I'm sorry to bother you, but is it possible for you to check the calls last night and help me reconnect with my sister?"

"I did that already, Kari. I spent a half hour after you left last night, but it was from a disposable cell, and maybe she chucked it. I tried calling the number several times." Megan spoke softly. "I'm so sorry. I would never have interrupted the call if I'd known it was from her."

"I understand. Can you give me the number? Maybe there's still a chance she'll answer if she knows it's from me."

"Of course. Here it is." She read it off. "Good luck. With everything."

Kari didn't have any better luck than Megan. She tried calling Jake a few times too. The two people she loved most in the world wouldn't even talk to her. Twenty-four hours ago, she'd been sitting pretty, on top of the world; now she felt like a leper.

She sat at the dinner table eating her Lean Cuisine, debating whether she should turn on the evening news. She could always check a rival's station. No one from PB News had a gun pointed to her head. As she flipped through the channels, she knew her loyalty remained with the station that had been paying her all these years, and that would not change. She might not trust as freely as she'd like or believe in miracles, but she did have loyalty.

Which was a heck of a lot more than she could say for Jake. Why hadn't he returned her calls? Had he turned his back on her too?

Jake had made her promise that she'd never tell Shane's story without his permission, and yet she'd done just that—blurting it out stupidly, without giving it a moment's thought.

Tears blurred her eyes. She loved him, and now she had destroyed their friendship and any hope that one day it could be more. She'd lost her job, lost Jake, and lost her sister a second time. She had nothing left worth fighting for.

∽

Jake made the multicity connected flight to Palm Beach on Sunday night, alone. Brent had convinced Shane to return to California, take care of his apartment, and see about getting a new position with CAL FIRE. Taking Shane to see Brent had been the best thing he could have done for his friend.

The weekend away had been equally good for Jake. It had been great to spend a couple of nights with his brother while he still could. It had also kept him away from Kari's door and helped him to cool down some.

He was still upset by what she'd done, but he knew it hadn't been malicious. It had been a desperate plea to save her career.

He arrived home at eight in the morning, after picking up Muffin from the boarder's. He headed directly for the shower, figuring he might as well go to work. But first, he had to see Kari and try to sort things out. His misguided memory had set this calamity in motion, and she probably didn't ever want to see his face again.

He'd come to a decision this weekend, and that decision required a move. He'd be out of her hair, and she could move on with her life as she'd wanted.

He put on his suit, grabbed a to-go cup of coffee, and headed down the hall to the elevator. He punched the button, and when the door opened, there was Kari, dressed in a skimpy halter top and tight jogging shorts. She had one leg on the railing, stretching her hamstring muscles. Her back was to him, and he admired the taut shape of her ass, her narrow waist, and her lean, lithe body.

"Kari. I was just coming to see you."

She dropped her leg and whipped around. "I'm going downstairs for my run." She eyed his suit and cup of coffee. "If you were coming to see me, wouldn't you be going up?"

"Must have pressed the wrong button," he muttered. "Did you have any luck finding Alaina?"

"No. The phone was a disposable, and she never called back." She bit her lip. "Where have you been? Why haven't you returned my calls?"

"I hoped you'd be having a happy reunion with your sister, and besides, I didn't think you'd have anything to say to me, not after I got you fired."

"So you thought I was calling to tell you that I didn't want to talk to you anymore?" she snapped. "How idiotic is that?" Her eyes glittered, looking angry. "Neither you nor my sister would answer your damn phone!"

"I'm so sorry, Kari. I really am. For everything. Mostly for your sister, but also for the trouble I got you into. You wouldn't have been in that situation if I hadn't told you that damn story."

"It's not your fault. And, Jake, I'm sorry I said something about Shane."

"You didn't do it to hurt either one of us," he answered.

When the elevator reached the lobby level, Jake reached out a hand. "I took Shane to see Brent this weekend. Brent convinced him to return to L.A. and take care of his apartment until he finishes his training and has to head overseas."

"That's good. I'm glad."

"While I was away, I made an important decision. I'm moving to Washington."

"You are what?"

"I want to make a difference, and that's where I need to be."

## CHAPTER THIRTY-NINE

Washington? He was leaving her again. Oh, dear God, how could she let him go?

Kari fought back tears and ran harder, pushing her endurance. Her lungs were bursting, and her heart was racing along with her feet. Maybe she was trying to outrun her thoughts, but they were keeping up. How could he walk away so easily? Did he care so little?

Her steps faltered, and she slowed to a walk, breathing hard. Jake, dear, beloved Jake. She'd never loved anyone more. And damn him to hell. He couldn't turn his back on her again. She wouldn't let him.

She'd been so busy chasing dreams that she had forgotten what was important. The people in her life were what mattered—they were all that mattered. And love. What was life without love? A few days ago, she'd lost her job through no fault of her own. Her sister had given her a moment of hope, then snatched it back, without any regard for her. So why waste a moment on them, why not win back the man she'd loved since she was a young woman?

Jake deserved someone who loved him completely and was not afraid to show it. She intended to be that person. She'd explain to him that it had taken her a long time, longer than most, to finally realize what she hungered for. Not fame. Not fortune. But love.

She knocked on his door at six o'clock, and he opened it wide. "Kari. Come on in."

"Jake." She ran to him and threw her arms around his neck, bringing his face down for a kiss. She kissed him sweetly and for a long time.

"What was that for?"

"For everything."

He took hold of her hands and unclasped them from his neck, taking a step back. "Kari. Why are you here? I didn't think you'd be speaking to me."

"I have something very important to tell you."

His face looked closed, his eyes distant. "What might that be?"

"I love you."

He put a finger to her lips and shook his head. "Kari, I'm leaving. I made mistakes with you, but they're nothing compared with the ones I made at war." He couldn't meet her eyes.

"No." She had to make him understand. "I finally realized what I want. What I need." She grabbed him by the hand. "You."

"What you want is your job."

She stepped closer and looked into his eyes. "I've wasted enough time searching for something to make me whole. I thought a career would do that, but it was never enough. Jake, you left an emptiness inside me, and only you can fill it."

"Kari..."

She put up a hand. She had to finish what she'd come here to say. "I've always loved you."

He was silent, and her gut twisted. Her eyes searched his face. Something was wrong.

"I want you, Jake. Please don't make me say it again."

His face softened, and he took a step closer. "Kari, you are the best thing that ever happened to me, and I was wrong to let you get close to me again. Things happened overseas, terrible things. You have no idea what I'm capable of, and I don't deserve your love, or your respect."

"I know you, Jake." She could hear the quake in her voice, but it didn't matter now. She was fighting for her life. "Whatever you did, I'm sure you did it for a very good reason."

He turned and walked away from her, his hands pulling at his hair as if he were trying to pluck out memories. Finally, he sighed, turned, and came back to her.

"I killed a woman and a child," he said bluntly. "Innocent bystanders." He closed his eyes. "A group of insurgents had blown up a gas station. When we got there, the terrorists were still there, shooting civilians as they ran." He sucked in a breath and released it slowly. His eyes opened, and she could see the pain in them. "There were mothers and babies, small children carried by their fathers, and these maniacs were shooting everyone on sight."

"Oh, Jake." She stood on her tiptoes and kissed his cheeks, his eyes, his mouth. She held his hands and squeezed. "You were defending the civilians. You didn't mean to kill anyone. The insurgents were killing the innocent people, not you."

"While the reporters were busy writing their stories and the cameramen caught it all on tape." He looked at her, and his expression chilled her. "That's why I'm not a big fan of journalists or their need for a good story."

"They were doing their duty, just as you did yours."

"You have no idea what it's like." He closed his eyes. "One terrorist grabbed a mother and a boy, holding them as shields. It was chaos, insurgents firing, soldiers shooting back. I don't know if it was my weapon or someone else's that killed that insurgent and shredded the woman and the boy."

She closed her eyes, envisioning it for a moment. How did one live with such awful memories? And she was sure he had many more buried deep inside him. "Jake, you were trying to protect them."

He wiped a hand over his face. "The military investigated and found that we all acted appropriately under the circumstances. We all received counseling afterward, but still, I can't get their faces out of my mind."

Something like that ate at a person, destroyed his soul. But it wasn't his fault, and she had to make him see that.

She led him to the sofa. "Jake. Forgive yourself. Please. You have to. You did what you were trained to do. Don't carry this guilt around. You're better than that. You're strong."

"Sometimes I hear a car backfire and I hit the ground. Stuff like that stays with you for a long time. I don't want you, or anyone else, exposed to my shit."

"Jake, shush." She kissed his cheek. "If you can't put this behind you, it'll destroy you."

"Kari." He pulled her into his arms, and she felt a sob wrack his body. "My sweet Kari." He kissed the top of her head. "I don't want to let you go, but I have to."

"Why?"

"I'm going to lobby for the homeless vets and get them the support they need. I don't care what I have to do or how long it takes, but I will see that they're not forgotten. We need more homes and shelters. We can't leave them to rot on the streets."

"I see." She spoke quietly, feeling her stomach roll. He didn't want her to come.

"I have to do this. It's the only way I can make amends for the wrong I've done. You understand that, don't you?"

She understood everything. He was a courageous, generous, honorable man, and she'd betrayed him. He didn't want her. The network didn't want her. Neither did Alaina. She was alone, as she'd always been.

"I do." She bit her lip to stop it from trembling. Her nails were digging into her palms, and she had a tight knot in her stomach.

"I have to be there. It's where the action is, and I need to be visible. This is a fight worth fighting, and I'm in for a long, hard battle."

"That day at your college, I came to see you…to tell you I was pregnant."

"Kari…" His mouth fell open, and he stared at her with shock and disbelief. "You had a baby? And never told me?"

Tears blurred her vision. "No. I saw you with that other girl, and I took off. Driving back to the airport, I couldn't see, I was crying so hard. There was an accident—"

"You lost the baby?"

"Yes." He pulled her into his arms. "That's why I hated you for so long. Now you know."

She pushed out of his arms and ran from the apartment.

## CHAPTER FORTY

He put his head in his hands and breathed deeply, trying to digest this new information. He would have been a father had he known. If she'd called and told him she was coming that weekend and not run off, the baby would still be alive, and he'd have dropped out of college and married her.

Oh, dear God. No wonder she'd hated him on sight. He'd taken so much from her, and now he'd done it again. She had accused him of ruining her life once, and now it was twice.

He couldn't go back to her and beg for her forgiveness any more than he could marry her. She didn't understand. No civilian could know what it felt like to kill innocent people, a mother and child whom he'd been trying to save.

There had been two separate attacks, occurring within hours of each other in Baghdad. Sixty-seven civilians were killed. Nine rounds of mortar hit a petrol station packed with motorists lined up for gas, and in another section of town, a fuel truck exploded. When he and his troops responded, insurgents were firing into the fleeing crowd of civilians, in one of the deadliest sniper attacks the city had ever seen.

That had all been in the official report, but what happened after was a part of him now. Like a cancerous growth, it spread into every cell, every molecule of his being, eating away at his heart and soul like a slow-acting poison.

During the chaos, Jake had lost it. Assault rifle in hand, he had blasted into the street, hunting the sons of bitches who had no regard for life. To this day, he didn't know if it had been his M4 or someone else's that had hit the mother and child, killing all three of them. But it didn't matter. He could not have allowed that jihadist to escape. No matter what.

He had to atone for their murders, but was it fair to ask Kari along his road to redemption? No, not really, yet how could he live with himself if he left her again?

∼

Kari unzipped the pretty sundress she'd worn for Jake and discarded it on the floor. After putting on a robe, she poured a glass of wine, taking it outside to the balcony. She had no idea how long she sat there, too numb to think, too numb to even cry. It was her own fault. It had taken her too long to realize she loved him. She had denied her true feelings and chosen her career over him, and he'd made a choice that didn't include her.

She thought about Alaina too. If her sister wanted to see her again, she knew where to find her. And if she didn't, well, then Kari would accept her decision. She was tired of searching and hoping. Tired of disappointments.

She returned inside, turned off the lights, and crawled into bed. The sheets were cool against her skin, and she shivered. The bed was so cold, and she knew it would never be warm again. Not without Jake. A fat, sloppy tear slid from under her closed lid and trickled down her cheek, landing on the pillow. It was followed closely by another.

She tossed and turned all night, drifting in and out of a troubled sleep. In her dreams, she was running down white corridors, searching, searching, but could not find what she was searching for. She awoke in the morning drenched, her sheets and pillow on the floor. She lay there for a considerable time, remembering everything, trying to convince herself that she would be fine and happy again sometime soon. But how could she be when Jake didn't love her?

Pain shot through her like a knife to the heart, and she knew losing him a second time would be far worse than the first.

For the next few days, she hunkered down in her condo, spending her time obsessively cleaning, working out, and sleeping. Jake was a warrior, and he had a new battle to fight. He intended to make some powerful changes in the government's responsibility to the country's veterans, and she wouldn't stop him if she could. But she'd miss him every day of her life and mourn all that they could have been together.

After three days, she decided she'd wallowed long enough. She dried her eyes, sniffed back her tears, and ventured out of the house. A day of shopping was what she had in mind. Kari stopped at a few of her favorite shops on Worth Avenue. She visited all the designer shops, and after trying on clothes and buying ridiculously expensive shoes, she temporarily forgot her worries.

It was late in the day by the time she finished her rounds, but she didn't want to go home. Instead, she decided to treat herself to an early dinner. Bice's courtyard had a Tuscany feel, with crisp white linen tablecloths on the small tables, cobblestone pathways, rich foliage, and discreet lighting. Perfect for dining alfresco.

By six o'clock, the bar was hopping and men were vying to send her drinks. She refused with gracious smiles, as she really did not want company. If she got lonely, there were several people in the restaurant she knew, some of whom had stopped by her table, eager to chat.

She wondered how long her celebrity status would last in this town once the news got out that she'd been fired. Replacements filled in for the regular anchors all the time, so her absence on the morning and noontime shows probably hadn't sparked any gossip. By next week, though, people would begin wondering. The TV set in the bar was tuned to PB News. She caught a glimpse of Jeremy and turned away. She much preferred her table in the courtyard, where she could enjoy the lovely setting and the warm evening air.

Enjoying the attention of her handsome young waiter, she followed his suggestion and ordered ravioli with crab and lobster. While she waited, she sipped her chardonnay and watched the parade of beautiful people coming and going.

After a few minutes, Kari became uncomfortably aware that people in the bar kept looking at her. Was it just because the news was on and people connected her with the station? Or was it something else? She beckoned to her waiter and asked for a favor. "Could you please find out why I'm the center of attention suddenly? Does it have anything to do with the news?"

She watched him talk to the bartender, who gestured to the TV. Then both the waiter and the bartender talked to two or three people at the bar. Finally, the waiter returned.

"Are you Kari Winslow, the TV lady?" he asked in a conspiratorial tone.

She nodded. "Yes. What are they saying?"

"I'm not entirely sure, but it seems as if the network announced yesterday that some show of yours had been canceled, and ever since, the station has been flooded with calls and e-mails."

"Really?" She licked her suddenly dry lips. "Do you think I could change tables? Is there a table available in the bar?"

"I can get one set up in just a minute, Ms. Winslow. Would you like to take your wine to the bar while I take care of that?"

"I would indeed."

She slid onto a barstool and looked at the TV. Jeremy was trading jokes with the weatherman. She turned to the older man beside her. "Excuse me, but did you catch the news report?"

"Sure did." The man shot her a glance. "That new anchorman said the station had canceled the Friday-night show about unsung heroes. Said it was going to be replaced with a new reality show, hosted by him. Then, before he said good night, he made another announcement."

"What did he say?"

"He said after announcing the cancellation of the 'hero' show, the station received hundreds of calls from people wanting it back on the air."

"Is that so?" Kari said. She was gratified at the support—but what would the station do about it? She smiled at the man and thanked him for his time.

"My pleasure. Not every day I get to talk to a pretty, young newslady like you. Now go get your job back."

## CHAPTER FORTY-ONE

Kari finished her dinner quickly and went outside to use her cell phone. First call would be to Jennifer, her right-hand assistant. The moment she turned the phone on, she noticed she'd already missed four calls. Before she had a chance to check to see whom they were from, another call came in.

Jake.

"Hello?" she answered cautiously. Her heart was hammering, and she didn't want to get her hopes up. She'd lived long enough not to hope for things she couldn't control.

"Kari, don't hang up, but I need to speak to you."

"I'm listening." The sound of his voice had her pulse humming. She missed him so much already, and he hadn't even left.

"Have you been watching the news?"

"No. I've been out all day, and I missed it. What's happening?"

"Where are you now?"

"Worth Avenue. I had some dinner."

"Can you sit down? You don't want to be standing when I tell you this."

Glancing around, she found a bench and took a seat. "Okay. I'm ready. What is it?"

"Ever since Friday night, the network has been besieged with calls and e-mails from servicemen and women, family members, and even people with no connection to the military."

Kari was glad Jake had made her sit. "I don't believe it," she whispered.

"Then tonight, Jeremy told the viewers that he'd be hosting a local reality show, only to later correct himself. He said the hero show was back on."

"But if the news department is taking this seriously enough to broadcast it, wouldn't you think that one of the news directors would have given me a call?"

"Didn't you just say you've been out all day?"

"You're right. I do have a few messages. Let me listen to them, and then I'll call you back."

"Good. Do that. I have something to tell you as well."

"What?" Her throat went dry. "What is it?"

"Not now. I'll tell you tomorrow. You're going to be busy tonight."

"Okay." Her palms were damp as she hung up. Jake sounded secretive, but in a nice way. Not like a man hell-bent on breaking her heart.

As she walked to her car, Kari listened to her phone messages. The first one was from Jeremy.

"Kari, I wanted to give you a heads-up. We've been getting calls for days about your show. Seems like that Friday-night disaster worked out for you after all."

The next call was from George. "I may have been too hasty terminating you. Come on in tomorrow, and we'll talk."

The third was from Tom. "Hey, congratulations. It looks like you pulled it off. Give me a call when you get this message. We've got things to discuss."

And Lisa. "Kari, did you hear the news? You're a hit. Everyone loves you and your show! I'm so proud of you."

Kari drove home with a dopey grin on her face. She felt dazed by this sudden turn of events. She wasn't a hundred percent sure that she still wanted the job, but it was nice to know that they wanted her.

Once she got home, she let out a whoop and danced around her living room. This time tomorrow, she'd be an anchorwoman again. If she still wanted it.

∼

The next morning at precisely nine o'clock, Kari walked into the station and headed straight for Tom's office. She knocked lightly on the door. He looked up, saw her through the glass, and jumped up to open the door.

That was a first.

"Kari. Thank you for coming in. Have a seat."

"Good morning, Tom. How are you?" she asked politely as she sat.

"Excellent. As you may know, we've been getting a lot of calls about this show of yours. Seems like you've got a hit on your hands. To make a long story short, the news department had a meeting yesterday, and we all want you back. The director himself said he made a big mistake in letting you go, and he wants to make it up to you by giving you a raise."

She nodded. "Money's nice, but I want the night anchor job."

"We'll see what we can do about that. Maybe you could coanchor with Jeremy."

"Not with Jeremy. I'd like to coanchor the five o'clock show with Maddie. I've always liked her, and we get along great."

"I'll see what can be arranged."

"And I don't like getting up at four. I'd like to keep my noon show and do the early-evening news. I've decided I want a life."

"Well, let me talk to George and see what can be done."

She stood. "Thank you, Tom. Call me when you've worked out the details."

She shook his hand and marched out of his office.

Damn, it was good to be in command.

Now, instead of slinking out of the station, she stopped to talk to the news reporters clamoring around her, welcoming her back. Not only was she back in the game, but she'd somehow arrived on top.

It was almost surreal. She belonged, and yet she didn't.

Her desk hadn't been reassigned, so she wandered over and sat down in her swivel chair. She knew many eyes were upon her, and she spun around in her chair, head back, waiting to feel exhilarated, happy…something.

The feelings didn't come. She'd loved working here, year after year. She'd given her heart and soul to this network, and they'd dumped her at the first hint of trouble. She had a right to be cautious. The old camaraderie, the respect, the trust, was gone.

She picked up her handbag, ready to leave, when Jennifer came running up to her. "Did you hear?"

"Hear what?" Bracing herself, she folded her arms in front of her chest. She simply could not take any more turmoil.

"The rumors, silly!" Jennifer shook her head, her red curls flying around her face, and laughed. "I see you haven't." She leaned in and whispered, "You are being considered by WNYW. How could you not have heard?"

WNYW was the number-one Fox affiliate in New York. Why would they consider her? It didn't make sense, but then, nothing in her life made sense anymore.

"Not only that," Jennifer whispered excitedly, "but the rumor mill has it that your hero show might become syndicated."

"No way. How did you hear this?" Kari looked around at the familiar faces of her coworkers and knew from their expressions that they'd heard the rumors too. "This can't be true. If it were, wouldn't someone have contacted me?"

"I'm sure they will. Probably today."

Jennifer danced off, and Kari walked slowly out of the building. She was excited, of course she was, but did she want it? Once, not long ago, she'd been so sure of her goals and dreams. Now everything was topsy-turvy, and the only thing she truly desired was Jake.

## CHAPTER FORTY-TWO

Later that afternoon, Tom called her at home. "Kari, I'm not sure if you've heard the rumors, but I don't want you to get ahead of yourself. You have a fine career here, and we aim to keep you."

"I don't believe the rumors, sir. I haven't heard a word from Fox."

"If you do, I hope you don't jump ship. George and I drew up the contract you wanted. You can have the two news shows you requested." He added, "And a ten percent salary increase."

"That is a very generous offer." She knew she'd be crazy not to sign on the dotted line, before they changed their minds. But without Jake here, she might be better off out of town, starting somewhere fresh, where she wouldn't have daily reminders of him.

"If you can messenger the contract to me, I'll have my attorney look it over," she said. "I can get back to you in a few days."

Tom grunted. Clearly, she'd caught him off guard. "You don't seem as delighted by all this as I'd expected."

"Yes, well, a lot has happened fast, and I'm simply trying to keep up." The idea of working with Tom, George, and Jeremy again gave her a headache.

"You'll make the right choice. You always do."

∼

A few hours later, Kari was still at home when the call from WNYW came through on her work line. Her pulse raced, and she took a couple of quick breaths, trying to steady her nerves. She used a tissue to wipe her damp palms, and was about to answer when she heard a firm knock on her door. Jake.

She looked at the phone, then back at the door. After a moment's hesitation, she picked up the business line.

"Kari Winslow speaking. May I put you on hold?"

Then she ran to answer the door.

"Jake, hi."

"Kari, I realize you probably have a million exciting things to take care of, but do you have a minute now?"

"That depends. I have Fox on the line, and they may want me in New York."

"Hear me out first." He sounded like his old self: confident, aggressive, the man she used to know. "I was a damn fool to leave you the first time, and no way am I going to make that mistake again."

"You're not going?"

"I have a secondary plan, if you want to hear it."

"Give me a minute. Take a seat." Smiling, she stepped away from the door and went back to her waiting call. "This is Kari Winslow. How can I help you?"

She listened to their spiel, made appropriate responses, but her eyes were on Jake as he prowled around the room, too impatient to sit. What did he want? He'd called himself a fool for leaving her. What did that mean? Her pulse raced and her heart did flip-flops.

She turned her back to him so she could concentrate on this business call. Finally, they said all they had to say, her questions were answered, and she could move on to more important matters. Like the man in front of her, who was wringing his hands and giving her pleading glances.

"Thank you so much for calling," she told the Fox general manager. "I will think about it and have my answer in forty-eight hours."

She turned to Jake. "You had something to say?" Her stomach was a tight, nervous knot, but she cocked her head, acting indifferent.

"I do." He stood next to her desk. "But first, what did Fox say?"

"They asked me to come to New York to have 'a talk.'"

"That sounds promising." He reached for her hand and pulled her out of her chair. "I'm really happy for you. It's what you've always wanted."

She felt a sharp ache inside. He didn't want her after all.

"It is," she said, "but I'm not so sure anymore. PB News has offered me the most amazing contract. And I love it here. Besides, if Alaina does decide to contact me again, she will look for me here."

"True, but this is New York, baby. Prime time. All your dreams come true."

"I've changed my dreams." She sat rigid beside him, waiting to hear him out. If he had something to say, then he needed to get on with it. "Why are you here? What did you want to tell me?"

He inched closer and cupped her chin, urging her to look at him. "I let go of you once, and I'm not going to make that mistake again." His fingers caressed her cheek. "Washington is important to me, but I can't go without you." He gave her a soft kiss. "I know it's corny, but you make my life complete."

He smiled, and she would have had to be blind not to see the love shining in his eyes. Her heart thudded in her chest, but she didn't reply. He still hadn't told her he loved her. She needed to hear the words.

He swallowed hard, and for the first time, she realized he was nervous. "I want you with me, but I know you need to take this job. It's too big an opportunity to pass up."

"I don't even know what the job is." She was getting impatient now. She didn't care about the job. She wanted to hear words of love. "Why do you want me with you?"

He gave a loopy grin. "Did I forget that part?"

"I think you might have missed an important step or two."

"I love you, Kari." His big hand curved around the back of her neck, drawing her near. He bent his head and slanted his mouth over hers. The kiss was deep, passionate, brimming with love and promise. She clung to him as tears slid down her cheeks.

"Don't cry." He kissed the tears away. "Not for me. Never again for me." His chest shuddered, and she could see his eyes were suspiciously bright. "I love you more than life itself."

"Jake. I've waited so long to hear those words. I love you too. More than you'll ever know." She looked at him with hope. Her career was no longer the driving force of her existence, but it might be possible to have both. "You'd be in Washington?"

"And you'd be in New York."

"Is that doable?"

"It is if we want to make it work."

"Oh, Jake. This is too much to take in. I was ready to give it up for you if you'd asked."

"I would never ask that. And I won't let you give up your dreams. So you go to New York and dazzle them, and I'll be nearby. Washington is an easy commute."

"Maybe Fox in Washington needs a new anchor," she said slowly. Then another idea popped into her head. "And I don't need to be in New York to syndicate my show."

"You see?" His arms slid around her, drawing her near. "When two people love each other, they find a way to work things out."

She rested her head against his chest. "Maybe it isn't so scary after all."

"When you get back from New York, what say we get married?"

She looked up at him, laughing. "Is that your proposal?"

"I could possibly make it more romantic, but the answer would still be the same."

"Pretty sure of yourself, aren't you?" She kissed his neck, then nibbled on his earlobe.

He gave her his old cocky smile.

"I'll do my very best not to let you down." His eyes were steady on hers. "I probably have years of therapy ahead of me, and I'm not going to be the easiest man to live with, but I'm sure going to try."

"I know you will," she said. "And I promise not to put my career first ever again."

He kissed her. "I love you so much, and you will make an excellent politician's wife."

"Politician?"

"Did I forget that part?"

"You might have. But then, the last few days have been full of surprises."

"I have one more." He reached into his pocket. "Close your eyes."

She did. Her heart was clamoring so loud, she was sure even Jake could hear it.

"Now hold out your hand."

She put both hands in the air and wiggled her fingers.

"Just the left one."

She squinted to see what he was doing.

"And no peeking." He kissed her eyelids, and she obediently kept them shut until she felt something slide onto her ring finger. Her eyes flew open, and she gasped with delight.

"You like it?" he asked. "If not, we can exchange it tomorrow. I thought you'd like the simple marquis cut, but if you'd prefer something else, just let me know."

"It's perfect and you're perfect." She admired the diamond ring on her finger. "How could you have known that this is what I've always wanted, when I didn't even know it myself?"

"That's my job for the rest of my life."

Their kiss was the sweetest, most meaningful kiss they'd ever shared. And she knew they were just getting started.

## ABOUT THE AUTHOR

Patrice Wilton knew from the age of twelve that she wanted to write books that would take the reader to faraway places. As a voracious reader, she gobbled up books, and her imagination soared. She was born in Vancouver, Canada, and had a great need to see the world that she had read about.

Patrice became a flight attendant for seventeen years and traveled the world. At the age of forty she sat down to write her first book—in longhand! Her interests include tennis, golf, and writing stories for women of all ages.

She is the proud mother of two, has three lovely granddaughters, and a wonderful man at her side. They live in West Palm Beach, Florida, where he teaches her golf, and she teaches him patience.

FICTION WILTON
Wilton, Patrice.
A hero lies within /
R2000307716 WOLF CREEK

ODC

Atlanta-Fulton Public Library

# Kindle *Serials*

This book was originally released in episodes as a Kindle Serial. Kindle Serials launched in 2012 as a new way to experience serialized books. Kindle Serials allow readers to enjoy the story as the author creates it, purchasing once and receiving all existing episodes immediately, followed by future episodes as they are published. To find out more about Kindle Serials and to see the current selection of Serials titles, visit www.amazon.com/kindleserials.